THE HAUNTER OF THE MOOR

AN IRISH GHOST STORY

JEFFREY KOSH

Jeffrey Kosh

The Haunter of the Moor

First Edition
Edited by Lorraine Versini
Cover art by Jeffrey Kosh Graphics
Published by Optimus Maximus Publishing, LLC

This book is a work of fiction. Names, characters, businesses, organizations, places, events, and incidents either are the product of the author's imagination or are used fictitiously. Any resemblance to actual persons living, dead, or otherwise, events, or locales is entirely coincidental.

ISBN-10: 1-944732-03-9
ISBN-13: 978-1-944732-03-5

To Kat Yares

To the Lady of the Moor and Phantom Hounds.
My work is finished, my duty is paid.
Now leave me alone, please.

Acknowledgements

Kat Yares, to whom this book is dedicated. Life isn't the same without you, my friend.

To Kevin 'THAT MAN' Yares, for allowing me to use his and his wife's names in the novel.

To Ireland, for whispering this incredible story to me while I was visiting the Malahide castle and gardens in October 2014.

To Lorraine Versini, for polishing and proofreading my story and for all the funny fights we had over it. I owe you a lot, Babe.

To Natalie G. Owens, for all the good advice.

To an unknown shape that visited me in my dreams at the age of twelve. Probably you're not going to read this, and perhaps you don't exist, but thank you.

And finally, as always, to all of you, my faithful readers.

THE HAUNTER OF THE MOOR

A Novel by

Jeffrey Kosh

I close my eyes then I drift away
Into the magic night, I softly say
A silent prayer like dreamers do
Then I fall asleep to dream my dreams of you

In Dreams – Roy Orbison

PROLOGUE
1778

November 1st, 1778
Glencree Valley, County Wicklow, Ireland.

At the end of a dull, dark, and dreary day, Hugh Nigel Talbot, Squire of Glencree, found himself yelling and cursing his driver. He understood the road was muddy and quite dangerous to horses' hooves, yet it was late, and it was of the utmost importance that he reached his destination before the day was over. It had been raining for weeks, and the snaking path had turned into a morass, threatening to rejoin the bog from whence it had been dug forth. Not without struggling – for a strong wind, full of water and dirt was scourging the hills – he poked out of the carriage's window and shouted to the coachman to go heavier on the whip.

The driver heard his master's order and reluctantly lashed the animals, forcing them to gain speed. A smirk of satisfaction formed on Talbot's face as he rejoined the comfort of the vehicle's interior. Nothing would stop him; the stone was going to be toppled today.

As soon as the coach reached the last bend, the view of the singularly gloomy landscape surrounding his property brought melancholy to Talbot's heart. And it was exactly because of this forlornness that he had so eagerly accepted his family's offer. Hugh knew that his family reviled him, nonetheless, he was still a nobleman and kin, and it was his right to be made part of the vast Malahide fortunes.

They thought they were insulting him.

They did him a favor.

Dorchae Bog and Glencree were exactly what he needed for his research. A cruel joke would soon turn into the greatest discovery man had ever made. And he, Hugh Talbot, would be forever remembered as the new Prometheus, for as the titan, he would bring the flame of knowledge that would forever dispel the darkness of ignorance. Thanks to him, superstition would be gone. Thanks to him, man's future would be unbound.

Unbound.

That word reminded him to check that all his orders had been meticulously followed by the men he had hired. A minimal error, an insignificant difference in the ritual, and everything would be compromised. The price of failure was too high to pay. Hence, his presence at the binding was essential. He had to be sure the men would be using the chains he had forged. He had to make sure they would bind the stone thrice. And finally, Hugh had to absolutely be there when the stone would fall down.

As the coach rounded the skeletal structure of his future mansion, Hugh fished an old book from his travel bag. Its yellowed pages flipped fast, revealing diagrams, geometrical figures, runes, and scrawled annotations. The leafing stopped after Talbot found exactly what he was looking for: surrounded by drawings of leering, demonic faces, there stood the Solomonian circle; the key to a power matrix that would force the Non-Euclidean into the Euclidean, and Man's ultimate arrow to pierce the Dragon's armor. Tonight, he was going to slap the gauntlet of knowledge onto the shadowy face of superstition. Tonight, alchemy and cabalism would join forces against the unknown. They had called him a warlock, a sorcerer, and a diabolist. They had looked at him as a destroyer, the ignorant fools. But he was none. He was an explorer and a benefactor. His quest was for knowledge and the power that comes from it. Because with knowledge comes enlightenment, and out of enlightenment comes truth. And truth may appear like madness to those who had no eyes to see, nor ears to hear. Others before him had suffered the same ostracism, the same isolation. Despised by the very people they wanted to help. If people feared that, so be it. If people feared him, so be it. Why would he have to suffer because the narrow-minded clung to the comforting darkness of ignorance? They had called him mad. Yet, was he?

On his book, he ran his finger around the painted ring, traced the edges of the etched symbols, caressed the texture of sigils and wards. His eyes darted to the fast-approaching hillock, and the standing stones coronating it like a Queen's crown. For as much as it was an important part of his project, that circle was far less concerning tonight. Because what he craved for was sitting on the top of a drumlin, behind that set of ancient standing stones. Finally, as the coach reached the top, the solitary menhir came into view. A group of six men, soaked to the bone by the savage rain, were binding the ancient pillar with heavy chains, while a couple of muscular oxen mooed nervously just below on the muddy pathway.

"Stop!" he cried to the coachman. He was eager to make sure that those illiterate had not damaged his precious diagram around the Cailli stone. Surrounding the ancient menhir was a large ring of dark metal, etched into the soaked ground. Hugh had crafted the ring in pure iron, for no other metal or natural rock had to interfere with its qualities. He trundled on the muck, his black shoes and grey stockings immediately turning reddish-brown with it. One of the men, a robust individual with a face more apt for the Dublin docks than for serving a gentleman, turned to him; his meaty left fist clutching one end of the chains, the right one fighting a losing battle to sweep rain away from his face. "We're ready, sir!" he shouted in the downpour.

Talbot ignored him, and the incessant rain. He circled the stone, examined every inch of the ring; its notches, its symbols, and the wards. Satisfied, he looked up to the menhir, checking the triple rounds of the heavy chains, and, when he was finally sure that everything was exactly as he had planned, he allowed a smirk to form on his lips. "I know you will try all the tricks to make sure I will fail," he mumbled, "but it won't happen."

The large man looked at him quizzically, sure the master had been speaking to him, but a quick gesture of dismissal showed him different. Then, Hugh opened the case he was carrying, and pulled out a large medallion. Made of a dull grayish metal, streaked with silvery veins, it was in the shape of a five-pointed star, surrounded by a ring. At the center of it, where the intersecting lines formed a pentagon, was a flame-enshrouded eye. Cautiously, Talbot placed the final ward in front of the menhir, inside the iron ring, then he stepped back. Signaling the men to start pulling, he began his mantra.

Acba Pein yin Keron. Acba Pein yin Keron. Acba Pein yin Keron...

The oxen pulled at the chains, prodded by one of the workers. The other men added their strength.

Acba Pein yin Keron. Acba Pein yin Keron. Acba Pein yin Keron...

The standing stone trembled, then tilted to the side.

Acba Pein yin Keron. Acba Pein yin Keron. Acba Pein yin Keron...

A blade appeared out of Talbot's cloak, then the sharp metal cut the palm of his left hand.

Come Infernal, Terrestrial, and Heavenly One. Thou of the broad roadways, of the crossroads. Thou who goest to and fro at night. Thou, enemy of the day.

Drops of blood mixed with the muddy water.

Thou who doest rejoice at the howl of dogs. Thou who art walking in the void between the stars. Come.

The rain worsened. The stone slid sideways in the mud. As a fang forcibly extracted from the jaw of a ferocious giant, it swung over the drumlin's edge, threatening to collapse on the pulling men. Quickly, the workers moved to the other side and pushed. The chains became taut to the extreme as the oxen moved further downhill.

Then, unexpected, the dry and sharp sound of cracking stone rang from the drumlin, and a large fissure appeared at the base of the menhir. The five men barely had time to react, for the long and narrow depression quickly wormed through the rocky surface and, inexplicably, caused the upper half of the stone to get free from its base and start sliding on the jagged remains of its root. Talbot watched in terror as the giant slab of ancient rock hit the ground, crushing the leg of the dour-faced worker under its weight, before rolling toward him. In that instant, he knew he had failed and was going to die for his insolence. He had dared to challenge a superior force. In his hubris, he had failed to foresee that outcome.

Amidst screams of pain, he closed his eyes and waited to die.

Unseen hands pushed him away with force and he found himself tumbling into a tumbling and blurry world of shadows and murky water. Then his head hit something hard and the blurriness was replaced by total darkness.

And in that darkness, the taste of his failure became bilious, turning truth into denial.

Later.

Hugh Nigel Talbot was a man of honor and generosity. Yet he could also be bitter and resentful.

He spared no expenses for the funeral of Niall O'Grady, the man who, with courage and promptness, had jumped into peril to save his master from certain death. And had lost his own life in this. Niall had been a loyal servant, an excellent coachman, and somehow, even if etiquette and bearings set them apart, a good friend. Talbot made sure that his family received a fair and substantial compensation for the loss.

This wasn't the case for Michael Drury.

Talbot accused the man of negligence, blaming him for the cracking of the Cailli stone and the consequent death of O'Grady, even if the poor man had lost his left leg in the mishap. Stubbornly, he refused to pay any indemnity, thus he gained a bad repute among the folk of Ballymoor.

Nonetheless, he didn't care. As he stood triumphantly on the top of Gorta cave, now orphan of its landmark, he had thoughts only for the next step of his ritual. He had ordered the fallen stone to be cut into pieces, and for the slabs to be used for decorating his house. The base, that insolent root which obstinately had refused to part from the ground, he had it dug out. It became the mantel of Talbot House's main hearth, to be bathed forever by warm firelight.

In his delusion, he had prevailed.

The slave had become the master. Deprived of its *Focus* stone, the henge behind Talbot House was no longer a gateway, but a prison.

Once the house was finished and Talbot could finally move in, he gloated in the power he had captured. But he needed to venture beyond: he had to have proof that he controlled that power, and not the reverse. As he studied the ritual of the *Bonds of the Black Dog*, he smiled, thinking about Annie Carrick. The ignorant woman had willingly accepted to become the puppet of the very power she had longed for. Though these powers lay in eternal slumber, their dark essence, inimical to Man, was splintered and brought into the world through terrible dreams. Dreams that reach out for the aching soul, that beckon to the lost, the greedy, and the vengeful, promising comfort in their darkness.

But Hugh was different. He had no dreams of greed, nor thirst for vengeance. There was nothing that the Darkness could offer him. So, in his wisdom and knowledge, he had enslaved the Darkness; he had chained the Beast.

It was too late when he came out of his delusion.

PART ONE: *THE JOURNAL OF PATRICK CONROY* 1891

CHAPTER ONE

April 25th, 1891
Bridge End Inn, Ballymoor, County Wicklow, Ireland.
Morning.

Dublin isn't the best for a young student of medicine to prepare his final examination. It offers too many distractions, especially to an American abroad. So, needing isolation for my studies, especially from my jolly peers, yesterday I decided to pack a travel trunk with all the clothes a gentleman could do no less and all the books I necessitated, went to the Westland Row Station, looked at town names on the timetable, and selected the first train to the Wicklow countryside.

Born in Marblehead, Massachusetts, I'm the last in line of a family of Irish immigrants who found their luck in the American fishing industry. Not respected for their roots, yet extremely appreciated for their money, mine is a good-hearted family that has never forgotten their less fortunate kin back in the motherland. When the potato famine struck Ireland in 1845, they sent money and shipped goods for those in need.

But I, well, I'm from a different pot.

Being the last in the Conroy bloodline, I have been pampered from birth and I'm still the sparkle in my family's eye. I'm used to comfort and beauty, and barely tolerate untidiness and poverty.

When I demanded to go and study medicine at the Royal College of Surgeons in Dublin – mostly for the thrill of having new adventures in a different country rather than for the school's prestige – my father felt so proud he immediately called for a gargantuan party, inviting all the Irish families of Marblehead, and, as Irish parties usually go, it lasted a whole day.

Alas, in Dublin, being a lover of gentle company and easy life, I allowed Dionysus and Aphrodite to be my companions more than Aesculapius and Panacea, and again, I spent more time partying with my pals than studying the mysteries of anatomy, so when the time of reckoning finally came I found myself in the desperate need to plunge my nose inside those heavy books and stuff my brain with their content. Hence my decision to find an isolated place in the countryside.

At the end of a pleasant trip, I alighted at Bray, then took the first coach to Ballymoor, a tiny hamlet nestled in the Wicklow moors. The journey to Ballymoor exposed me to much of the beauty this land offers and I feel myself impatient to start the long, solitary walks I have planned during my sojourn. After a stop at Anniskerry to rest the horses and pick up other passengers (though none came aboard), we finally arrived at Ballymoor. It's a charming, picturesque village that doesn't offer much to the adventure-seeker, but, I'm sure, it will help me focus on my studies. Immediately, I booked room at the local inn, had a hearty supper – followed by a not so good tea, I must say – and went straight to bed.

The innkeeper's wife, Kathleen Yares, insisted on helping me with my heavy travel trunk, though I staunchly refused.

What kind of gentleman would have a woman hoist such a heavy hog!

She is a nice and helpful lady and only has good words about her peers. Although born down the ladder, she is surprisingly well-educated, speaks with no accent, and seems to be more worldly than you could expect from a countrywoman. She told me that her husband, Kevin, was asleep, and she didn't want to wake him up because he had had a terrible day working hard to fix the inn's roof.

I could see in her eyes that she loves the man heart, body and soul.

I hope that when I fall under Cupid's spell (as far in time as possible, may God help me), I will find a woman like her: devoted, lovely, and helpful.

This morning, rested and full of goodwill, I opted to mix with the locals in the common room, and after a full breakfast, decided to approach the innkeeper – a burly man, simple but well-mannered – to inquire about anyone willing to rent a cottage or a house in the countryside. This man, Kevin, told me there was not such a big choice in a place as Ballymoor, but he remembered a mansion that would surely suit the city gentleman I am. He said he was given duty by a local landlord, who now lives in Cork for he has no interest in this forgotten village, to rent his property for seasonal or yearly inhabitation on his behalf. Nonetheless, the innkeeper was sure he would not truly mind having a rich stranger lining his pockets for a shorter stay. He said it is an old but magnificent house set in the lovely Pooka hills, a stone's throw from the village, which was built by a formerly influential family in 1780. However, its isolation and ill repute had scared off any potential lodger or buyer. Excited, especially by the word 'isolation', I completely ignored the 'ill repute' and enthusiastically offered him enough money for a three-month rent, though my intent is to spend just one month in there. Surprised by my eagerness, the good man emphasized that the place, known as Talbot House, was quite lonely and a young man like me would certainly fare better in a bigger town; after all there aren't many amenities to entertain and distract a man of my age in the moors. Smiling, I told him that distraction was the thing I was escaping from, and that isolation was what I fancied as I needed its dour companionship to complete my studies. I still do not understand what happened next.

Kathleen came out of the kitchen and gifted him with one of those burning gazes that had the man fry on the spot. His usually placid lineaments filled with concern. It was as if a ghost had passed through him, and taken by some inexplicable regret, he said that it would be better for me to be told about the bad repute Talbot House had gained through the years, and why it was shunned by everybody.

At that, I immediately lifted my hand, rebuking that, being a man of science, I didn't want to listen to local superstitions and tall tales. Still smiling, I added that as much as I appreciated his concern, I didn't want my mind to set sail on such nonsense: a house is a house, a shelter built by man, not by fairies and bogeys, and that knowing any fantastic tale about alleged dark deeds or events that happened in, or around, that building would just make my already creative mind wander to places I didn't have time to visit.

So, with a swift move, I grabbed the man's hand, slapped a large number of notes in his palm, and then asked for the keys and directions to the place. Befuddled, but unable to fight back, the innkeeper gave me all I needed. However, he informed me that finding anyone in the village to come over there for housekeeping or cooking would be near impossible since many of the oldest families distrust Talbot House. I replied that I don't believe in the impossible and that money would surely cast the mists of fear away, replacing them with the golden sunshine of good Irish whiskey. That said, I slapped another note on the bar and offered a free drink to all the patrons. Cheers of joy and blessing filled the inn's air, and after gulping down one myself, I winked at the innkeeper and merrily strode out of the tavern.

As I crossed the threshold that would lead me into this new adventure, I heard Kevin Yares shouting, "May ye be in heaven half an hour afore the Divil knows ye're dead, lad."

CHAPTER TWO

April 25th, 1891
On the road to Talbot House.
Afternoon.

To some, the road to Talbot House might hardly be called a road as it wounds through large patches of muddy moorland, bends around a fast-flowing stream, then narrows and almost disappears in the mire. Here and there you can spot the solitary cottage, but the rest is all a desolate landscape of low, damp hills made even more forlorn by the dense mist hugging them.

What follows is the *extraordinaire* experience I had this afternoon while traveling on that twisted path.

After leaving the Bridge End Inn, I rented a cart, pulled by a strong draft horse named Bertha, from a local, so I could reach my new residence – and carry my heavy travel trunk – alone and before sunset. The vehicle is old and uncomfortable, and the draft animal is quite temperamental, yet it is sturdy and its wheels seem able to tread on the occasional hard rock jutting out of the mud.

After one hour on the trail all signs of human inhabitation disappeared, leaving me and the horse alone inside that pearly fog. The pounding of the horse's heavy hooves grew inside that sea of whiteness and dampness invaded my clothes, causing me great discomfort. Except for the *cloppity-clop*, there was a stillness in the air, as if the whole area had silently been waiting for my arrival. A negative sense of anticipation took home inside my heart, and for a moment, my firmness to go and spend a month inside that mansion faltered and I almost ordered the horse to stop. But then my rational, modern mind kicked back like a bewildered donkey, and I incited the animal to proceed.

Once that moment of weakness was over, I noticed that even the pea-soup fog was parting ways; the oppressive vapors had begun to fade and were now crossing the path in strands and patches similar to a flock of migrating birds. Amidst that haziness, I spotted something on the left side of the road: a tall stone standing upright against the dull sky, with strange engravings marring its surface. I recalled something about *broad stones* my grandpa talked about: stones planted by the *Fomorians*, a race of giants who lived in Ireland before the coming of the *Fir Bolg* and the *Tuatha de Danann*. Having never seen one before, I resolved it was an excellent opportunity for me, so I pulled Bertha's bridles, stopping the beast. However, it was far too distant to leave the safety of my cart, and hazarding an excursion into the very moor without proper knowledge of it was out of discussion. Besides, the stone stood atop a low hill, and the strands of fog – paired to the perennial low-lying mist that seems to cling onto the ground in this region – hindered most of the visibility of the eventual crag or peat bog, and it was not in my plans to mar my precious tweed suit and country boots with muck or worse. Especially without a good cleaner available.

That made me think about my main problem: finding a cleaner, and a cook possibly, to help me out in duties I have nor the time nor the will to partake.

While I was looking at the stone and thinking about the housekeeper, something happened. I spotted the outline of a couple of strange figures coming into view at the base of the broad stone. There was something queer about them, and they unnerved me as they, presumably, looked down the hill. Their heads seemed grotesque and too big for any human. More, they looked far from human. One had the shape of a bull, complete of horns and a ringed nose. The other was shaped like a cone with a tuft of hair descending from the top and dangling by the side.

What was I seeing? Were my eyes playing tricks on me?

Bewildered more than scared, I tried to understand what I was seeing, so, remembering my binoculars inside my trunk – the ones I use for bird-watching – I hastily opened my travel companion's lid and jumbled through my clothes and personal effects till I found my trusty helpers. Unfortunately, by the time I returned my eyes to the top the hill, the figures had vanished. Disappointed, I scoured the landscape for traces of the uncanny duo, but I found none. However, this gave me the opportunity to look at the engravings on the stone. Indented cup marks, and abstract shapes and spirals, covered most of the west side while the opposite one was relatively smooth. I intend to visit that megalith one of these days, during one of my planned excursions. I also want to know more about the broad stone and the engravings, so I will ask the villagers when I go back to Ballymoor for food and other supplies.

That was just the first of my encounters today.

The next one was surely more lively, but no less startling.

With time, as the sun reached its zenith in the heavens, that pugnacious fog finally gave up and disappeared, replaced by a dull haze that blurred the distances, but, at least, was no longer sullying my humor. I found myself forgetting about the queer figures and happily whistling a made-up tune. A large bird, a raven or a rook, I suppose, burst out of a bush, protesting about my lack of skill, I think, and I shook my fist at it yelling, "You haven't heard me sing after five rounds at O'Hara's with my whooperups!"

I laughed at that silly joke, reprimanding myself for such nonsensical absurdity. I'm supposed to be a doctor. Well, not yet one, but as a student of natural sciences I should always behave in a rational way. Yet there was no one there listening to my ludicrous tirade. Or so I thought.

In fact, after regaining my composure, I became aware that something or someone was spying on me. I was under the spell of that curious sensation that makes you *feel* someone's eyes on you. Science hasn't found yet an explanation for this phenomenon – maybe it is a yet undiscovered gland in our brain providing us with a sense of warning from predators – but it is a proven thing that we *perceive* being watched. Embarrassed by my previous infantile behavior I shouted a 'who's there?' to the wall of tall bushes on my right where I guessed my peeping Tom was hiding. No answer came. Yet I could hear a distinctive panting and the sound of grass being crushed as something moved behind the wild hedge at the same speed as my trotting horse. It was the horse that startled me, when, for no visible reason, it sunk its hooves in the muck and neighed, shaking its large neck, then snorted as if challenging whatever was out there.

Wolves! was my first, stupid thought. Then, I recalled that my father used to say that no one had seen a wolf in Ireland since the times of Cromwell. Still, I was worried, so I shook the bridles, commanding the stubborn animal to continue our path home, this time faster. But the beast refused to comply; instead, it lowered its head, flared its nostrils, and started digging the ground with its right front hoof.

Bertha is a Clydesdale mare, bay in color with white markings on the face and legs, with an extensive white feathering on the fetlock that almost covers the hoof, and weighing around two thousand pounds. She's a big lady and doesn't like to be threatened, as I learned today. More, when she feels danger she doesn't flee, but stubbornly stands her ground ready to charge and kick whatever gets closer.

This reminds me to tell Mr. Flanagan, her master, that he rented me a warhorse and not a placid dray.

I yelled, yahooed like those cowboys out in the west do with their horses, kicked her in the backside, but nothing. She just got more nervous and kept pawing the ground and shaking her head. The situation began to be a little tedious rather than scary, and, in frustration, I reached for the whip.

It was at that moment that the first large canine came out of the bushes, snarling angrily. The sound of its growling froze the blood in my veins and my heart skipped a beat or two. I watched in terror as the large shaggy beast feigned a bite to the mare's front right leg, then backed off, exposing its glistening sharp teeth. It wasn't a wolf, but worse: a ferocious Irish wolfhound.

Bigger than a wolf, dark gray, and with strong jaws, that animal looked dangerous. I had no weapons with me, as I'm not in love with hunting, yet even if I had one, I doubt I would be able to stay calm enough to hit the beast in such a way to cause it any considerable damage. As if not enough, another one, smaller, but still threatening, came bounding down the hill, barking and showing its teeth.

I dare to say I felt like a poor piglet left alone in a wolf's den; I couldn't move and Bertha was surely showing more bravery than me. She reared, then started to kick the empty air as the two dogs were smart enough to stay away from such a combative behemoth. Problem was, Bertha was attached to the cart, and I was on the cart, so when she lifted from the ground the vehicle tilted in accordance and I found myself losing my balance and falling off the deck straight into the rear. I lost grip of the whip and used my hands to land safely into the van. When Bertha returned her hooves to the ground, the cart jolted back horizontally and I was hurled toward the headboard, whilst my heavy trunk rushed toward me. Again, I used my arms to dampen the impact with the rushing box, and I cursed myself for bringing along that gravid hog of a trunk as pain flamed in my hands.

My tragedy turned into comedy when I heard the horse and dogs squaring into a bloodless standoff while I was fighting to regain my footing and keep my own travel trunk away from me. Then, out of thin air, I heard a stern but clearly feminine voice shouting something incomprehensible at first, but it soon became clear she was calling her dogs.

"Adair! Kalie! Come!"

I peeked out of the cart and saw the two dogs begrudgingly walk back up the hill, tails guiltily between their legs, toward a black haired young woman whose features I couldn't see. She was wearing a long, front-buttoned, embroidered white dress, and a brightly-colored scarf around her waist. Her curly hair fell in waves about her shoulders, disappearing behind her back.

While the dogs reached their master – and Bertha relaxed – I, not without difficulty, regained my balance and a more elegant posture. I dusted my jacket off, retrieved my hat, straightened it, and then ran my hands on the back of my trousers to wipe off the dust that was surely clustering on my backside. And, to my horror, I found out I had a large rip in the fabric!

"Are you well?" demanded the young woman, while getting closer. "I apologize for my hounds' behavior, it was not my intent to cause any damage." With every step she took, I became more aware of her beauty.

Sparkling jade gems.

That was the first thing that came to my mind the moment I saw those gorgeous green eyes. Her skin was a bit darker than the porcelain tone many of the island's girls sport, nonetheless, her cheeks showed the radiant blush that only a cool, moist climate can bring. She wore no makeup; however, a couple a silver earrings paired with a necklace holding a heart-shaped locket gave her a bit of female vanity.

She was the jammiest bits of jam.

"I'm fine," I said, one hand desperately clutching the torn fabric of my pants as if, by pinching it, I could somehow mend the atrocious gap. "I'm sure your dogs aren't so used to strangers in such a place." Etiquette and gallantry required that I dismounted the vehicle to be at the same height of the lady, but I was afraid that by doing so, I was going to show her the sad and inopportune sight of my knickers peeking out of my lacerated trousers. So I stood there like an idiot, smiling and evidently poked up. She noticed my awkwardness, but thinking I was afraid of the dogs, she commanded her hairy companions to go back to the *vardo* (the meaning of this word, I discovered later). They growled at me despite her protests, but, at last, still grumbling, they climbed up the hill and disappeared in the underbrush.

Maggie (that's her name) is a smart lass.

In fact, she soon noticed my distress – and my queer stance – and with a wry but benevolent smile, she pointed at me and said, "I don't think you can continue in your voyage in that condition, my good sir. It would be nice of me, and the least I can do to apologize for the accident, to invite you to my vardo, where you can ease your bones with the warmth of a good tea and have me repair the damage that occurred to your trousers."

I felt myself turn red, but, also, couldn't refrain a chuckle.

"I reckon you are a bright, if rather forward, dame," I said. "Nonetheless, I must decline your – even if tempting – invitation." I looked at the sky, eager to be at the mansion before dark. The dogs and the strange figures had upset me, and, I'm not ashamed to say, the dreariness of the moor was playing on my nerves.

"I insist," she said, coming closer as if to bar my way. "By not accepting my hospitality you are not only insulting me, but my whole clan."

A *clan*? What was she on about? Yes, I knew that in Ireland there were families that could trace their lineage to ancestral clans of the island, but in these modern times, clans were seen as things of old; a vestigial appendage that Cromwell, and later the British Empire, had gone to great length to amputate from the proud heritage of Irish folk. The clans, like in Scotland, had been a major source of upheaval in this country. They weren't just outlawed. They were wiped out.

Anyway, I didn't want to offend anyone, especially such a lovely lady, so, with embarrassment on my face, I proffered my apologies, "In this case, I must accept." Then, I moved to the box seat, careful to not show too much of my indecorous predicament, and offered her my hand to help her climb aboard. The warmness of her hand surprised me, and I found that her brief, gentle touch somehow dispelled the dreadfulness that had taken home in my heart.

She is of pleasant company and of joyful demeanor, in plain contrast to the land she lives in. During the trip to her vardo (she explained to me that's the way her people, the Travellers, call their wagon-homes) she giggled at my jokes with the intimacy of long-time friends. I know most men would find such behavior a bit too inconvenient for a lady, and would surely misjudge her friendliness, but, as I discovered later, the nomadic folks of Ireland have a much relaxed attitude and are quick to friendship and slow to anger. I will write later about the Travellers and their customs, as well as about their exceptional hospitality.

She introduced herself as Maggie Blair, granddaughter of Siobhan of clan Blair. She lives with her old grandmother, her uncle Ben, and her two dogs in vardos close by the trail, and, it appears, they are all that is left of their clan. In the past, they had been part of a larger tribe, the Szeks, a mixture of local Traveller families and gypsies from Eastern Europe (hence the use of 'vardo' in their slang), but some bad happenings had caused the families to split, and now her family survives as tinkers, fixing pots and pans, buying old horses and breeding dogs. They are looked with suspicion by the village folk of Ballymoor, who often accuse them of trespassing and stealing. However, they do not disdain their simple but precious craft, and regularly employ them with menial tasks like restoring a malfunctioning hand pump or cleaning soot from chimneys.

Their vardos are colored affairs, encrusted with decorations and rather picturesque. It is inside such a mobile home that I'm writing now while I'm waiting for Maggie and her granny to be back from Uncle Ben's wagon. The poor guy is suffering from a nasty bronchitis, with a strong fever, and I'm worried he's verging on pneumonia. I suggested he was hospitalized as soon as possible, but his mother, Maggie's granny, strongly declined my offer to pay for transport. She said she knew what he needed and that she would take care of him. Siobhan is a stubborn woman, proud of her heritage and suspicious of townspeople. More, she doesn't trust modern medicine and thinks that everything can and must be cured by herbs. I'm afraid such an attitude is going to cost poor Ben his life, but I'm a guest here and I can't intrude too much.

Side note: I'm wearing a pair of Uncle Ben's trousers Siobhan kindly offered me while Maggie fixes mine. They are large, faded, and look like a couple of hay sacks sewn together.

I'm feeling quite uncomfortable.

April 25th, 1891
Talbot House.
Night.

Finally at home.

It has been a long and wearing day and I'm glad to finally rest my tired legs and enjoy the comfort of my bed.

Still, I can't sleep: I'm too excited by this afternoon's events, my meeting with Maggie Blair, and all the extraordinary things I've learned about the Travellers. My new home ended up being a real disappointment. It is a magnificent mansion indeed, but left in such state of neglect and disrepair that it looks like a renovator's nightmare.

But I will write about it later.

Now I want to pen down what I learned about Maggie's people, the way Siobhan Blair told me.

The Travellers or *Pavees* in their own language – the *Gammon* – are small family groups who travel the length and breadth of Ireland in horse-drawn wagons. Though leading a nomadic lifestyle similar to that of the Romany gypsies, they are of an unrelated breed. Their origins are surrounded by legends and myths. One of them states they are what is left of the vanished clan Murtagh O'Connors. This clan, though one of the numerous branches descending from the High King of Ireland *Toirdelbach Ua Conchobair*, somehow decided to adopt nomadic ways. Another, more plausible story reckons they descend from those Irish families who were made homeless by Oliver Cromwell's military campaign in the 1650s. The problem lies in the fact that they have no written records, as they prefer to verbally pass on their history. They are known for mending pots, pans and cutlery, so they are also called *tinkers* by townsfolk, and sometimes, unflatteringly, *knackers* because they buy dead or old horses to slaughter them and then sell the by-products. They also breed dogs, notably wolfhounds and greyhounds, especially for hare coursing. One source of conflict with the settled population lies in the fact that Travellers do not respect borders and governance and often set camp in privately-owned land. Considering themselves as outsiders, they tend to stay away from political upheavals, though most of them are devout Roman Catholics and wish Ireland to be freed from the yoke of Britain.

All of this I learned in my conversation with Siobhan, head of the Blair family.

This woman is something to be seen.

Her face is strong, almost hawkish, with a high bridge on a thin nose, a sharp forehead, and a big mop of stark white hair growing barely at the sides, yet copiously elsewhere. Her bushy eyebrows surmount watery, blue eyes, and thin lips scarcely hide her decaying teeth. Her colorful clothes, golden jewelry, and exotic bangles add to the stereotypical fairground gypsy appearance I suspect she built for herself on purpose, as she likes to act in a theatrical way. Her voice crackles like dry weeds, with a thick Irish brogue. Nonetheless, she is a good-natured woman, with a strong respect for hospitality. In fact, she treated me like royalty during the time I spent at her camp, offering me a dark – but pleasant – slightly tangy tea, which came with a few dry biscuits I had never seen before. She had Maggie take care of my torn trousers, and asked me many questions as to my journey from Dublin. The woman showed interest about my studies and seemed curious to know more on the lifestyle of the Irish living in America. I told her about my family and what they do, about my dreams and my failures. I don't know why, but I spoke to her like she was *my* grandma, and in more than one instance I found my tongue loosening and blurting out beans I should have reserved for private cooking. Withal, she never showed disrespect, nor did she scoff about my plans for the future.

Time passed so fast inside her cozy wagon, that I noticed lunchtime had been and gone. The grumblings from my irreverent stomach were pressing me to say good-bye, but Siobhan acted before I could start my polite leave-taking.

"Ye haft to be hungriest than wolf, me dear," she said. "Plaze, furgive tis nozy ould woman, that puts her curiosity afore good manners." Then, she quickly snapped something to Maggie in their cryptic language and the lassie hastily disappeared behind a curtain. Again, having guessed her intention, I tried to protest gently, but the sweet lady interrupted me in the same way my granny would do. "I'll not let ye go widout a sup. Do ye want me to be branded a deshpicable host? Phat wuld yer family tink av me?"

"I ..." I hazarded a weak objection, but she wouldn't listen.

"I pray ye to stay set down wor ye are, me good sir, an' at as much as ye plaze," she smiled, then moved toward the curtain. "Ye'll axcuse us fur not sharin' yer table, fur we are afastin' to honour our gone ansisthers."

"It is a holy day for your clan?" I inquired. Behind the drapery I could hear the sound of dishes and cutlery. "I think I've abused too much of your kind generosity."

Siobhan reappeared, stone faced. "Ye're me guest, Mr. Conroy, so, plaze, behav as wan. Tis not America. Tis not Dublihn." She looked offended. "Our ways might seem queer to ye, but thim are always behnevolent. Iverything we do is done wid our heart, an' wid no harrum intended."

This practically closed the conversation as she disappeared behind the drapery. The pair didn't come out until they had finished their task, leaving me in an embarrassing solitude, sporadically interrupted by Siobhan as she set up the tableware. The white, embroidered cloth was spotless, and the cutlery looked like genuine silver. As for the glasses, they were exquisitely crafted out of the finest crystal, and so were the water jug and a decanter full of golden cider.

When Maggie finally emerged from the wagon's private section, she came forward, smiling, laid a ceramic dish on the table, and ceremoniously took the cover off, revealing a delectable roasted chicken surrounded by a sea of green beans. This, along with goat cheese and dark bread, was my lunch today. And the leftovers became my soup tonight, for Siobhan insisted I should dine in a proper way because she found me quite underweight for my age.

Later, I recalled the strange figures I had seen around the standing stone and, hesitantly, asked Siobhan if she knew what they might be.

"Oh, those," she said cackling like a crow. "Those have to be certainly Mummers." As if that explained everything. She must have noticed my befuddlement for as she soon added, "Mummers are like actors. Thim frolic masked folk plays durin' the winter months an' particularly over the solstice. In fact, Beltane is approachin' an' the Ballymoor Mummers are surely rehearsing at the feet av *Ould Lugh*."

Clearly, I know nothing about pagan customs, my family being a devout Catholic one. However, Siobhan explained to me that these plays descend from the Celts and are a reenactment of the struggle between the light of summer and the dark of winter. The Mummers hope to gain the favor of the goddess, and to end the dark of winter and have spring reborn. They wear straw and wicker masks representing strange characters with obscure names, like the Captain, the Green Knight, Brian Boru, and Devil Doubt.

I asked what '*Old Lugh*' was and Siobhan told me she herself can't remember why that standing stone bears that name, but she thinks it is connected with Lughnasad, the summer solstice. As for Beltane, she told me it is an ancient festival celebrating the turning of seasons and the possible coming of summer. It is celebrated on the 1st of May and folk believe that the night before it, much like Halloween, the otherworld is particularly close and denizens from that realm can be easily contacted. Siobhan, who has traveled extensively through Europe, says that it is called *Walpurgis nacht*. At Beltane, huge bonfires are lit on prominent hills across the country and cattle is driven between them to be purified.

People also walk between the fires to be cleansed, or dance around them in a clockwise direction to bring luck.

Time soon came for me to thank the Traveller's hospitality and say farewell, as I didn't particularly fancy a journey in the dark, so I told Siobhan and Maggie I really appreciated their company but had to leave as soon as possible if I wanted to be at Talbot Mansion before sundown.

At the mention of that name, the old woman froze; the joviality that had kept us company in the two or three hours we had spent together vanished, replaced by a cold and dreadful silence.

Then, Siobhan broke it. "Do ye know wor ye goin', young man?"

"Yes," I said. "I know that people in Ballymoor consider that place cursed, but I don't believe in ghosts, or curses, or the evil eye. I'm a man of science, and as such, my trust resides in knowledge, not in legends."

"Ye're new folk, lad," she rebuked, then grasped my hand in such a way that, for a moment, I really thought she was my granny. "Ye belave only in phat yer eyes can see. Mind ye, heed my words: there are things that can't be seen, but still axist." Her hand was becoming a vise around my wrist. It was ridiculous and ominous at the same time, and I wasn't feeling comfortable. I didn't know what to say; I couldn't offend her beliefs after being treated like a long lost son.

"Answer, jintleman," she demanded. "Do ye know why we keep those dogs?"

"For breeding? To sell their pups?" I hazarded. I was frankly surprised by the question; I couldn't see the connection between fairy tales and their dogs.

"Nay." She looked at her granddaughter as if begging her to try and put some reason in my empty American head. "Dogs can see things fur phat they thruly are. It says iven childher have that gift till the age av twelfe, then the veil av ignorance falls on thim eyes. Childher, as do dogs, have an intensely curious mind, wide open to ideas that adults would rayject. To thim, the world is wan wundrous place, wor iverything is possible. Thim can see the lil' folk livin' under the mound. Thim can sense the monster under the bed." She smiled trying to look more convincing. "Dogs can iven see phat's invisible to human eyes. An' those things out there, those things that come out at night, know tis. Thim hate an' fear dogs as thim can see the decepshun. Especially sight-hounds. An' our wolfhounds," she pointed outside, "know exactly what's out there, prowlin' the peat bog behind Talbot House."

I tried to gently get free of her grasp, and said, as kindly as I could, that I appreciated her concern, but I was no longer a child, so, whatever her dogs could see it was not my vexation. Again, I didn't want to offend the good woman who had been so kind to me, but at the same time, I didn't want to be afflicted by local superstitions. As a Catholic, I have been taught to regard superstition as idolatry, and as a student, to treat it as primitive and obscurantist.

"Moreover," I scoffed, "I'm going to spend the nights inside the mansion, not wandering in the moor. And by day, as you said, these things, whatever they are, will not bother or harm me."

She wouldn't listen. "Aye, it is bad av me to insist, but the mere thought av ye, a young jintleman, goin' to live there all alone make the hairs av me shtan' up like a mad cat's tail." Then, she released my wrist. "Wor ye av me blood ye wudn't sleep in such a tainted plaice a single night!"

She was so unmistakably worried that, although amazed by that scene out of a penny dreadful, I felt touched. So, I took her hand back and smiled. "You see, my dear Mrs. Blair, you need not be concerned over me. A student who is delving into the anatomy of man has no time to be disturbed by these mysterious apparitions. Veins, arteries, and blood circulation have sufficient mysteries to keep me busy during the days I'm going to spend there." I kissed her hand, then, bowing, I moved to the entrance, ready to continue my journey.

"Nayther make nor meddle with the sper'ts." Siobhan recited. "If ye're goin' along the lonely boreen at night and ye hear, from a mound or a stone, a sound av fiddles, or av pipin', or sweet voices singin', or av lil' feet pattherin' in the dance, don't turn yer head, but say yer prayers an' hould on yer way. Fur the plazures the Good People'll share wid ye have a sore sorrow hid in thim, an' the gifts they'll offer are only made to break the hearts."

"You forget the leprechaun, Granny," irrupted Maggie, smiling and winking at me, "You can't deny that to catch the little fellow is great luck. It says that if one only fix the glance of his eyes on him, that look makes the fairy guy a prisoner."

I smiled back and added, "And he'll give you three wishes to buy his freedom, right?"

Maggie nodded, and so did Siobhan, however, there was no trace of a smile on her face. She turned to her granddaughter, admonishing her, "An' may the Lord help ye, child!" Then, she eyed me. "Fur around the favours av thim same three wishes lies a bog av tricks an' conditions that'll defayt the wisest. Iven whin he does grant the wishes, ye're not safe, fur, if ye tell annywan ye've seen the luricawne, those favours melt like snow on the stove, or if ye make a fourth wish that same day – swoosh! They turn into smoke. So, heed my advice – nayther make nor meddle with the fairies. An' that's the trickiest lil' divil that iver wore a brogue, mind ye."

But Maggie insisted. "And what about Darby O'Rourke of Cork? It is said he captured one and never had to work a single day of his life. He died rich. And what about the magic purse with the charmed shilling? Only one shilling, but the wonder is, no matter how often you dig from it, there'll always be one inside there."

"Tis be thrue," admitted Siobhan, but also added, "But fur wan who git it right it don't mean that's the rule. Tink about Dennis O'Bryan av Tipperary."

I was charmed by their exchange. I was there listening to true Irish legends (or stories), inside a mobile home in the middle of nowhere. Though it was late, I couldn't resist but listen to the story Siobhan offered to narrate as a moral tale.

Here I pen it down the way she told me.

The Tale of Dennis O'Bryan and the Leprechaun

"Tis Dennis was a young, lazy lad, always apeepin' undher the hidge fur to ketch a luricawne, fur he hated work worse than sin. Wan day he was comin' home whin he seen the lil' fellow. Quiet as cat he jumped on him, an' grippin' him be the collar, he thin pushed him on the ground.

"Arrah, give up yer goold, says he, I've got ye at last!

"Begob, I've no goold, says the luricawne, an' begs, an' scritches, an' cries, an' says he's not a rale luricawne, but a jintleman midget that hadn't anny goold.

"But Dennis didn't belave him, an' wudn't let go av him. Thin outs wid yer magic purse, says he, or by jakers I'll choke the life out av ye, says he, shakin' the luricawne an' squeezin' him so hard till the lil' man's eyes stand so out ye cud knock thim off wid a shtick.

"At last, the luricawne gave in, an' in exchange fur his life he offered his magic purse to Dennis. The man tuk the purse, looked at it to make sure it was av red shilk, an' had the shillin' in it, but the minnit he tuk his eyes off the luricawne, away wint the rogue wid a laugh that Dennis disloiked much.

"Annyway, Dennis is feelin' comfortable be havin' the purse, an says to himself, I'll dhrink till a pump can't squaze wan dhrop more down me neck, an off he goes fur Miss Clooney's tavern. In he goes, an' there wor his friends, an' he pulls up a sate an' down he sets, a-callin' to Miss Clooney to bring in the best.

"Where's yer goold, says she to him, fur he didn't use to have, barrin' a tuppence or so.

"Do ye have no fear, says he, I'm a jintleman av forchune. Come jintlemin, dhrink at my axpinse. An' so they did, an' Miss Clooney brought dhrink and dinner, the best of the house. As he ordered more, Miss Clooney dimands to see the money, so he pulls out the magic purse to show at thim and told thim phat it was an' where he got it.

"An' was it the luricawne gev it ye? says they.

"It was, says he, then he fishes out wan shillin' fur all to see. An' thin, he puts his fingers afther another, but none was there, fur the luricawne made a ijit av him, an' instid o' givin' him the right purse, gev him wan just like it, so as onless ye looked clost, ye cudn't make out the differ betune thim.

"To the divil wid ye an' yer luricawnes, an' magic purses, an' pots of goold, screams Miss Clooney. Ye're a thafe! says she, an' she hits him a powerful crack on the head wid a bottle. An' the other fellas got on him an' belted him out.

"There, a polisman comes along, an' hearin' the phillalloo, comes in.

"Lave off. Phat the matther here? says he. So thim told him an' he suspected Dennis shtole the purse.

"Lave go, says Dannis. Phat the harrum o' gittin' the purse av a luricawne?

"None, says the polisman, but av ye projuice the luricawne an' make him teshtify he gev it ye, says he.

"But Dennis cudn't do it, so the polisman tumbled him into jail. From that he got thirty days at hard labour, that he niver done in his life afore, an' afther he got out he left lookin' fur luricawne forever."

Charming, isn't it?

I thanked Mrs. Blair for sharing that tale and asked permission to write it down in my journal.

Subsequently, I remembered about my need of assistance. "Dear ladies, if you really want to help me, I'm in need of a maid and a cook. Maybe even a factotum. Can you help me find a skillful and willing aide?"

At that, courageous Maggie broke in. "I'm ready and willing!"

Her grandmother looked at her with brazen eyes, and then she said something in Gammon I, naturally, couldn't understand, but it was enough to put her back in line. Thinking that Mrs. Blair's preoccupation was about having her young grandchild alone under the same roof with a young man, I intervened and explained that I just needed someone to clean the house and cook for me in my absence, as I would spend the daylight hours walking the countryside and studying under some tree, so that no inconvenience would be caused. Yet Siobhan wasn't listening to me as she was too busy arguing with her granddaughter in their obscure language.

Oh, wish I could understand it!

Again, I explained my reasons and offered Maggie – and Mrs. Blair – a large sum of money, more than local landlords offer for menial tasks. Now, I don't know if it was my generous offer or something else that helped change the old woman's mind, because, suddenly, she turned to me and, in plain English, said she accepted the deal. Amazed and confused at the same time, I paid a full advance – which Siobhan immediately pocketed – then I kissed Maggie's hand and finally went out of the wagon. The two women followed me to the cart and, before I could leave, Mrs. Blair had me swear on my honor that Maggie would be allowed to be back home long before sunset, and that she could bring the dogs with her. I wasn't too happy about having those snarling pests around my 'haunted house', but I wasn't in the position to refuse, so I conceded her request and finally resumed my journey.

I saw the house for the first time when the sky was turning a russet color, and dark clouds, promising rain, were gathering on the horizon. Silhouetted darkly against the rusty sky, the three-story house looked magnificent. However, once I got closer its picturesque decoy was soon replaced by the forlorn truth.

Surrounded by a tangled garden, which itself is bordered by a high stone wall, it stands partially masked by dead and dying trees. Silent it stands; withdrawn, brooding, cobwebbed by wild ivy, and exposed to the wind. Coming closer, the remains of the whitewash that once protected its wooden clapboards, along with the last remnants of paint blasted from its surface by the harsh Irish winters, can be spotted. The windows, thick and substantial, are sealed by hinged, wooden shutters, closed against the outside world as if privy to the secret stories the place hides. Yes, it is large, well-constructed, with high ceilings and thick walls and doors. Nonetheless, from the outside, an acute observer can't fail to notice the queer, slightly tilted appearance; the foundations seem solid enough when viewed closely, yet, the house itself stands oddly crooked. The extensive garden, with stone benches, planters, and a fountain, has now become a wild expanse of dried foliage, overgrown with rampant weeds and scrub grass. The front door waits atop a columned porch, accessible by a short flight of steps. There, the door is carved oak, surmounted by a wide fanlight, with a fine iron knocker, cold to the touch.

When I opened the door, I discovered that inside, it was worse than I had imagined. The light from my lantern, piercing the darkness filled with whirling dust dancing in the beam, revealed the sad condition of the interior. Everywhere I swung my lamp, the appalling view of thick coats of grime and cobwebs, stretching across archways and hanging from furniture in sticky strands, awaited me. As I stepped through the door, a huge, wet chunk of plaster showered me in fine powder. The odor that pervaded the structure hit my nose; a nasty, moldy smell of dampness.

After exploring the house, I came to the conclusion that it has been plagued by humidity: the whole ceiling in the hall is moist, large cracks mar the walls, and water damage is noticeable in several rooms. Loose plaster, sometimes in chunks, sometimes in drifts, covers the floor at the base of the affected walls. In places, the wallpaper sags, pictures hang at odd angles, and there's a green coating on the wooden panels. However, the roof doesn't seem to leak.

With all the shutters closed for so long, it never benefitted from the sun's healing rays.

Still, I don't care that much. I'm here for its relative isolation, not to buy and renovate it. Luckily, the salon seems to be in a better state. Expensively furnished, it contains a large fireplace that keeps me warm and provides the light for me to write my journal right now.

Speaking of which, this is indeed a gigantic hearth. It dominates the west wall of the hall and it could hold a log up to six feet in length. The mantel is a single piece of rough grayish stone. Its surface bears petroglyphs, of the same kind seen on the standing stones. The pit itself is made of sandstone blocks; once dark brown in color, they have long been blackened. Above it, shadowed by the tall ceiling and covered by strands of cobweb, stands a large oil painting depicting a craggy landscape at night.

Queer thing: when I entered the room, I saw trickles of gray smoke dancing inside the obviously dead fireplace. Upon closer examination, I found nothing. No ashes, no cinders. Actually, the pit was clean, except for the usual dust and webs. I'm tired and my over-active imagination is playing tricks on me. Also, there's a cold breeze coming from somewhere – I will investigate the source tomorrow – that chills my back. I think it's time for me to go to sleep.

CHAPTER THREE

April 26th, 1891
Talbot House.
Early Morning.

I'm awake again.

It's almost six in the morning and, though the fire has died in the hearth, I'm covered in sweat. I feel I must pen down what just happened because I'm sure later this morning, when rereading it, all of this will sound ridiculous. After all, it was just a dream. A bad dream.

Still, it felt real, so real that I can't fall asleep again. In the dream, I awoke at the feeling of not being alone in the house. I remember jumping out of bed, as if I had heard a sudden loud sound, the nature of which I couldn't fathom. The room was dark except for the glowing red of the dying embers, thus I lit up my lamp and moved toward the source of disturbance. As I opened the door leading to the balcony that overlooks the hall, I heard the distinctive snarling of dogs. My heart jumped at the revelation, and memories of my recent encounter with Maggie's wolfhounds resurfaced, forcing my thoughts to wander down unwanted and irrational paths.

The dogs had somehow broken in, and were now stealthily climbing the stairs; their mouths slavering, ready to pounce on me!

Wolves had made a den of the abandoned mansion and, returning from their daily errands, had found signs of my intrusion!

Uncle Ben had turned into a werewolf and was coming after me!

All of this nonsense crowded my dreaming mind while my feet refused to obey me and kept walking, boldly, toward the balustrade. I felt like a stranger in my own body.

Unexpected, a sudden draft of chilling wind extinguished my lamp, and for a moment, I found myself in complete darkness, until my eyes adjusted to a feeble luminescence coming from downstairs. I got closer to the edge of the stairway and noticed, in terror, that that glow was coming from the main entrance's threshold, as the door was wide-open and allowed the feeble moonlight to shine through. No, it wasn't open: the door had been completely torn asunder!

Nonetheless, I had no time to wonder too much about it as growls from the yet unseen beasts attracted my attention to the right.

There, the most horrible of sights was waiting for me.

Scattered around the hall like fragments of a torn rag doll, human limbs and entrails were littering the room; copious amounts of blood had darkened the old carpets and its smell quickly irritated my nose. Then, I saw Maggie's wolfhounds ravenously nuzzling on what was left of their prey. One was gorging on the soft viscera it had so diligently dug out of the corpse's abdomen. The other was happily chewing at the woman's face. With horror, I observed the last one tearing away a strip of wet flesh from what was Siobhan's cheek. It came off with a sick sound, and I tasted bile in my mouth. Shocked by the unbelievable sight, I gasped, and that attracted the dogs' attention. Promptly, they lifted their heads and spotted me.

Holy God, I'm still shivering at the memory of what happened next!

As I tried to back up, the rabid beasts sprang on me so quickly I barely had the time to lift my arms to protect my neck. To no avail, as I felt their hot breath on my skin, soon followed by the agonizing pain of their jaws puncturing my throat!

Then, I woke up screaming and fighting my sheets to try and free myself from the grasp of the nonexistent canines.

Dear God, it felt so real! The smell, the pain ...

I figure this afternoon's emotions did carry over into my dreams, causing a nightmare so vivid in its details that I surprised myself looking for wounds on my neck, checking the lamp on my nightstand, and even going downstairs to be sure it had only been a bad dream. Obviously, there was no trace of the dogs – nor of their victim – and the door stood solidly in its place.

It was a dream. A horrible dream.

P.S. : Just now, while I was writing the last sentence, I heard a dog howling in the distance. Perhaps it was one of the wolfhounds at the Blair camp, or the wind – which has grown in intensity now – whistling through a fissure in this old house. Whatever it was, it certainly upset me.

Tomorrow I shall tell Maggie to not bring her dogs along.

I do not want to see dogs for some time.

April 26th, 1891
Pooka Hills.
Late morning.

The Pooka Hills are magnificent.

After last night's terrible experience, this outdoor excursion into the glens around Talbot House is certainly reinvigorating my spirit and lifting my humor. County Wicklow is known as *the Garden of Ireland* for good reasons, and when the sun shines bright, like today, its majestic beauty is evident. Though the remains of winter are still lingering, green sloping lands full of dense woods can be seen from the hills, extending to the large granite ridge of the Wicklow Range. On steep hills, often crowned by farmhouse or cottages, and around the river Glencree, it's quite common to see dense thickets of wild cherry, beech, larch, aspen, and Douglas fir. Cranberry, bog myrtle, honeysuckle, and heather bushes, all dormant and waiting for spring to release their treasures, dot the base of the u-shaped valley, while an incredible variety of sturdy grasses – from sedge to rush – cover the ground despite the cold. I have recorded and catalogued some interesting herbs growing in this area, including St. Patrick's cabbage (a *Saxifraga*) and *Veronica officinalis*, also known as heath speedwell. Lichens are also common, along with mosses and some kind of spongy mushroom I was unable to identify.

The remoteness of the open hills is rewarding to bird lovers. I've spotted skylarks, pipits, merlin falcons, and ravens. Near watercourses, I've seen snipe, curlew, and a red grouse. And I've spotted some kind of deer, of a breed I've never seen before, which is smaller than the common red one and has a very dark gray-brown pelt. The animal I saw was making a lot of noise; a pitched, whistling call that turned into a short, bark-like sound after I was spotted, and disappeared, with the deer, into a dense coniferous forest.

All this beauty starkly contrasts with the bleak peat bog bordering the west side of Talbot House. Bogs, of any kind, are not the best of places for a walk, and the forlornness of the landscape certainly doesn't help the sullen spirit. However, *this* bog has a malignant nature; its brackish water is browner, almost black, and the short skeletal trees protruding from the muck bring images of drowning giants to the mind. I haven't seen a single animal in that sad mire; even the ubiquitous raven shuns it. It's malodorous, and covered by *Sphagnum moss* and dark peat.

I suspect the Talbot family erected their house here to make profits from the stripping of the bog for fuel, but it doesn't seem to have brought them great fortune. I've heard stories of mummified human remains found in bogs, the bodies preserved by the peat to such an extent that the hair, clothes, and even the facial expression of the corpse remained intact. People say they were victims of Celt sacrifices.

However, I do not want to cloud my mind with such dreary thoughts, not now that I'm enjoying this pleasant day.

Speaking of pleasant and unpleasant, I must pen down my second meeting with the lovely Miss Maggie Blair.

She came early this morning, accompanied by her grandmother and her dogs.

After my horrible dream, I was more than happy to see the old woman alive and well, but I didn't feel the same about the hounds. Just the sight of them, jumping and frolicking in the tall grass of the garden, made me uneasy and edgy. I was sipping my morning tea – a fine Earl Grey I bought in Dublin – in the study: a dark paneled room, sparsely decorated, with a large roll-top desk and matching chair, plus a dusty armchair by the tall French window. From there, I could see the two women approaching the gate and finding it open. I don't have the key for that gate, and although this is a sparsely populated area, I don't think it's wise to leave it that way, so I'll provide it with a lock and chain after I've been to town for provisions.

Anyhow, Maggie swung the gate open and let her granny go first. It was at that point that I noticed the wolfhounds as they hastily ran past the women and chased one after the other. To my surprise, my hand holding the teacup started to shake and I spilled some of the liquid on the armchair. Not a big damage considering its condition: it's a dirty contrivance, standing askew on the left side, worthier for the fireplace than for resting one's posterior. Still, that show of cowardice made me nervous. I'm an adult, no longer a nipper!

Thusly, disgusted by my infantile reaction, I replaced the cup on the desk, straightened my vest, and went to the foyer, where I retrieved my Chesterfield overcoat, my Deerstalker hat, and my Inverness cape. Once I was sure of being properly attired, I opened the door and stepped onto the porch.

Unfortunately, all my resolve faded away in an instant as the two animals spotted me and started barking like lunatics. Hearing the fracas, Bertha, whom I had left grazing in the backyard as the carriage house is a total wreckage (sagging just like the mansion, and the pressure of the bowed roof making it impossible to open its jammed doors), whinnied in protest, then started thumping around to try and get free of the rope I had secured around one of the porch's columns. Suddenly, I became aware of the danger her behavior posed and of my stupidity. What if the columns there were in the same poor condition as the rest of the mansion? That demon of a horse could surely bring the whole house down!

Immediately, I rushed to the backyard, but in doing so, I provoked the dogs' chasing instinct and the two hounds ran after me. As the devilish duo appeared onto the porch, I panicked. Remembering my terrible dream, I started shaking, yet at the same time I felt a rage take hold of me. As a human being, I felt indignation at the animals' impudence, for Man was meant to rule those beasts, not fear them. My resolve found again, I shouted at them, "Hold off, you villains! This is my house and you're not going to bark at me like that on my property. I am the Master here!"

I still don't know where those words came from, and I feel stupid just thinking about them now. Nonetheless, it worked, as the hounds froze on the spot, stopped their chase, and then dug their muzzle under their paws as if ashamed of their impertinence.

Maggie and Siobhan climbed to the porch, both worried and surprised at once.

"Are you well, sir?" Maggie demanded, while her grandma took hold of the dogs' collars and forcefully dragged them back to the yard.

I was still shaking, but feeling better, as if that show of willpower had finally dispelled that bad dream, sending it back to the place it belonged: the misty realm of ephemeral fantasies. "Yes, I'm fine," I said. "However, I beg you to keep those animals out of these premises for the time I am here."

Her face reddened and I felt regret for my harsh censure, but there was no need, for soon I discovered the source of her embarrassment when the girl, hardly suppressing a giggle, pointed at my waist, keeping her eyes low.

God Almighty! I was wearing no trousers!

I don't know how that happened, but it seems that, in my state of nervousness, I had put on my shirt, vest, and jacket, forgetting my trousers. Thus, I was standing there, showing my woolen union suit, my drawers and my socks through the opening of my overcoat.

"Ye haven't shlept well, me dear," I heard Siobhan say while she walked back to the entrance. From my position, I could see the familiar colors of her wagon just beyond the gate. "I'll latch those imps at the vardo, thin, if ye allow, I'll drive it through so that we can bring in all the goodies we made fur ye, young man." She cackled like a witch, until she disappeared inside her mobile home. I excused myself to Maggie and rushed inside the house, eager to retrieve my trousers.

How did that happen? How could that be possible? I remember waking up in my underwear, performing my ablutions, a long toilet session, and ...

Nothing else. Everything from the moment I came out of the bathroom to the time I was sipping my tea in the study has completely disappeared from my mind. It has never happened before and I must check my medicine books to find about similar cases. Or maybe I'm just stressed.

Anyhow, while I was in my bedroom, still fuming and worried about my sanity, Mrs. Blair and Maggie came inside the mansion and proceeded to arrange matters. When I came downstairs, I found them in the kitchen and saw that, with much kindness, they had brought from their own larder sufficient provisions to last a week. I thanked them profusely and apologized for the earlier inconvenience. Also, I offered them money in repayment, but Siobhan strongly refused.

"Ye shall pay us as charwomen. We don't usually sell our food. These goodies were made be Maggie as a sign av sympathy an' affectshun. An' the goold ye paid in advance is far more thin phat is axpected. So, I've decided to lend a hand to my Maggie, an' fur phat I see, it was a wise decision as tis house needs more thin wan pair of hands."

The woman's kindness dissipated my dark mood.

I'm really glad to have such friendly neighbors.

Later, while the two women were busy with their chores, I decided to have a look at the backyard. And what a surprise awaited for me there!

Just coming out of the back door, one is astounded by the sight of a peculiar, if not prehistoric, marvel. Standing on a hillock and surrounded from west to east by the peat bog, a circle of megalithic stones amazes the unwary observer. It's not as complex, or as large, as the more famous Stonehenge in England, but it is charming nonetheless. The standing stones are set twenty-five feet apart, in radius, with the tallest one measuring no more than twelve feet. A rough path of flat stones, now completely invaded by weeds, leads up to the circle's main entrance, which is highlighted by two of these pillars being surmounted by a lintel. All the stones appear untouched on the exterior side, but once you look from the inside of the circle, you can clearly see etchings and markings similar to the one I saw yesterday.

Obviously, I couldn't resist its attraction, and immediately set to climb the serpentine path. Once I was right under the lintel, I noticed an inscription, far more recent and written in familiar characters. It is in French and says:

Fais ce que tu voudras

Do whatever you want.

What a curious inscription for a place like that. I presume the carving was made in the last century, maybe by Talbot himself, as it looks cleaner and less weathered than the mystical inscriptions observed on the inside of the megaliths, which, on the contrary, look faded and cluttered with dark moss.

Grass seems reluctant to grow here, leaving a bald patch of dried dirt and sand all around the circle, and this patch gets darker – as if bog water is seeping underneath – at the center.

There, I found something that still befuddles and chills me at the same time.

Right in the middle of this prehistoric construction, erupts from the ground an evil-looking iron spike, four feet tall and covered with markings even more bizarre than those on the stones. Four heavy yet rusty chains are welded (or the queer contraption was already cast like that at its creation, I can't say) to the spike, and end into rudimentary, but still effective, cruel-looking manacles, whose purpose remain a mystery to me. It's easy to imagine someone being bound to that device; forced prone and enduring whatever fate its gaoler had reserved for them. Yet, I'm sure, that was not the purpose of the artifact, but just my mind going to morbid places, maybe under the influence of that strange motto etched under the lintel stone.

Yes, that motto, for I now remember where I saw it the first time.

It was while visiting Mount Pelier Hill, County Dublin, with a couple of college friends.

One evening, while we were batty-fanging yet more traditional Irish songs in our weekly whooperups at the Eagle Tavern on Cork Hill, my chuckaboo Liam O'Brian came out with the story of the Hellfire Club and how the Eagle used to be their public meeting place. I had never heard about such a club, so, naturally, I pressed him to reveal more. Liam said that the Hellfire Club was a common name for several exclusive social groups reserved for high-society rakes established in Ireland and Britain in the last century. Such clubs were rumored to be the meeting places of *'persons of quality'* who wished to take part in immoral acts, and the members were often very involved in politics. They are said to have undertaken all kinds of drunken debaucheries, prayed to the devil, and sacrificed animals to pagan gods. Mostly, they were rebels for the sake of it, enjoying pranks and libertarianism. Still, there were dark rumors talking of human sacrifice, cannibalism, and other unspeakable acts. The club was officially disbanded in 1800, but rumors abounded of wealthy Irishmen holding secret Hellfire meetings in out of the way estates and remote villages, and some still go round even to this day. He said that their secret meeting place was at Mount Pelier Hill, in a hunting lodge built around 1725 with stones taken from a cairn – which surmounted a prehistoric passage grave – and that shortly after its completion, a sudden storm blew off its roof, causing locals to attribute the accident to the work of the Devil as a punishment for interfering with the cairn. Today, it is left in a complete state of abandon, even if, nominally, it's property of the Massy family of Duntrileage.

The following Sunday, Liam O'Brian, Hugh Fitzpatrick, Lawrence Cabot and I (plus a lovely trio of indulgent dames I will not name) went visiting the place. It's a sad place indeed, pervaded by a feeling of decadence and giving the morbs to those who look at the magnificence of a past gone. The ruins face to the north, looking over Dublin and the plains of Meath and Kildare. To the front, there is a semi-circular courtyard enclosed by a low stone wall and entered through a gate that was supposed to stay locked, yet, someone had provided to it by forcibly removing the clasps. Inside the grounds, only squalor, and rubbish from past illicit visitors, greeted us; no ghosts or demons. The lodge's entrance, which would have been on the upper floor, was reached by a long flight of stairs which is now destroyed. There, above the missing front door, I saw the inscription.

I will spare myself the memories of that gloomy day, because if not for the joyous company of some fine poitín (a potato brew well-known for its strength, often reaching ninety-five percent proof, and illegally produced by many night distilleries) and that of the merry ladies, it would have been completely erased from my mind.

Fais ce que tu voudras.

Is it possible that Hugh Talbot was a member of that debauched club?

That would explain his bad repute and why the locals shun this place.

I must peruse his personal library – barring the inheritor didn't sell all of his collection – and see for myself what kind of studies and interests kept him busy here, all alone in the countryside.

CHAPTER FOUR

April 27th, 1891
Talbot House.
Early morning.

Now I'm worried.

Whatever happened just minutes ago can't be real, and I'm really afraid for my own sanity. That's why I'm going to pen down my experience now – even at the cost of my own reputation – so that I can reread it after having slept some more, and when sunlight has improved my emotional state and cast away the shadows of irrationality. I'm feeling like my brains have been unhinged and I'm under the spell of some kind of illness.

I will start with the facts, and will not confuse them with experiences, as they are based only on my own observations and my memories.

After my pleasant day in the countryside, and with my mind wondering about the mysteries of the human body – since I had carried the anatomy book along to study while I walked – I found Talbot House in a different state. The place had been swept and tidied, the cobwebs removed, there was a jolly fire burning in the living room's hearth, and an oil lamp lit and set on the table, which had been spread for supper with Maggie's delicious stew. A wonderful sight, indeed.

Once I finished my supper, I moved the lamp to the living room, got my books out of my trunk, rekindled the fire with fresh wood, and immersed myself back in the ways of veins and blood circulation. I carried on reading – and taking notes – till about half past ten, when I paused to feed more wood to the hearth and indulge myself to a cup of hot coffee.

Staying up late and drinking coffee just before going to bed is a habit I have taken up at college. Some physicians discourage it, saying that the substance is going to disturb your sleep pattern, but I've found that it actually relaxes me and help me focus on my activities.

Then, glancing out of the kitchen window, my eyes went to the hillock. The moon was shining just above the lintel stone and brightening it with a silvery aura. Looking at the henge reminded me of my desire to explore Hugh Talbot's library, so, cup of coffee in one hand and lamp in the other, I crossed the parlor and tried to open the library's water-damaged wooden door. I found it unlocked, but still, it refused to give in, wishing to remain untouched. The wood, warped by seepage and by the growing mold, had become misshapen and jammed it tightly against the floor. After some rough shoving and banging, it finally stopped its sturdy resistance. The door swung open, and my nose was immediately assaulted by the nauseous smell of moisture mixed with rot. Intellectual sadness took hold of me once my lamp illuminated the room, as it is a sin in the eyes of knowledge to allow the booklice and the deathwatch beetle to feed on human wisdom.

The library is large; its walls covered by floor to ceiling bookshelves of what was once polished mahogany; the rows interrupted by three boarded up windows. A huge iron chandelier – whose candle stubs have never been replaced since the times of its master – dangles over an ugly chestnut table. Everywhere, dust, spider webs and crumpled plaster hold dominion over this fallen kingdom. Books are still present, but they are all damaged by excessive dampness; I think less than twenty-five percent of the whole lot can be salvaged. It seems Talbot was a cultivated man, as his tomes deal mostly with poetry, grammar, rhetoric, history, and classical languages.

Nothing esoteric there, and not a single reference to religion or the occult.

After a cursory examination of the room, I convened I was just wasting my time, so I shut the door tight behind me and returned to my own books.

However, just when I was crossing the foyer to fish an anatomy text from my big travel trunk – I have left it in the sitting room, just to the right of the main entrance, for convenience – I heard the sound of footsteps right above my head. I wondered if Maggie or Siobhan were still here, maybe finishing their daily chores in an overzealous act. Smiling at the thought of catching another pleasant look at the jolly girl, and with the intention of sending them off for the day, I went upstairs. The steps creaked under my weight, and the beam from my light fell upon the huge portrait at the top. The cobwebs that covered it yesterday had been removed by the charwomen, and I could now see a strong man posed at the wheel of a ship. His eyes looked sad, and behind him, out at sea, a storm was growing. A brass plaque at the bottom simply stated, *'Captain Roy Cooney – 1838'*.

I couldn't see any light in the hallway, still, I could hear a soft creaking noise coming from beyond the wood-framed archway leading to the long and extremely dark east hall. That area of the mansion has four rooms: three are bedrooms, and one used to be the sewing room. It was from there that the pesky, rhythmic sound was coming from.

Creak, bump, creak, bump, creak, bump.

What on Earth was it?

"Maggie? Siobhan?" I called aloud.

No answer came, but the bumping sound ceased; only a soft, rocking creaking remained.

Rats? A trapped bird?

No light shone from underneath the door. I tried the handle, but it didn't move. The door was locked, or so it appeared. I wondered if it was just the wind playing with a loose shutter, so I went outside to check. The air was crisp, but there was no wind. Looking up, I saw that the front windows at the second floor were all closed; the heavy shutters firmly in place. So, it had to be something from inside the sewing room. Yes, it surely had to be rats. Yet, the sound was familiar. It was a sound I had heard when I was a child.

Creak, bump, creak, bump, creak, bump. What was it?

I tried to focus, but the only thing that came to my mind was my grandma knitting. I went back inside, locked the front door, and whisked my book from the trunk. I decided I would explore the room tomorrow;

after all I was sure the key to that room was hanging on one of the hooks in the study.

I was deeply immersed in the book, the rats forgotten, half an hour later, when the noise came back. This time, preceded by the nervous whinnying of Bertha; a pitched neighing that chilled the blood in my veins. Then she snorted as if annoyed.

Do horses have nightmares? I wonder.

I was thinking about going to check on her, but changed my mind when I heard the creak – followed by the bump – again. This time, I went to the study, grabbed all the brass keys from the hooks, armed myself with the fireplace poker, and quickly climbed the stairs. The sound was louder now. Almost furious.

Bump, bump, bump.

The creaking was gone and the bumps were deeper.

I tried four keys before I found the right one.

Once I opened the door, the bumping ceased. There was still the creaking sound, but it too was dying. Inside, my lamp brightened the small room. No one was there, except for a pair of rocking chairs, one of which was slowly coming to halt after being rocked by an unseen force. An unseen force that was clearly a rat, for I spotted something skittering into the small fireplace.

A rocking chair.

That was the sound I remembered from my infancy; my grandma sitting there, knitting, and rocking the chair back and forward. Oh, how much I miss her!

I stopped the chair's momentum and looked around. The room had not been cleaned by my servants and long strands of webs covered everything. Except for the rocking chairs. Queerly, they had been avoided by the spiders.

Having solved this little mystery, I resolved to go back to my studies and ignore the pesky rats with a need for lullabies.

At half past eleven, the fire was dying, my lamp sputtered – murdered by the lack of fuel – and my eyes were fighting a losing battle against Morpheus, so I retreated to my bedroom and called it a day.

And that's fact.

However, here I must enter into the realm of the unthinkable and the unimaginable, where the walls of rationality crumble against the force of dreams or insanity. For I'm still shaking at the memory of my horrible experience, and for as much as I try to shake it off as totally incoherent and implausible, I can't deny it appeared – and sounded – as real as my trembling hand.

I must have fallen asleep almost immediately after climbing into bed, and had been carried away to the lofty realms of dream on the swift wings of tiredness. I was dreaming about things that are best left out of this journal (but they were certainly pleasurable and regarded Maggie Blair), when I was vehemently dragged out by a loud sound coming from the main floor. At first, I couldn't fathom what had awakened me, but soon, the violent banging repeated itself. Alarmed, I stood silent in my bed, my ears trying to locate the provenience of the disturbance. Then, as my mind came out of the slumber, I realized someone was knocking at, or was trying to forcibly open, the main door. Understanding that, perhaps, Maggie or her family could be looking for my help (maybe Uncle Ben had worsened), I jumped out of bed, put on my night robe, and stormed onto the balcony, forgetting the now dead lamp. But, as it had happened in my previous nightmare, there was no need for it anyway as the lower floor was again brightened by that weird luminescence, and my eyes easily adjusted to the dimness.

Yet, this time, the door was intact.

The light was coming through the wide bay window, and, again, it looked as if someone had put the moon on fire. Pale, yet too bright even for a full moon, that unpleasant aura made the living room appear of a yellow-greenish color.

It is the color of death, and that of rotting things.

This sprang into my mind; my thought, yet not mine.

I heard the silvery voices of children singing a rhythmic melody out in the garden, then their chorus died abruptly when, again, the door banged under the unknown force, and, as irrational as that macabre thought of earlier, a new one took shape: it was not Maggie or any other friendly visitor battering the oaken door. No, it was someone – or something – dangerous. An unknown enemy in the dark of the night.

Assaulted by that dreadful feeling, I felt unconfident, unable to act.

Had I to face whatever it was out there? Or had I to lock myself inside the bedroom and wait for dawn? Better to look for a weapon to defend my very life, or flee like a panicked rat into the moor?

As my confused mind analyzed those conflicting thoughts, the banging stopped and I found myself cowering as a child. The stillness didn't last, for soon the unknown visitor changed its strategy. I heard the sound of something metallic sliding inside the keyhole, then the lock unlatched and the handle turned.

Oh, Holy God! The stranger had a key!

Scholars say there are two ways of reacting to fear and danger: fighting or fleeing. My instinct dragged me to the middle ground, because I rushed down the stairs and jumped against the door, using my body to force the door shut just an instant after I saw a blade of light cutting the floor's darkness as the door moved inward. The wood released a dull thump under my weight and my shoulder protested to the impact. I heard another, faster bumping, but soon realized it was the sound of my heart drumming into my ears. Only that, because the invisible opponent had ceased its intent. I lay there, quiet, unable to think about my next move.

Then, I heard that horrible voice.

It sliced through the wood, grating, unhuman, like the voice of the *Big Bad Wolf* in the *Three Little Pigs*' story.

"For now, I'm only dream, but soon, I'll be there with you."

Those words, spoken by a cruel, invisible mouth, sent shivers through my spine, and even now, while I'm writing them, I can feel the chilling fingers of fear clutching my heart.

I can't recall how much time I stood there, pressing my body against the door, too afraid to release my pressure on it. The next thing I remember is that I woke up in my bed, covered in cold sweat. After a moment of disorientation, I rushed out to the main floor to be sure the door was locked. It was. A sigh of relief escaped my mouth when I convened I had just had another bad dream. Shaking my head, ashamed of myself, I moved back to bed, but that was the moment when dream and reality mixed together, and got me to doubt of my mental health.

As I turned my back, a piercing howl erupted the other side, soon followed by an evil snarl. Fear returned, but this time it was quickly replaced by anger. Anger directed at the Blair wolfhounds. Anger directed at my neighbors for bringing those dogs to my property once more. I was not going to be scared again by those stupid mutts, so, grabbing a poker from the fireplace, I rushed to the door and opened it.

Nothing was out there. Only the moonlit moor.

Then, I realized the door's lock had been unlatched though I was sure I had locked it when I had returned from my daily excursion. Nonetheless, I could possibly be wrong. Still, inside of me, I felt something was amiss. There was something I couldn't figure out, something in my memories yelling at me that it wasn't a dream. Or it wasn't completely a dream. Whatever I had experienced was like a doorway between the dreaming and waking worlds. Shaking in anger and fear, I left the porch and went back in.

Here it was when my mind remembered. Here it was when I saw those things.

As I closed the door behind me, a memory of what I had seen crawling through the threshold, trying to force it open, flashed inside my brain. White – yet darkened as if burned – things similar to a large crab's legs had slithered across the doorframe, brightened by that eerie light. It had only lasted an instant, the moment when I had hurled myself against the door, but I had seen them.

My eyes ran to the floor and, in horror, I spotted them there.

I was taken by an uncontrollable terror as I comprehended what my eyes were seeing. Shaken, I crouched to look closer and I couldn't refrain from gasping as those horrible, impossible things dissolved into thin air.

And here I am, writing the impossible, for I know something unnatural just happened, something that defies rationality and casts dark shadows over my sanity. I can't explain it. I can't find a logical explanation to it. And most of all, I almost prefer that something is wrong in my head rather than to accept the existence of a world denied by science.

What is dead stays dead.

There are no ghosts, no lurking monsters. Monsters don't hide in darkness, but inside our mind. Nonetheless, whatever happened tonight surely left a scar of doubt in my soul as it left a physical proof of it being real. When, in the dream, I had slammed the door shut, the heavy door frame had sliced through the appendage that was trying to force it open.

And I know that appendage was a hand.

For on the floor, close by the door's threshold, my eyes have seen those terrible, blackened, and severed finger bones.

CHAPTER FIVE

April 27th, 1891
Talbot House
Later.

I'm still shaken.

After my queer experience last night, it took me a long time before I finally succumbed to slumber. I slept heavy, but uneasy. Obviously, I don't feel too well this morning and I made myself a strong cup of tea to freshen me up.

As intended, I reread my last entry in this journal and tried to rationalize last night's uncanny events, but this just brought me to two possible conclusions, none of which soothe my sullen spirit: haunting or insanity.

If what I experienced was a real manifestation of the unnatural, I'm in dire danger, because whoever or whatever was out there clearly showed their intention to cause me harm.

If the experience happened only in my mind, I'm equally doomed, as this shows symptoms of mental instability and it is notorious that insanity is hereditary. My great-grandmother died of brain fever in an asylum.

May God have pity of me.

April 27th, 1891
Pooka Hills
Afternoon.

More queer stuff for my feeble mind.

Apparently, I fell asleep again, and I slept so soundly that I didn't hear Maggie and Siobhan coming for their daily chores. It was Maggie's gentle touch that woke me up from a dreamless rest. I found myself lying on the beige couch, the one close by the main entrance, my journal kissing the carpet. At first, I was startled by that intrusion and I wondered how she'd come in. Then, I remembered the spare key I had given Siobhan so they could come in after I had left for my daily walks. Maggie looked worried about me and searched my face for signs of illness. "You shouldn't overwork yourself, sir. You look paler than you should be. Are you staying up late because of your studies?"

I tried to smile and reassure her that I was not putting too much strain on my mind, but I didn't convince her. "Or is it something else?"

I didn't know what to say. Immediately, I rose from the sofa, rescued my journal, and, excusing myself, retreated to my chamber. I didn't want her to read my last entries. More, I started wondering if she and her grandmother could be behind the strange happenings. After all I didn't know much about them. What if they were trying to scare me away? Maybe, being nomads, they didn't like my presence here. Perhaps, they looked kind and helpful, but they were hiding something dark under their sunny facade.

Later, properly dressed, I went downstairs to fix myself some breakfast. Maggie and her grandmother were there, whispering about my state of health, but they immediately fell silent once I stepped through the kitchen's threshold.

"Good aft' noon, sir," said Siobhan, "hope ye had a good night." There was no irony in her statement, but I was still reeling from my dark thoughts, so, quite rudely, I snapped. "No, I didn't. Thanks to your dogs and whoever had planned to play unpleasant tricks on me!"

Both women stared at me, like they had heard the Devil speak.

After an embarrassing moment of silence, I felt regret and tried to apologize, but Siobhan interrupted me. "Tricks? Phat tricks, son?" She didn't look angry; quite the contrary, she looked sincerely concerned. "Plaze, have a sate whilst I serve ye breakfast, an' tell me phat darkens ye."

"I'm just tired," I mumbled. "I'm sorry for venting on you the spell of a bad dream."

Yet the old woman didn't eat that. "Ye're not afoolin' me, son. Something is causin' ye to lose yer shleep, an' I disloike it. I've told ye tis house is no good, but ye won't lissen. An' now," she pointed outside, "that something is hintin' ye, like it did to all the other guests afore."

What *something*? What was she on about?

"I do not want to listen to more nonsense, Ma'am." I rebuked. "I have enough trouble discerning what is real from what is fantasy. I'm worried about my sanity."

A shadow fell on her wrinkly lineaments. "That's exactly phat *IT* wants. Shroudin' yer mind wid doubts." She underlined that 'IT', as if she knew what it was.

"Please, sir, listen to my granny," irrupted Maggie. "I know you are a student and an educated man, but sometimes, there are things that science cannot explain. Things that could hurt you because of your ignorance."

"I said ..." I started, but couldn't finish.

"It's the hound, is not it?" Siobhan blurted.

That blunt statement had the effect of chilling me on the spot, my mouth agape.

"Here, young man," said the old lady, grabbing my arm and gently leading me to the sofa, "set down an' I'll tell ye phat is that *thing* an' phat it wants from ye. There's reason to be ascared, but not all hope is lost. Fur the unnatural is weak. It is us who giv it strength. It is us that giv it shape."

Again, there's something in that woman, some kind of uncanny strength, an invisible force, or an aura that makes it impossible for me to fight back. So, I did exactly as she asked and, after gulping down the delicious breakfast Maggie had prepared for me, I patiently listened to her story.

Here now I report it exactly as she narrated it to me.

The Tale of Hugh Talbot
As told by Siobhan Blair.

"Wan hundred years ago, 'twas tis Hugh Talbot, a deshpised an' disinherited member av the Talbot av Malahide. 'Twas a nashty man, tis Talbot, an' only liked the company av dogs. It says he possessed such a cruel heart that, some times, he let his favoured hound, a large black mastiff named Arawn, hunt down intruders into his land or iven, thim say, chase an' kill servants who'd dishpleased him.

"Obviously, no wan wished to serve under such a deshpicable master, so the man spent more time alone, isolated be the rest av the community, than in the company av other human bings. Strangers who'd came to the village seekin' fur imployiment wor ofthen warned to accept not Talbot's offer, but not all av thim wud lissen.

"It says, a conshtable wance wint to Talbot House to inquire about the worabouts av a lad from Galway who'd last been seen workin' at Hugh's home. Whin he returned back to the village, he looked pale, he looked, an' clearly upset, an' still, he refused to disclose phat had happened at the mansion. He only says the man he was lookin' fur had been laid-off be Master Talbot an' his fait wor unknowned.

"More queer things happened in the years, yet the villagers wor too afrightened to act. Evil or not, Talbot was a nobleman, an' at those times a commoner word had no weight againsht that av gentry.

"However, the forchunes av Hugh Talbot wor adwindlin'; havin' no servants an' no work force he'd no way av making new goold. So, wan day, here he came to the village lookin' fur men to work in the peat bog. He offers thim iven access to his well-known wine cellar. But no wan stepped afore.

"At those times 'twas custom fur real ould Irish families, especially those wid thrue Milesian blood runnin' in thim veins, to be hospital to strangers, whether jintle or simple, an' put on the table aplenty to at an' dhrink fur those who worked fur him. It says, Talbot Home had a cellar crowded wid bins av foine wine, long raws av pipes, an' casks, that it wud take more time to count than any sober man cud spare in such a plaice. T'was also thrue that the man was not known fur his hospitality

an' that he was quite tight on his sper't. So, naturally, no wan accepted his offer.

"He stormed out av town, black as the Divil an' agrumblin' as a pig.

"Now, t'was a lad, a Jack O'Leary, bright not av mind, but av good heart, that ivery an' wan luveth in Ballymoor. Tis Jack had grown a sailor somewor north, an' had returned home to stay clost to his dyin' mama. He was a brave boy, he was, an' always helpful an' ready fur annywan in need, so iverybody luveth him as thim childher.

"'Tis a mighty queer thing, surely,' says Jack wance the man is gone. 'How's no wan man wants to content himself wid the best plaice in the house av a good master!'

"'That's no good master, son,' the folk say to him. 'He's the old Divil hisself, an' it's better fur you to stay away from him.'

"Yet, the lad was stubborn, an' the luv fur good sper't drove him aknockin' at Talbot House. He became Talbot's butler an' fur some time things looked fur the best, as it seemed that, somehow, Jack had alighten'd Hugh's heart, an' he hisself was seen comin' to the village fur news or supplies.

"Thin, wan day Jack O'Leary disappeared. The good folk av Ballymoor started to wunder why the lad wasn't coming to town annymore, especially now that his mama was at death's door an' had asked fur him. So, they send a local hunter, Ian Mulholland, that was his name, to bring the bad news to Jack. An' twas tis Mulholland who found Jack's mangled body in the moor. The large slash around his throat lave no doubt he'd been thrashed be Talbot's dog.

"In Ballymoor, the news av Jack's death brought pain an' rage to the whole village, fur as I said ivery wan luveth the boy. Finally, tired av Talbot's reign av terror, unable to have the law lissen to thim, the God-fearing people av Ballymoor took things in thim hands. Torches alight an' armed wid iverything – from pitchfurk to shpade, from knife to pishtol – thim marched up tis very house. Yet, afore they cud git clost to the great gate, Talbot, who'd been warned be the barkin' av his hinting dogs, armed hisself an' started ashootin' at the mob.

"It says, the showdown lasted all night, till at dawn, havin' spent his last bullet, Talbot fled his home keepin' Arawn at the leash. He flew into

the bog, he flew, hopin' the townsfolk won't dare to follow him there, but in doin' so he got trapped in the mire.

"The villagers heard his shouts, beggin' fur help. An' indeed they came. Yet, no wan lifted a hand to pull him out av the peat, fur they saw it as a sign av the Lord, finally deliverin' thim av the evil man.

"Slowly, Hugh Talbot an' his dog were drhagged down be the mud, but afore both wor completely swallowed be the bog, he spat a curse:

'Bog take me bones an' keep thim. The hound is forever yers'

"Now, the legend goes that the ghost av Arawn, evilest than afore its death, hints tis very land, an' that some nights it comes out to hunt an' kill those who cross its path. Furever tied to the bog, it can't lave tis plaice, as it can't cross the standing stones. From the times av Hugh Talbot, ivery wan who tuk tis house and made it its home disappeared like mist."

April 27th, 1891
Pooka Hills
Later.

After Siobhan finished her story, it seemed like she had more to add.

"An' that's the thrue shtory av Hugh Talbot an' his mastiff, Arawn, me lad," she said, while Maggie refilled my cup of tea. "However, 'twas not the end av it."

"I don't believe in ghosts, Ma'am." I replied, but my staunchness wasn't as strong as before. "Dead is dead. The soul goes to Heaven, that's all I know. Or Hell ..."

The old lady smiled sadly at me. "Aye. But, dear boy, phat happens whin a sowl is so evil, so full av hate? It can't go to Heaven, fur sure. An' the Divil hisself is alighted to let it linger into tis world an' spred more havoc an' sufferin'. An' phat about a dog's sowl? Do dogs have an aftherlife?"

That theological conversation was going too far for my weary mind, so I lifted my hand. "I don't know if dogs do have souls. However, if all dead dogs had no place to go after their demise, I figure they would all be here. And that's not the case. So, I suppose there's a place for animals too."

"Have you ever heard of the *Barguest*?" Maggie interrupted.

I lifted my eyes to her, puzzled. "No. What's that?"

She sat beside me and took my hand. The smell of her fresh skin reached my nose and somehow relaxed me a bit. I must confess I have a fondness for this girl.

"A *Barguest*," she said, "is the ghost of an evil dog. It stays invisible most of the time, but it can assume corporeal form if some conditions arise. And when it does, it doesn't look like a real dog, but like a huge, monstrous version of its former self. Its eyes and jaws glow with the fires of Hell. And only its chosen prey can see it."

"What are these ... *conditions* you mentioned? What have I done to attract this most foul creature?"

Siobhan broke in. "Not a thing. Ye just stumbled in its hunting grounds. Ye're treshpassing, me dear."

"What am I supposed to do? Leave the house?" I replied. The situation was getting weirder and weirder. "If all ghosts can force the living out of a place, there won't be a house or a land left to inhabit."

The old woman shook her head. "Nay. It don't work like phat."

Maggie continued. "You see, the Barguest can't take shape, usually. It needs first to locate a suitable victim to haunt, then it needs to fill its target with terror. It starts by entering your dreams and creating nightmares about dogs. Night after night, the chosen victim is forced to dream of being pursued and torn apart by packs of hounds, or by one large black dog. Once the dreams put the poor soul in the proper mood of fear, the Barguest can finally manifest itself. And attack."

I remembered my dreams and shuddered. Still, my rational mind fought fiercely against this irrational legend. I didn't want to believe that the ghost of an evil dog was haunting me. "I'm having nightmares about dogs every night ..." I heard myself say. It was as though no matter how hard I was fighting irrationality, my simpler side – the one that grew up with fairy tales and legends from Ireland told by my grannies – was seeking help.

"That's axactly phat happened to me son," Siobhan said.

"What?" I exclaimed, perplexed. Was she saying that poor Uncle Ben was lying there, in his vardo, because he was a victim of the same ghostly creature that was driving me insane?

"How's him?" I asked, sincerely worried. I had forgotten about the poor man.

"He's recovering, but he's not safe yet," said Maggie. "The dogs have helped, but he still needs to fight his fears."

"The dogs?" I was even more confused. Now, what was that about the dogs?

"Raymember I told ye that we were keepin' those wolfhounds fur protection?" Siobhan was staring directly at my eyes now, as if she was looking inside me to see if, finally, I was coming to reason. "Barguests fear alivin' dogs. I dunno why. Maybe it's because dogs can see thim. Always." She paused, took a sip from her cup, and then continued. "Annyway, dogs, even lil' puppies, fear not the Barguest. On the contrary, thim bark an' run afther it, should they spot wan."

"How come your son was targeted by this beast? It looks like the dogs didn't help." I replied.

"We have had those dogs for a week now. We didn't have them when the Barguest started hunting my uncle." Maggie said.

There was a logic in their tale. I had to admit it. Still, I didn't accept it. "So, you bought those dogs to keep the Barguest at bay, right? And how comes that this ghostly hound hasn't fled these grounds? You brought your dogs here, and they seemed to be more interested in scaring me than anything else."

Siobhan shook her head again. "They worn't afther ye. They wor afther the thing that is always wid ye. Iven now, the Barguest is a'here. Invisible. Awaitin' fur whin ye'll be alone an' manifest anew."

I rose from my seat, to point out that the conversation was over. "I appreciate your help, ladies. However, I really must go. I have books waiting for me, and I've already wasted enough time with legends and bogeys. Yes, I admit there have been queer events since the moment I set foot in this house, but I still believe the best way to fight nightmares is to stop thinking about them and keep your feet firm on the ground. No Pindaric flights. No faes. No goblins."

I caught Maggie looking gravely at her grandmother, sincerely concerned about my fate. I felt bad about it, as it looked like they truly believe this nonsense. Yet, honestly, I must preserve a sound mind. So I grabbed the lunch basket Maggie had prepared for me, retrieved my books, and went for the door.

"Have a good day, ladies. And thank you for trying to help. I shall see you tomorrow morning, and I promise you will find me in a better state than today."

That said, I left.

Now, I'm sitting here under a tree, enjoying the pleasant countryside, and the way it contrasts with the dark tales I've heard.

I think I should pay a visit to Uncle Ben soon.

P.S. : I forgot to mention that while going out on my daily excursion, I discovered a series of tombstones in the back garden. Standing far back on the property and obscured by tall weeds and overgrown shrubs, it is surrounded by a low, rusted fence; more for decorative purposes than anything else. The tombstones are weathered and hard to read; some are tilted at odd angles; the paths among the graves are clogged with grass and undefined.

Here's a list of those buried there whose name I was able to decipher:

Gregory Campbell	*1740 – 1818*
Maura O'Shea Cooney	*No birth date – 1825*
Unknown	*No birth date – 1827*
Andrew Cooney	*1828 – 1829*
Beulah Quinn Cooney	*1803 – 1829*
Dermot Cooney	*1807 – 1830*
Seamus Cooney	*1768 – 1845*
Angela Reilly Cooney	*1824 – 1852*
Roy Cooney	*1804 – 1853*

There's no marker for Hugh Talbot.

CHAPTER SIX

April 27th, 1891
Talbot House
Night.

I'm back from my excursion and I am more distressed than before. I expected this day out in the countryside to relax my nerves and calm my galloping mind, yet to no avail, as the news I've just heard from the village have sunk me in a state of anxiousness.

A gentleman has been murdered.

And in a horrible way.

It appears this happened three days before my arrival in Ballymoor, and an investigation is still underway, yet, most of the villagers became aware of it just two days ago when Father Earl Wales of St. Kevin's Church returned from Anniskerry with the news. It has clearly created an upheaval in the hamlet, and though Constable Smale thinks the murderer is surely one of the deceased's hired workers from Bray, locals whisper about the curse of a *fuath.*

A *fuath* is a vicious *cailleach*, some kind of hag or witch linked to a bog, who doesn't like trespassers, especially those who disrespect the ancient ways.

Nonsense, superstition, I would normally say. But I must admit that here, at the foot of the Wicklow mountains, surrounded by the mysterious relics of pagan times, it's easy to suspend disbelief and wander into the unthinkable. I confess this is happening to me. For as much I try to rationalize all the weird events, there's something more that calls to my primal instinct and makes me nervous.

This afternoon, after trying to dive into the study of the nervous system – and failing – while sitting in the shade of the stone henge, I decided to stretch my legs and wander about.

Just down the hillock, on the side sloping to a wild path in the bog, I noticed a little drumlin. More like a mound than one of those elongated hills in the shape of a half-buried egg for which Ireland is famous. Though we know landforms like these were created by receding glaciers, commoners in Ireland believe them to be the entrance to the world of the Shee, or faeries. The Shee can be divided in two courts: the Seelie (beneficial and predisposed to kindness) and the Unseelie (cruel, mischievous, and evil). Both are sensitive and easily offended, bestowing curses, ill luck, or even death upon those whom they dislike. Legends say they inhabit halls built under the drumlins, and that, at certain times of the pagan year, they can be seen dancing on the top of the hillock.

Finding a bit of comfort in the memories of my grandma's tales, I went, a childish smug on my face, exploring the faerie fort, half-hoping to find a leprechaun to whisk me away from the ominous thoughts of this morning. What I found, instead, was something that left me even more puzzled. At the base of the drumlin, surrounded by half-buried rocks, stood an entrance. I had no light with me, however, the daylight was enough to brighten its interior, as it was not so large as a mine entrance or a cave system, more like the abode of a bear. Luckily, that was not the case – as bears have been extinct in Ireland for a long time – and it didn't show signs of inhabitation. And, apparently, there was a reason for that, as I will explain later.

It had a low-ceiled entrance, framed by strong roots, and it curved immediately, ending into a roughly round cul-de-sac. There, though the sunlight dimmed a bit, I was able to see this stone slab. Shaped in a rough triangle, it rested at the center of the cave; a flat, thick and heavy stone slab which bore a faded inscription. I could discern a cross on it, but also a warped, five-pointed star with a flaming eye at the center, and some unintelligible Latin words surrounding the engraved symbols. I ran my fingers around the borders, trying to determine its thickness, but the ground was too hard to dig it out with simple tools.

It looked ancient and gave me the creeps.

Later, I remembered the fact that monasteries, being the target of Viking raids in the ninth century due to their wealth, used to hide their treasures in natural caves. What if that slab concealed the lost fortune of forgotten monks? As a matter of fact, we are not that far from Glendalough, the monastery founded by St. Kevin long before the Viking invasion of Ireland.

Perhaps I had found my leprechaun's pot of gold after all.

Anyway, after a while, tired of wasting my time with something I was not properly equipped to deal with, I left the cave and decided to go to the village for some supplies and ask about my finding.

This time, I optioned for a secondary path, which crossed the moor and snaked up to the hills, ending into the Old Military Road. In 1798, following the example of France and the American Colonies, the Irish attempted to set up a republic. The effort was doomed, but it caused the British Army to create a supply route to pursue and capture Irish rebels before they escaped into the Wicklow Mountain glens. It starts from Rathfarnham, County Dublin, and stretches down thirty-six miles to Aghavannagh, County Wicklow, passing Glendalough.

While the nameless path to the military road was bleak and a bit treacherous, the road itself offered an astounding view of the countryside. Seen from the hills, the whole landscape was a study in brown: chocolate brown peat; black brown water; light brown grass; dark brown mounds of packed peat. Must say that from afar, the bog looked charming.

Trotting north to Ballymoor, I spotted a grassy field straight ahead and a large mansion, surrounded by carefully tended lawns, flowerbeds and a small ornamental pool on my right. Now I know it to be Moorcrest Downs, the estate of Squire Edgar Douglas, and that the field I crossed to reach Ballymoor belongs to this gentleman and his family. From *Cailleach Cnoc* – as the locals call the tallest hill on the road – I also could see, in the distance, the standing stone I had spotted the day I moved to Talbot House, and the Rathmoin Bridge, a little arched, stone bridge that crosses the Glencree river. Beyond that stood Ballymoor; the tall bell tower of St. Kevin standing out over the low roofs of the village. Down the *cnoc*, looking toward Talbot House, amid the tall, dry grass, I caught sight of another standing stone; this one, no longer standing, but laying on one side, as if it had been toppled. In fact, as I discovered later, the stone had been upturned by men hired by Squire Douglas (who's the owner of this tract of land, called Gob's Field) because he wanted the ancient relic moved to somewhere else. This monolith looked different from Old Lugh – the one on the way to Talbot House – as it was crudely shaped and bore no sign of carving. Nonetheless, the grey boulder was clearly man-made. As it wasn't that far from the safety of the road, I left my cart and went for a closer look.

The earth just beneath and around it looked blackened and burned, as if it had caught fire. However, upon closer examination, I discovered that even the side of the stone touching the ground had been scorched, for I found black, powdery soot caking the rough rock. Moreover, starting from the top and trailing down both sides, there were some dark stains that made me feel uneasy. I recalled an image of ancient pagan rites where maidens were sacrificed on stone altars; their heart removed; the blood flowing copiously down the rough altar …

Oh, how much closer I was to the truth.

Because it seems that Squire Edgar Douglas has been killed in that exact fashion atop that ancient rock!

This, I discovered later during my brief visit to the village.

In fact, when I reached Ballymoor, I noticed quite a commotion around the Bridge End Inn. There was some kind of town gathering inside, and I spotted Mr. Martin Flanagan, the man who is renting me the cart and Bertha, coming out with a dour expression on his face. He also spotted me and immediately forced his face into a smile, as if he didn't want me to know the whatabouts. I tipped my hat, then asked him what was going on. He said that the constable from Anniskerry was in town and he was conducting some kind of investigation, then he apologized for being in a hurry and immediately went his own way. I heard loud voices coming from the main hall, so, puzzled, I stepped inside the Inn. As soon as I crossed the threshold the ruckus ceased. All heads turned to me and I felt like I was the uninvited guest at a local secret ceremony. That wasn't the case, obviously, but the good folk of Ballymoor just didn't want to involve a stranger (and a foreigner, as I am) into that bad story. However, there was a man who was clearly interested about my presence: Constable Thaddeus Smale.

Smale is a red-haired man, with a face marred by freckles, mutton-chop sideburns, a big handlebar moustache, and a thick British accent. He was born in Somerset, and represents the Crown here in the Glencree area. The valley's climate hasn't been fair to him, for his skin – especially his face – looks wind-baked.

He immediately stepped forward and introduced himself, then asked me the motive of my presence in Ballymoor. Must admit the man did his best to act mannerly, yet his behavior was a bit rough at the edges. He clearly doesn't like living here, and I also suspect he thinks little of Irishmen. He reminds me of a Roman legionnaire sent to live among conquered barbarians. I can see he considers himself the last pillar of civilization at the edge of the empire. Honestly, I can't say I don't like the man, for he's not unpleasant. Nonetheless, his deeply repressed racism can be seen blowing out of him like smoke from a pipe.

By the time I had told him where I was living, why I was here, and where I came from, he had already blurted the beans out. Not a good tactic when one is conducting a murder investigation, I think. It would sound comical if it weren't for the horrible deed that was committed in Gob's Field.

In the morning of April 23rd, just two days before my arrival in Ballymoor, George Yates, gardener at Moorcrest Downs, discovered the abominably burned body of his master, Squire Douglas, laying atop the *Shamna* stone (that's the name of that toppled monolith in Gob's Field). Constable Smale didn't reveal all the details, but it seemed the poor man had been savagely treated and was already dead before the flames consumed his body. Smale, in light of Squire Douglas' clear opposition to Irish Home Rule and his disrespect of local traditions in favor of a modernization of County Wicklow, suspected a political instigant might have been responsible. He pointed to the fact that the gentleman had been forced to hire men from Bray to tear down that stone so he could have Gob's Field plowed; a task no locals would carry out because of superstition.

When the local smith, Bruce O'Reilly – a gruff man and a regular at the Bridge End – heard the word 'superstition', he became red on his face, slammed his pint on the counter, and roared something unintelligible at the policeman. Mrs. Yares tried to calm him down, but the man would have none of it.

"Ye don't understand, Constable," he said. "Ye come a'here from a different land, with different customs and beliefs. Ye judge, ye make yer own mind. Ye think ye know it all. Yet, ye know nothing!"

Smale ordered him to restrain himself and to remember he was talking to a police officer.

"Do ye know what's that stone?" the smith insisted, "Do ye know who owns it?"

"The fairy folk?" I chimed in, to divert his attention to me. I didn't want that poor man, a hard worker and father of three, as Mrs. Yares told me, to get in trouble.

"Nay," he shook his head, "Shamna was the stone of Dark Annis."

The constable rolled his eyes and muttered all his contempt for such nonsense. "*Black Annis* lives in Leicestershire, England, good man. And it's a fairytale to scare children, not reality, for goodness' sake! Ought to be ashamed of yourself; you are acting silly."

"I didn't say *Black Annis*," he hollered, "I said … *Dark Annis*!"

I could see the patrons' faces turning white. They really believed in that stuff; whatever it was.

"She's real, I say," continued O'Reilly. "I told Sir Douglas to stay away from the stone or he would suffer the consequences. I warned him. He wouldn't listen and look what happened! We're all cursed now. She will get her revenge."

That confrontation was quickly becoming dangerous for the smith. Soon, he featured as suspect number one on Constable Smale's list. "When was that? When did you talk to him? And why did you lie to me when I asked you before? Is it the alcohol loosening your tongue?"

I felt out of place. Clearly, it was not right moment to ask around about my findings. Upset by the news, and eager to get back home before dark, I moved to the exit.

"What was the reason of your visit, good sir?"

That came from Father Earl Wales.

Father Wales is a nice person. An old man, he has been a minister of God for over fifty years. Though a new addition – he came here six years ago – he takes great pride for what he has done for the community, yet at the same time, he seems a bit bored of speaking always to the same people, over and over.

"Oh, I came for some supplies, but I think I'll pick another time," I said.

"No need. Shops are still open," he insisted, almost begging for company. "Here, my good fellow, I will be glad to assist you."

I think he was quite happy to leave the pub and join a stranger for a bit of chit chat.

"I would be honored," I said, and we hastily left together.

During our rounds, Father Wales showed interest about my studies and praised my idea of finding isolation in the countryside to better focus on my disciplines. He also invited me to drop by for tea and biscuits from time to time. He told me that the first 'civil' inhabitants of the area were Ui Maol clansmen who had moved from the coast to escape Lochlannach raids. The Lochlannach being what we call the Vikings today. Viking raiding parties began to sack Ireland's coastal villages in the year of Our Lord 490, and some of the Gael tribes moved inland. According to Father Wales, these clansmen founded a settlement, called Rathmoin, in proximity of the two lakes.

Oh, I forgot to mention that down south, beyond the bog and the Pooka hills, there are two small lakes named Lough Bray Lower and Lough Bray Upper. They are encircled by the slopes of Mount Kippure and there's an interesting outcrop, like a real-life widow-peak, soaring above the two stretches of water. This outcrop is called Eagle's Nest and is a good point to get a breathtaking view of all the valley. Father Wales strongly suggested a field trip over there.

Sadly, nothing is left of the Gael settlement. From time to time some relics of the past were found; nothing precious, just simple tools and some bones. Father Wales suspects Vikings eventually found Rathmoin and burned it to the ground. It seems the area was resettled in 1605, when the village of Ballymoin was created to benefit from the peat trade. However, this hamlet didn't last much, as it was completely destroyed by Oliver Cromwell's army during his campaign to pacify Ireland in 1650. All that remains of the original Ballymoin is Rathmoin bridge. Ten years later, plantation immigrants, mostly from Scotland and Wales, created the village of Anniskerry, but strongly refused to settle in the Glencree vale as they were afraid of a local legend. When I asked Father Wales about this legend, he said it is exactly the one O'Reilly was barking about. It is the story of Annie Carrick, the *fuath* (bog hag).

It seems that in 1640, just prior to Cromwell's invasion, there lived in Ballymoin a woman suspected of practicing the dark arts. In truth, Father Wales thinks she was just a wise woman with a strong connection to nature and Irish traditions. Her entire life was devoted to her spouse and her children and she also acted as a midwife for most of the villagers. However, one day, her husband returned home with a younger and prettier woman. Annie had been beautiful herself once, but the hard life she had led for her family had taken its toll, robbing her of her beauty. Shortly, the man cast her out of his home, proclaiming that he had a younger and healthier wife now while she had become a hideous crone. Annie begged him to reconsider, then turned to her sons, but they too spurned her. Sent off, Annie Carrick wandered around Ballymoin asking for help, but everybody shunned her, calling her a witch or worse. Starving, she moved into the moor and the hills, feeding on what she could find or trap. Father Wales believes she died in the bog, however, local folklore says that she found refuge in a cave in the moor. The legend says that, alone in that dark place, she begged the Morrigan to help her, and the goddess answered back. The Morrigan took pity on the poor woman and offered her the opportunity to get revenge. Annie accepted and she became a real hag. From that time on, children disappeared from the village, men were found butchered in their beds, and bad accidents happened to those women who flaunted their beauty. Father Wales says that it seems that after ten years of this, the villagers, who were living under the terror of Annie Fuath, as they called her, finally took arms and boldly confronted the hag in her cave. Stories say that they found her rocky abode furnished with human skins and bones, but Father Wales suspects these bits were added later to the legend by the Scottish immigrants who connected her to the British Black Annis. Hag or not, Annie was dragged out of her lair, rope-bound to a standing stone, and burned alive.

Indeed. Like Squire Douglas.

Therefore, I see Constable Smale's reason for suspecting political foul play. Folklore says Dark Annis was burned while tied to a stone. And Sir Douglas, an opponent to local traditions and superstition, was treated in the same way. Easy to find a connection.

However, Father Wales isn't sure if Shamna was the stone where Annie Carrick was burned. He said that it was recorded that Annie Fuath was often spotted dancing around it, but some stories say that she was bound and set on fire at Cailli stone, a menhir that has long disappeared.

While rounding the village pond – a beautiful, well-tended little garden in the hamlet's center – I heard a child singing a ballad that sounded weirdly familiar to me. In fact, it was the same one I had heard in my dream! I froze there and listened carefully at the creepy rhyme.

She had a knife long and sharp, weile weile wee.
She had a knife long and sharp, down by the Glencree

She stuck the knife in the baby's heart, weile weile wee.
She stuck the knife in the baby's heart, down by the Glencree.

Father Wales noticed and, with a smile, told me that was an old nursery rhyme, or murder ballad, that kids in the Glencree area sang by generations. It is usually sung while jumping rope, or skipping as they say here, or when playing pat-a-cake. He said that rhymes like this were quite common in the countryside, often referring to horrible events. This one was somewhat connected to the legacy of the great famine, when extreme hunger and poverty denied families the ability to feed all their children.

I didn't tell him the first time I had heard it had been in a dream, sung by unseen tikes.

He pulled my arm, dragging me gently to the grocery store, saying that we had to hurry up if I really wanted to buy supplies. But I could see in his eyes the need to not discuss the argument further.

This reminded me about my extraordinary finding: the slab.

When I asked Father Wales if he knew anything about it, his face turned to stone. Funny, he had been telling me legends of witches, spellcraft and social injustice with a jolly attitude, smiling all the time and adding his personal suppositions, but the moment I named the slab, his demeanor changed.

"That, my son," he said, "is a different thing. Yes, I know about the slab under the hillock and it has nothing to do with Dark Annis or Annie Fuath's tale. That slab is older. And it was placed there by Saint Kevin himself."

I thought he was pulling a prank on me, so I hazarded a chuckle, but his expression didn't change. I invited him to tell me more, and he was reluctant at first, insisting it was late and he had to go back to Church for the evening service. However, he promised to tell me the whole tale the next time I visit him for tea.

Now, thinking about it, the murder of Squire Douglas could hold more than mere superstition or politics. It could be about a treasure.

I'm getting tired and I think I had my full share of emotions today, therefore, it is better if I go to sleep.

Tomorrow I will try to find more about St. Kevin's slab.

April 28th, 1891
Talbot House
Later.

I'm awake and shaking in the aftermath of yet another bizarre dream.

I swear the Almighty, I've just checked the house for signs of intrusion; for as irrational as it sounds, the dream appeared so real that it left me breathless and in pain. Now, it is entirely possible that a suggestion has been implanted into me by Father Wales' tale, mixed to the anxiety caused by the news of an iniquitous murder. I must also admit having overindulged on the scrumptious apple crumble cake made by Maggie. And my, if that was some heavenly food: the apples and blackberries just make you melt.

It didn't help shake off the feeling that there was more to the nightmare.

After my delicious supper, and my ablutions, I prepared for bed, then resolved to add my previous entry in this diary.

From where I lay – with the heavy curtains wide open, so that the soft moonlight soothes me – I can see the wide expanse of the moor, crowned by the dark hills, and this gives me a sense of relief from the oppressive mood of the master bedroom: dark mahogany furniture decorates this room, and the drawings – also dark – of stormy seascapes just add to the grievousness. The only reason I selected this room is because it allows me a pleasant view of the Pooka hills, that, frankly, are quite impressive in their morning beauty.

After writing down my last entry, I felt sleepy, so I replaced the journal and the pen on the nightstand, then killed the lamp's flame.

I came out of my sleep with a start. There was a shuffling sound, like of dragged – yet light – footsteps coming from the hallway. Patently, I tried to lift my body up, but to my amazement, and then horror, I found myself unable to move. Even turning my head was impossible. I struggled, but I was paralyzed. I could feel, breathe, and see; nonetheless, all my muscles were seized by immobility. Panic assaulted me in chilling waves and my mind frantically galloped in search of an explanation.

Had I been I poisoned? Had the still-at-large killer selected me as his next victim? Maybe, the cake had contained a powerful paralyzing venom that would have allowed the malicious murderer to kill me without a fight.

Yes, this sounds irrational now, but I can't forget the sense of paranoia which gripped me in, what I suppose, was just a nightmare.

The only parts of my body I could move were my eyes, and they darted from window to door, from the edge of my bed to the blackened corners.

Then, I realized not being alone.

As the footsteps came closer, a darker, hazy human shape, outlined by the pale moonlight, appeared through the door, which, I'm sure, I closed behind me before climbing into bed, but was now standing ajar. The dream felt so real, for all the room's details and smells were present, not as blurry as they are in my usual dreams. Then, the shape crawled onto the bed. Moving like a cat, it slid across the blankets, until it came to sit on my heaving chest. At first, I couldn't see the assailant's face, as the only visible thing was the outline of its wild mane, but then, as it bent over, the disturbing vision of something wicked faded in from the dark. Behind the cracked – and blood-stained – white leather mask of an unsmiling child, loathsome eyes, reddened and apparently sightless, shone with the light of madness. As the thing came closer to my face, I could see that the mask had been nailed to her head with rusty spikes. The hot breath coming from its mouth stank of rotten meat. Yet, this was nothing compared to the horror that was her face. Her face, yes! For soon, with a sickening sound, the figure peeled off the mask revealing the feminine terror behind it. Flesh the color of a deep bruise, as that of a woman skinned alive or burned by great fire, covered with warts, blisters, and open sores. She opened her mouth, slowly, and the myriad of thin, yet unnaturally sharp teeth glistened with drool. What I had believed to be a mane turned out to be a wig: a mish-mash of scalps and hair of different colors. Grinning malevolently – mere inches away – she cocked her head to the side, in an alien and disturbing way, while her hands – oh, my God, her hands! – ran to my neck. Long-fingered, inhuman, veined, and of the same color and texture as her face, those claws circled my neck, sinking their blackened and sharp nails into my skin.

In the distance, down in the garden, I could hear the children singing the nursery rhyme.

There was an old woman and she lived in the moors, weile weile wee.
There was an old woman and she lived in the moors, down by the Glencree.

She stole a baby three months old, weile weile wee.
She stole a baby three months old, down by the Glencree.

She had a knife long and sharp, weile weile wee.
She had a knife long and sharp, down by the Glencree.

She stuck the knife in the babys heart, weile weile wee.
She stuck the knife in the babys heart, down by the Glencree.

There were folks come a'knockin on the door, weile weile wee.

There were folks come a'knockin on the door, down by the Glencree.

They caught the woman lying on the floor, weile weile wee.
They caught the woman lying on the floor, down by the Glencree.

They bound the woman hands and feet, weile weile waile.
They bound the woman hands and feet, down by the Glencree.

They set her on fire and she went crisp, weile weile wee.
They set her on fire and she went crisp, down by the Glencree.

And that was the end of the woman in the moors, weile weile wee.
And that was the end of the baby too, down by the Glencree

As she bent over me, I felt like she was draining my very vital force. Overwhelmed, I closed my eyes, eager to remove that terror from my view, and waited for death to come. Then, while my vision became blurred due to the lack oxygen, I woke up from my ordeal, gasping for air.

After regaining my strength, I immediately lit the lamp and searched proof of the monster's visitation. I found none; the door was locked, same for the window. No stranger's footprints on the dusty carpet. I went down to check the front door, then every room in the house.

Realizing it had only been a bad dream, I resolved to go back to bed. Yet, I can't sleep: the crone's horrible face still dwells in my mind's eyes.

And that horrible nursery rhyme …

CHAPTER SEVEN

April 28th, 1891
Talbot House
Evening.

A day full of emotions.

Oh, dear journal, were you a person, I would feel the need to apologize for forgetting about you today. I use you as a physician (to not say an alienist): I promised myself to pen down everything I experience here, so, that when I reread it, I can evaluate my state of mind. And what a good commitment is that, for, after today's events, I'm more than convinced there's foul play going on among the people of Ballymoor.

The hag attack I suffered last night could be more than a nightmare. Same goes for the other queer occurrences; lest no forget the murder of Squire Douglas. These are dark days here in Ireland. A never sated need for rebellion against the British crown is coming ablaze again. It grows in the underworld, feeds on the commoners' rage – especially in the countryside – and skulks within unthinkable halls. Laying behind national heritage and tradition, the smoking coals of independence, hidden under the ashes of unionism and the common wealth, are fast to rekindle and hard to dispel. While I will not discuss the right – or not – for an independent Ireland, I strongly condemn the nefarious manipulation of superstitious villagers to trigger an uprising. For I'm sure a conspiracy is underway in the Glencree valley.

How I came to this conclusion? Simple: by the application of logic and rationalization. It comes a moment when a man must step out of the circle of darkness he fell into, climb the tallest hill, and, once at the top, look down with a brand new perspective.

And this new perspective I gained by looking at history.

Since 1874, agricultural prices have been dropping in Europe, followed by some bad harvests due to wet weather. This has been having a strong negative effect on many Irish farmers, who found themselves unable to pay the rents they had agreed on, particularly in the poorer and wetter areas. It was out of this desperation that the Irish National Land League was born, and that led to the ‘Land War’.

This ‘war’ was fought in the countryside from 1879 to 1882 in pursuance of the ‘Three Fs’: fair rent, fixity of tenure, and free sale. The League organized resistance to evictions and reductions in rents. Landlords' attempts to evict tenants led, naturally, to violence. When Ashbourne's Act in 1885 made evicting tenants unprofitable for most landlords, this violence was supposed to end, yet tenants found that holding out communally was the best option. Upheavals continued. Accompanied by several years of bad weather and poor harvest, the agitations, and subsequent evictions, led to a rent strike. Although the League, nominally discouraged violence, agrarian crimes increased widely. The rent strike was followed by eviction by police officers and bailiffs. The tenants who had continued to pay the rent were subject to boycott by local League members. This created a great divide among the farmers. Political elements have easily infiltrated this strife, and now, after the Land League is officially suppressed by the authorities, they have broadened the issue to Home Rule. A renewed Land War is going on, yet, this time, it is more subtle, and its covenanters are using national pride and tradition for their own means. Anarchists, independentists, and ruffians of all sorts are joining this hidden game.

In my case, there’s a supernatural smokescreen set around me and the good folk of Ballymoor. After today’s events – and encounters – I will be more careful about my acquaintances and I will not allow my goodwill to cloud my eyes. At the moment, I’m not in physical danger, for whoever is behind this plot to scare me out of Talbot House has showed no intent to kill me. No, they just want to frighten the meddling foreigner away. And I don't like it.

More, I have found a new resolve in my affection for Maggie Blair.

Let's start in order.

This morning, sweet Maggie came alone. She said Siobhan had gone to greet a tribe of blood-related gypsies who had just set camp at Lough Bray Lower. These aren't Travellers, but true *romany*: a *kumpania* (or company) of Szek families led by a matriarch. Maggie said it was great news, as this kumpania's goal is to restore the diminishing mana (the world's inherent magical energy) into the faerie stones. She appeared excited and was like a stream awakening in springtime, when the waters, frozen by winter, happily burst out of the thawing. Without doubt, she lifted my sullied humor. She spoke of portents, faerie forts, and wondrous places, and I, while looking at her, could not avoid being charmed by her mirth.

"They are going to restore the land, sir!" she said, pirouetting; her red skirt lifting so high it exposed her beautiful calves!

My eyes widened at the sight, and she must have noticed, for soon she calmed down, then, bowing, apologized for her excesses. I smiled and reassured her that she had not offended me; on the contrary, I was in need of some good spirit. Also, an idea occurred to me.

"It is such a wonderful day, isn't it?" I said, peeking out of the window. The morning sun was painting the hills in magnificent gold and vibrant green.

"It surely is, sir," she concurred, as she came to my side. "Are you going out again?"

"No," I said, looking at her. "*We* are going out." I took her hands, "The house doesn't need your attention today. But I do."

Perhaps, I showed too much audacity, for immediately she blushed and her eyes fell to the floor. Still, she didn't retract from my hands.

"Moreover, I need your opinion on something I discovered yesterday. It's hard to describe and I think it's better you see it with your own eyes."

She lifted her head, "What is it, sir?"

"Well … actually it's more than one thing. There's a hole, just on the other side of the hillock. But the most peculiar thing is this … this stone slab I found inside the cave. Have you ever heard of that?"

Maggie looked out with a puzzled expression, then her fine lineaments twisted in the grin of a child trying to remember a poem learned at school. A shadow crossed her face before she shook her head. "No, sir, sorry."

"Does that mean you're not coming?"

Maggie smiled, "No, I mean I know nothing of that place. I've heard stories about a witch living in a hole in the distant past, but I've never seen that place." Then, she immediately added, "And yes, I'm coming with you."

Oh, if I had known in what sort of additional worries I was putting myself I would have surely shelved the idea. I should have listened to the symptoms of my fast-racing heart, of the excitation at the idea of spending my day out with her. But I didn't, and by consequence, I'm in trouble.

I decided it would be better if we circled the hillock with the trap, so that if we found something inside the hole, it would be easier to transport it back home. Also, I could use Bertha's strength to uncork the stone from the earth. Later, we would continue for the toppled stone, and by afternoon we would reach Ballymoor, just in time for a tea with Father Wales. He still owed me the story of Saint Kevin and the slab. So, while I fastened Bertha to the cart and loaded the necessary tools, Maggie took care of preparing the necessary for a picnic.

Before going, I had breakfast with Maggie, who, though shy to share the table with me at first, ended up enjoying my company.

The food was delicious; the conversation even more.

Maggie asked to know more of me, my family, how life was in America, and about my past. I answered each question sincerely, until it was my turn to know more of her story. And what a story it is.

Maggie Blair wasn't born a Traveller, or, more aptly, she was born half-blood. Her father was Lazaros Strazi, also known as 'the Fabulous Lazaros', a knife-thrower at the Rovers Carnival. Her mother was Milena, daughter of Siobhan. While attending a fair in Dublin, Milena fell in love with the dashing Lazaros. He was, it seems, a charming man, renowned for his throwing skills and his silver tongue. Siobhan disliked him, being a *gaje*: not of the blood. Gypsies value their bloodline. They believe they must maintain purity in their race in order to keep the gift of the Sight. Especially the women.

However, so strong was the attraction of Milena for Lazaros that she had a fight with her mother, left her kumpania, and joined Strazi as her assistant. Maggie was born out of that love and she lived with her parents up to the age of nine. Then, tragedy struck.

Milena doubled as a fortune teller at the traveling show; wearing flamboyant – and revealing clothes – she lured clients to her tent where she predicted their future. Though she had no true Sight, according to Maggie, she was skilled at a scam called *bujo* or swindle.

In this scheme, a Gypsy woman looks for a likely (read: gullible or desperate) victim to con. She uses sleight of hand to replace one of the tarot cards she is reading for her client with a scorched version of the same card. Then, she cries out and acts worried. When the target of this scam demands to know what's wrong, the fortune teller tells the client that the news is not good, but perhaps she's wrong. At the client's insistence, the prognosticator will reveal that she sees terrible luck befalling the client. Then, she explains that the possible source of this misfortune could be some cursed money. Thus, she will hastily return any money the customer has paid for her services as she doesn't want to be contaminated as well. After a bit of talk, she will ask the person to give her some small notes or coins so she may determine if the money is indeed cursed. Naturally, she will find out so. And, of course, she can remove the curse. The hitch is that all the client's money has probably been infected by the curse, and so the victim should bring the Gypsy a suitcase filled with money. In order to undo the curse, some of the money must be destroyed. Once the client has brought as much money as the fortune teller can convince them to bring, she performs a great ritual that ends in the burning of much of the 'tainted' money. Obviously, the money will not be destroyed, for, at the first opportunity, the con artist will switch the bag full of money with one containing papers.

However, sometimes the scam turns on the scammer.

Lazaros had always been a jealous and possessive man. He regarded Milena Blair as a property, and had more than one fight with other artists at the carnival when he spotted a gaze lingering for too long on his wife's graces. There were rumors that he had killed a roustabout when he overheard the man complimenting, in a lewd way, Milena's figure. Though no proof was ever found.

Maggie remembered that when her mother started to work as a fortune teller, her father was always in an ill mood and took every opportunity to wrangle with his wife. Strazi was a violent man; full of rage, and consumed by it. He steamed it off by sharpening his skills at throwing. And by verbally attacking his wife.

Milena, however, would not back off. Being an Irish-blooded Rom, she had a fiery temper, too. Theirs was a stormy, but passionate relationship.

When Maggie was nine of age, the carnival was touring the province of Munster. And it stopped in Crosshaven, a beautiful village overlooking Cork Harbor. It was in that place that Milena met Arthur Fitzhugh, the son of Lord Chesterton of Balcombe, West Sussex. Lord Chesterton and his family were guests of the Earl of Cork, and were enjoying the summertime at Crosshaven. Young Arthur became attracted to the beautiful Milena and started to visit her every evening. Maggie's mother immediately targeted him as the right man for a bujo, for Arthur was as intelligent as a rock. Unfortunately, Lazaros mistook his wife's interest for the young man as something more. He spied on Milena while she received the gentleman in her privy. Upon hearing the stranger complimenting his wife, he became scarlet with rage. However, what sent him beyond the edge was the bag of money. Believing it to be payment for Milena's 'favors', he went mad. That night became the Strazi's – and the Rovers Carnival's – last show.

Better I describe what happened by transcribing it the way Maggie told me.

"The lights were bright in the big top, the smell of greasepaint, candies, and horses assaulted my senses like every time. I loved the circus, but now I can't stand it anymore. I was standing behind the main curtain, the one leading to the ring, close by Mr. Errol Pierce. He was the founder, along with his brothers, of the Rovers Carnival. A portly man, with receding ginger hair, Pierce had been like a grandpa to me. He always said he had great expectations for me; like he knew I was of special blood. Errol spoke high of my real grandma, Siobhan, and how much he missed her. I think he was in love with her. I don't know all the details, as granny never talks about him, but I know the two used to be friends before my mother married my father.

"Errol was the sole owner of the show, after Samuel and Duffy – his brothers – were called in the Lord's embrace. A good man.

"That night, he spotted a shadow on my face and asked to know why I was frowning. I said I was worried about my parents because they were always fighting. I remember him smiling and grabbing my face with affection. He said I didn't need to worry for my dad and my mom had always been like the sea: stormy one moment, calm and beautiful another. But I think he just saw the professional side of their relationship, for, you know, even after a bitter fight, my parents were like one when performing in the ring. You could see the trust in my mommy's eyes as my father threw blade after blade at her on the spinning wheel.

"But Mr. Pierce hadn't seen my father's face while he was practicing in our tent. Early on, I had stumbled in while he was honing his skills throwing knives at my mam on the rehearsal board. With them there was this man, Rudolph, a stage magician. He was one of those kind of men that's not happy unless he has someone to needle. And my dad was one of his favorite targets. So, while he was about to throw the fifth dagger, Rudolph said something I didn't understand at the time. And my father's knife went wild. Luckily, my mom ducked out of the way in a split second and the blade buried itself in the board mere inches from her face. At that, Rudolph blurted that sawing somebody in half was his act, not my dad's. I saw my father's eyes turn dark, and I think Rudolph saw that too, because he excused himself and left the tent. My mam hadn't heard what Rudolph had said, so she asked my father what was wrong. He shook his head and told her to get ready. The show was about to commence. Then he noticed me. He smiled sadly, caressed my hair, and told me to go to Mr. Pierce. I will never forget his face. Though I can't forgive him for what he did, I have pity for his soul.

"During the show, he missed his third throw. The knife sank deep into my mam's heart, killing her on the spot.

"Later, knowing the facts, I understood what Rudolph has said to my father. Like a whispering imp he had told him that the young Chesterton was here to see Milena again. And in fact, he was there, in the first row.

"Completely maddened, what was once my father but had now become a murderous monster, threw two daggers at the Lord's son. One missed. The second found its mark into the gentleman's right eye.

"As you can imagine, the carnival erupted into chaos, police were summoned, and the traveling fair was closed. My father was arrested, but he never reached the prison. He died of a stroke in the police wagon. So the officers said. I was sent to an orphanage in Dublin and it was there that my grandmother found me.

"As of that day, I can't stand fairs and circuses."

What a terrible tale.

I saw tears taking shape in her eyes as she recalled the last night she saw her parents, so I decided to shake her out of it by returning to the subject of our awaiting adventure. I told her about my plans for the day.

Thusly, we circled the house, and when we reached the little drumlin, I pointed it to her. "There! Can you see the cave?"

She was still upset by the bad memories and I regretted inquiring about her past. I jumped down the trap, then looked for two suitable trees to create a high picket line. This is something I learned from a Texan friend. When a horse is tied to a tree for a long time, the surrounding ground is pawed away from the roots, the tree's bark is damaged, and the adjacent ground cover is broken and torn. More, it makes the horse nervous. Horses are relaxed and content when tied to a high line. They seldom pull against the line because there is nothing solid to pull against. With the knot above their heads even the most skilled horses cannot untie their lead ropes or slip their halters. This high picket line, approximately seven feet above the ground, must be tightly stretched between two trees. Lead ropes are then tied to the high line at the drop knots. Maggie, obviously, wondered what I was doing, and I told her that after my bad experience with Bertha and the dogs, I didn't want to take risks. I helped her down the cart, and at that moment, when her body was so close to mine, I lost myself in her perfume. My eyes met hers and something passed between us.

She's the most beautiful woman I have ever seen.

Embarrassed by the contact, she gently pushed me away, then went for the lead rope, ready to fasten it to the closest tree.

"No, I don't want to tie Bertha that way." I said, then I explained her my intent.

She looked at me quizzically. "Well, you are full of surprises, sir. It would never occur in my mind that a gentleman like you possessed such a wisdom about the wilderness."

"Please, Maggie, call me Patrick. I'm no sir." I said while climbing the first tree.

Again, she blushed, but said nothing. She helped me make the high line, and watched as I fastened the ends with Dutch's knots.

"And about me knowing of the wilds: yes, I know more than I show. Though I'm a city slicker – as my good friend Jim MacFarlane likes to remark – I'm not wet behind the ears. To be honest, one of my dreams was to go exploring the West."

"Oh, I've heard about that!" she exclaimed, "Is that due in Edinburgh?"

I frowned, trying to understand. Then, I remembered.

Since 1887, Buffalo Bill's Wild West had become a popular attraction in Europe. A pitiful thing of 'tame' Indians, where even the proud, but now broken Chief Sitting Bull had performed.

"No, not that," I said with disdain, "the *real* West! What is left of the true frontier."

"It is really that wild?" She moved toward me. I took Bertha's lead from her hand and secured it at the high line. Again, her smell invaded me, transported me. I felt hot. In that precise moment, I knew I wanted her. I'm aware there are certain rules a gentleman must abide by, but I can't deny that my thoughts were far from pure. I couldn't remove the vision of her calves from my mind. She was there, swirling in her red skirt, the white blouse revealing too much of her soft skin. The jingling of her wrist bangles. Her corvine hair dancing in the air …

Bertha interrupted my daydreaming with a snort.

"Well, I will tell you what I know of the real Wild West once we are finished with this." I pointed to the tools, "Please, help me with those. You take care of the lamp. I'll carry the rest."

We climbed the hillock until we reached the cavern. And immediately I noticed something was wrong. Or different.

Someone had been there.

Footprints of at least three men were clearly visible about the entrance. I didn't wait for Maggie, but rushed inside like an idiot. I was concerned about my *treasure*. Luckily, I found no one, but I found signs of a recent attempt at removing the slab. Someone had dug all around the triangular slate, exposing the thick border. Yet, it was still deeply encased in the ground, sign that the intruders might have been disturbed during their work.

Maggie's voice, from behind my shoulder, startled me. "Is that what you were talking about?"

Not saying a word, I grabbed the lamp from her hand and lit it. Under the light I could confirm my hunch: those words were written in Latin. They are faded and some letters are scratched. More, on the north side, there's a crack, as if some kind of accident happened to the slab in the past, or someone scraped it. I studied Latin at university, as it is good care of a surgeon or a generic practitioner to understand the works of our Greek and Roman predecessors.

And I'm sure it reads:

Coemgenus Glendalochensis declarat nemo movere lapidem ne erumpere tenebras.

'Kevin of Glendalough declares let no man raise this stone lest he unleash the darkness.'

Coemgenus was the Latin name of Saint Coemgen, which was then anglicized to Kevin. So the priest is right. This slab was posed in the name of St. Kevin. Or better, it was set by the saint himself!

Sadly, it doesn't sound like I've found a leprechaun's treasure vault, but whatever it is, it obviously comes with a warning. And it is surely older than the story of Dark Annis, for St. Kevin lived in County Wicklow in the sixth century. If authentic, that stone must have been placed there around one thousand and three hundred years old.

Maggie knelt beside me. She ran her fingers on the letters. "That symbol in the center," she murmured, "I've seen it before."

She touched it, then retreated her hand and screamed, as if that flaming eye was the real thing. Immediately, she passed out. Luckily, I was close and grabbed her before she hit the ground, however, the lamp slid off my hand and, after rolling loudly on the floor, died. Alarmed, I gently patted her face. I had no salts with me, and I have no experience on how to revive someone who lost their senses, but of one thing I was sure: better to bring her out of the cavern, as the fresher air and the sunlight might help. I lifted her in my arms and carried her out. In fact, as soon as I stepped into the light, she came about. Dizzy, she murmured something. I didn't feel like putting her down, so I carried her over under the trees, where I gently lowered her to the ground.

"What happened? Are you all right?" I asked, while fetching the canteen.

She didn't answer, but looked into my eyes. Her pupils were wide and she was shaking. Unexpectedly, she threw herself at my neck, and then kissed me. At first, I was so stupefied by that reaction that she met only my half-closed lips. But then, overtaken by desire, I responded. I kissed her back, deeply, holding her tight. We forgot about everything, the cavern, the slab, my nightmares. It was just us.

I didn't know what had caused that reaction, and, honestly, I didn't care. I was so absorbed by that moment, by Maggie's angelic face, her jade eyes, the softness of her porcelain skin, and, mostly, those lips. Those lips I had desired since the first day I saw her. A mouth made to drive a man crazy. And I indulged on those lips, I ate them like Adam bit the apple: without thinking.

She is a Traveller, part of her is Rom. I'm a gaje. We come from different worlds.

Yet, I can't stop thinking about her. Even now that she's gone.

After that kiss, we stood there, in each other's arms, not saying a word. A silent bond was forged from a passionate wind that swept away all the differences in a single, but powerful blast.

"We should go back," she said, breaking that silence. Her cheeks were red, her gaze avoiding mine. It was like she had just come out of some sort of spell. "We should stay away from that place."

"What's that?" I asked. "What happened in that cav-"

“I don’t know!” she cried. “There’s *something* down there. *Something* horrible. *Something* buried. I don’t know what is it, but for a moment, when I touched the stone, I felt *something* invading my mind, as if trying to take hold of me.” She rose to her feet and started the descent.

I ran after her. “Tell me. What did you see?” She was going fast and I was worried she could tumble and get hurt. “Slow down, Maggie, please!” But she wouldn’t listen. To the contrary, she lifted her skirt and sprinted down the hill. I quickened my pace, still paying attention to the rocks, and soon reached her.

“Maggie!” I yelled, “Calm down. I’m here. Whatever it was, it’s over.” I grabbed her shoulder and turned her toward me. She struggled a bit, but finally gave in. I pulled her into my arms, and she allowed me to hold her tight, then, she started to cry. I caressed her hair, while her body trembled, consumed by fear.

“Patrick,” she uttered among the sighs, “please, let’s go. I don’t want to talk about it. It was horrible.”

“All right,” I lifted her chin. Her beautiful face was streaked by tears. “We will not talk about it. I just want you to relax. We’ll go back home and I’ll make you a nice tea.” She nodded, then started again for the trap. Holding her hand, we went down together.

We didn’t talk during all the trip back to Talbot House. She just huddled into me, and after a while, she fell asleep, as if the emotion, whatever it was, had been so strong that it had completely drained her. I can’t figure what she must have felt, or experienced inside her mind. Maybe, as her grandmother believes, she is a Seer, one of those people able to see things that other’s eyes can’t, like those that conduct séances and claim to see the dead. Or, maybe, she is just the victim of a plot, like me.

As I wrote before, today I have collected some – even if circumstantial and purely deductive – proof that a supernatural smokescreen has been set up to scare me away. And to keep the curious far from that cave. But I will write about that later.

Once we arrived at Talbot House, we found someone waiting for us.

Siobhan, in the company of three shady and unkempt gypsies, greeted us with a red face. She was angry at Maggie for going out with me, a *gaje*, without her consent. I tried to calm her down, telling her that Maggie had simply helped me look for some herbs. Obviously, I lied, for somehow – and luckily so – I didn't want the gypsies to know about the cave. Siobhan, ignored me, and started spewing forth a stream of questions at her granddaughter, in her unintelligible language. Maggie stood there, eyes to the ground, unable – or unwilling – to bark back. After a while, annoyed by this ugly episode I was forced to watch, I raised my voice, reminding my visitors that they were standing on my grounds and that I expected them to behave in a proper decorum or I would have them leave. At that, two of the gypsies moved toward me in a threatening way.

I didn't like it. I didn't like it at all.

The tallest one told me to keep my mouth shut and go inside the house. I stared straight into his eyes and stood firm, rebuking that he had to force me to do so, if he dared. My resoluteness didn't seem to dissuade him, and he got closer, towering above me. The other, a shorter, but stocky individual, stepped sideways and came behind me, while the third one, a weasel-looking fella, retrieved a whip from his own cart and cracked it to the earth, smiling in anticipation for a good fight. Things didn't go for the worse, luckily, for Maggie shouted something in Romany, and Siobhan snapped an order to them. Immediately, the two goons backed off: the tall one keeping his dark eyes on mine, and the weasel replacing the whip back. Then, the old woman told Maggie and the men to go to the vardo and wait there. The gypsies seemed reluctant to do so, but a stern look from Siobhan was enough to have them comply. Remembering everything nice this woman had done for me, I didn't want to argue with her; after all, I understood her concerns over her granddaughter. I tried to reason with her, but she cut me short.

"I've seen ye. I know phat ye did wid me, Maggie." She spat out those words with animosity. "Be lucky I don't curse ye. Yet, be warned: stay away from Maggie."

She turned and went to the wagon, ignoring my protests and my attempts to dialogue. Maggie glanced at me, looking guilty, but didn't say a word. Then, at the crack of the driver's whip, the two black horses pulling the gypsy wagon bolted down the road. I watched them disappear from my sight, my anger still seething. I felt offended, and, at the same time, sorry for Maggie. There was nothing I could do, so I went inside the house.

However, it soon came to my mind that I still had time to visit Father Wales and find out about the slab. Also, I wanted to know more about the nursery rhyme, for it was now clear that it didn't refer to the great famine, but to the deeds and eventual fate of Annie Carrick. I felt that Father Wales had deliberately lied to me about the ballad's origins. Besides, after my bad encounter with the gypsies, and the way they had looked at me, I thought it would be a good idea to speak to the constable too, if he was still in town. Thus, I mounted on the trap and sped down to Ballymoor.

I found out that Constable Smale was visiting Squire Douglas' widow and wouldn't be back at the inn until late. Yet Father Wales was at home when I knocked at his door. He looked quite surprised to see me, nonetheless he invited me in and asked his housekeeper to make some tea. It was a nice one, accompanied with scrumptious cookies.

We were enjoying this dark tea in Wales' study when I told him about the slab, and my rough translation of it. He almost choked, then put his cup down, spilling some of the content, and instinctively touched the silver crucifix dangling from his neck. He tried to evade the conversation; again proof that although he doesn't believe much in Dark Annis' legend, he's afraid of speaking about that slate. He asked me if I knew about the gypsy camp at the lakes. I told him what had happened this afternoon, and how it was my intention to report their unwanted, if rude and threatening visit to the constable. He looked shocked, and convened to report the trespassing as soon as possible, since many others in town had been complaining about the gypsies skulking around their homes. However, I didn't want the conversation to rail off, so I quickly went back to the slate. Cornered, Father Wales understood my determination to know more, and he promised to tell me the whole story once back from a certain duty, and, excusing himself, he disappeared into the church.

While waiting for him I took the opportunity to check out his library. The shelves are full of religious texts, of course, but I also spotted some books on history, poetry, and Irish folklore. I pulled out an old tome, titled *A Guide to the Folk of the Hollow Hills*, and to my surprise, I discovered a smaller book laying behind it, flat against the wall. What a discovery!

This book is *Ars Goetia,* based on the infamous grimoire *The Key of Solomon.* It refers to practices which include the invocation of angels and demons, to the binding of infernal creatures under the subservience of a wizard, and it includes the description of spells and wards. An occult book written – or translated – by an unknown author. The book is leather bound, small – roughly an octavo size – and heavily damaged. Its pages are yellowed and some of the illustrations have faded. However, what made this an important discovery is the fact that it had belonged to none other than Hugh Talbot. On the first page, handwritten in black ink, spidery letters declare his ownership. Inside, there are dozens and dozens of annotations, addenda, queer drawings, all scribbled around the pages. Just behind the back cover, there's a note, written by someone else, for the hand is clearly different.

It says:

'Bless the sun, for the Darkness cannot stand bright light.'

As I read this, I heard someone calling my name in a hushed, almost hissing tone. I turned my head. It had come from the window. And there, on the outside, a shadow crossed the frame. More confused than scared, I replaced the book in its hiding place (I didn't want Father Wales catching me in the very indelicate act of intruding into his secrets), then moved to the window. No one out there. Except an ugly blackbird, a crow, or a rook, probably, perched on one of the tombstones lining the church's yard; its silvery eyes like mirrors in the dying sunlight. It moved its head nervously, looking at me one eye at a time. Then, it cawed and burst into a sudden flight. Straight toward the window's pane. Instinctively, I backed, startled by that irrational attack. The bird hit the glass, bounced on it, and fell to the ground, where it writhed and jerked before finally ceasing to move. Incredulous, I looked at the glass, stained with blood. I couldn't believe my eyes.

The voice of Father Wales shook me out of my stupor. I didn't understand at first what he was saying, then I realized he was asking me if I wished for more tea. I pointed to the window and told him what had just happened, but when my eyes returned to the glass, there was no trace of blood. And outside, no dead bird.

Now I have to stop my narration to explain exactly why I think this was an hallucination caused by drugs put in my tea. I honestly don't know if Father Wales is part of this conspiracy, for he seems willing to share information with me, but his housekeeper surely is. Miss Henrietta O'Reilly is cousin to Bruce, the smith. Yes, the same man who had warned Squire Douglas to stay away from the standing stone. I believe some of the locals are up to something. Maybe, the slab hides a secret meeting place for covenanters; the last vestiges of a failed revolt. Or worse. One thing is for sure: they don't want me here. Especially in Talbot House.

However, then, at the church, I wasn't thinking about a conspiracy or spiked tea. I thought what I had seen *was* real. Scared, I decided I had enough, and thinking that, after all, none of this was my business, I resolved to pack my stuff and return to Dublin.

I believed the priest had been looking at me as if I were either pulling a prank or being truly insane. Thus, in order to dismiss any ill thoughts, I said that the light had played a trick on me and that, probably, I had seen a large moth hit the glass. I feigned an embarrassed laugh, then sat down, prompting the priest to tell me the slab's story. Father Wales chuckled along, then he questioned if it was opportune of him to tell me such a grisly story just before sundown. Nervously, I insisted, and finally, he complied.

"It is known that after being ordained by Bishop Lugidus, Kevin moved to a cave in Glendalough in order to avoid the company of his followers. There, he was rumored to have banished a monster that lived in one of the lakes, and to have accomplished other miraculous feats. He had an extraordinary closeness to nature; his only companions the animals and plants around him. In Glendalough, he lived as a hermit for seven years, wearing only animal skins, sleeping on stones, and eating very sparingly. He went barefoot, and spent his time in prayer.

"Despite his will to remain alone, disciples were soon attracted to Kevin and a further settlement was established near the lakeshore. Saint Kevin became their teacher, and by the year of Our Lord five hundred and forty, his fame as a holy man had spread far and wide. Many people came to seek his help and guidance. In time, Glendalough grew into a renowned seminary of saints and scholars. It became the parent of several other monasteries.

"By the sixth century, most of the Leinster region had been converted to Christianity. However, some isolated, rural communities still held strong to many ancient and pagan traditions. Such was the case of a tribe of *Cruithni* savages who lived in the Glencree valley."

I had never heard of this tribe, so I interrupted his tale to know more.

It seems that the Cruithni were relatives of the Scottish Picts, and, like them, they have been completely eradicated from history; their existence signaled only by the chronicles of more civilized people. Father Wales, being a passionate historian, has collected notes and tales on this vanished tribe. They were simple, living in crude dwellings made of wood and animal skins, so, obviously, no trace has ever been found of their villages.

Father Wales continued, "The Cruithni of Glencree, like the ravenous wolves in whose skins they were clad, used to raid upon the Gael farms, raping, looting, murdering, and, so it was said, consuming the flesh of their victims. On learning of these godless acts, Saint Kevin rallied an army of true believers and marched to holy war, to rid Ireland of these devil-spawns."

"In this book," he showed me a large and antique tome, apparently written by one of St. Kevin's followers, "Breanainn, one of the Cenobites – monks who lived in a monastery, as opposed to the Anchorites, who lived as hermits – that accompanied Saint Kevin to Glencree, recounts that the Cruithni lived around a stone henge. Aye, the same one which sits behind Talbot House. Not built by them, they revered it as a place of communion with their goddess: Morrioghain, the Queen of Shades.

"Saint Kevin's army fell on the marauders, surprising them at dawn. Amid the bog, the two forces clashed in a bloody battle until sundown. By day's end, Kevin's forces were victorious and the holy cross stood tall on the ashes of the Cruithni village. Those pagans not killed in the brutal fighting were dragged before Saint Kevin to receive his judgment. The holy man offered them redemption and salvation if they would accept the cross and convert, but to the last one of them they refused.

Like rabid dogs, they barked and howled, cursing the Gaels and their god.

"Now, just beneath the stone henge lay a cave. Inside this cave, there was a deep hole, which the Cruithni proclaimed it reached into the very bowels of the earth, where the goddess' offspring were supposed to thrive. Unwilling to order the arbitrary execution of the prisoners, evil as they were and heinous as their crimes may have been, Kevin ordered the savages to be thrown into the hole, along with the corpses. Of the sixty prisoners taken that day, no man, nor woman, nor child was spared this judgment. Because they worshipped the darkness, they became part of it. Saint Kevin ordered the hole to be sealed with a flat stone, upon which he placed a mark: a magical ward able to keep the darkness away. The saint's idea was that the degenerated would die of thirst or starvation, thus leaving no blood on his hands. And that was the end of it"

However, I felt he was purportedly hiding the rest, for that story, true or not, would not explain why no one had ever tried to remove a holy relic attributed to one of the most revered saints of Ireland in centuries. And this, I questioned.

Father Wales admitted that there was more.

"Legends say that the marauders didn't die." He moved to the library and showed me another book. "This document is from the time when Vikings began to settle on the coast." This tome was even bigger, and had pictorial illustrations of strange creatures, half man-half dog, dining on human bones. For as crude as they are, these medieval drawings have certainly upset me, because I can't shake them from my head.

"By the seventh century, the Lochlannach had a settlement where Bray now stands. It was named Dun Laoghaire, even if some historians confute this, for they say that the port was actually an Ui Brian outpost. But this isn't what's important here. In this book, written by Guire mac Domhnall, an inhabitant of Rathmoin, who later took his vows and joined the monks at Glendalough, it is recorded a series of terrible events that befell Glencree in the year of Our Lord eight-hundred and forty, and how the Gaels of Rathmoin, who had founded the hamlet to escape the Lochlannach raids on the coast, ended up joining forces with the invaders against a terrible menace from the dark."

He showed me an illustration depicting a tall, bearded man, with an axe and a great sword, fighting alongside a shorter, red haired one armed with a large, knotted club. The two figures, back to back, were desperately hacking and slashing at a multitude of those dog-men, who were surrounding them like wolves.

"Guire says that a band of Lochlannach, led by Ketil Flat-Nose, scoured the moor for signs of Christian monks' hidden relics. They found the capstone engraved with Saint Kevin's ward and bearing the sign of the cross. While removing the stone, they damaged it; a large crack separated the ward in two. Having no respect for Christian icons, they cast the two pieces aside out of the cave, then they gazed into the pit. A dozen Viking warriors, used to fierce battles and afraid of nothing, descended into the dark. No one saw them ever again.

"Then, the grave-robbing, the disappearance of infants, and the assaults on lonely women began. No one had ever witnessed an attack from these mysterious marauders, who acted as wild dogs. Villagers in Rathmoin were at a loss; they didn't know the source of their invisible enemy. Until one night, when Guire himself spotted one of the creatures skulking among the tombstones."

"Excuse me," I interrupted, "are you telling me that those *things*", I pointed at the illustration, "were the descendants of those savages?" I couldn't believe that. How was that possible?

But he lifted his right hand. "That's the way Guire depicts them. I'm not saying I do believe they truly turned into werewolves." He chuckled, then poured some more tea. "At those times, it was easy to believe in goblins and leprechauns. But let me finish the account, then I'll give you my opinion on this."

I refused to drink more, and allowed him to go on.

"The Gaels of Rathmoin knew about Uath Hole – that's how they called that pit at the base of the henge – and Saint Kevin's tale. They suspected the Cruithni to have been members of the Little People, and that the saint had driven them underground. They were Red-Caps, to them, and Hobgoblins, and Knockers. So, they prayed the Almighty to deliver them from evil. And, according to Guire, the Lord sent Olaf One-Eye to them.

"Olaf was the older brother of Ketil Flat-Nose, and thane of Dun Laoghaire. He came investigating his sibling's whereabouts in the company of twenty warriors. When they arrived in Rathmoin, they found a dying village. Guire says that the Gruagach, as he called the monsters – meaning hirsute ones – had got bolder night after night. Olaf's conquest of Rathmoin was an easy one, as none opposed the invasion; instead, they begged their new lord to help them against the Gruagach. The Lochlannach demanded to know what befell his brother, threatening to burn down the village. Guire, speaking for his people, told him that he had probably been eaten by the Gruagach.

"The next day, Guire led Olaf and six of his men to the cave. They found the broken slab. One man went down the pit. He found the helms and weapons of Ketil's band, but not their bodies. Olaf insisted to send his men down to search for his brother, but Guire convinced him that it was of the utmost importance to have the slab restored and blessed by a holy man. Olaf didn't believe in the Christian god, yet he believed in magic. Fearing that the hole led into the bowels of the underworld, where the goddess Hel reigned, he decided to help the Gaels.

"Now, here, it's not stated how they repaired and blessed the stone, but Guire tells of the final battle against the Gruagach and of their queen, a Cailleach called, Gorta – famine or blight – and how, in the end, they captured such a queen, killed her, and caused the Gruagach to swarm back into the earth."

He stopped, then replaced the book in the library. "What I think," he said, returning to the table, "is that those Cruithni that were cast down by Saint Kevin were already accustomed to eating human flesh. They heartily fed upon the rotting bodies of their dead comrades. Water they found in abundance, for there's a subterranean stream flowing under the moor. Once the corpses were picked clean they turned on each other; the stronger killing the weaker. And they mated."

"Still, I think it's highly unlikely that the tribe survived for almost three hundred years. And what about the light? How could they survive in the dark?" I replied.

And here came his unbelievable answer.

"In another book, I've read that the Devil favors on those who dine on their brothers' flesh. Like Cain, who spilled Abel's blood and was cursed for eternity, those who partake on such unholy feast are rewarded with immortality, yet at the price of their souls."

"So, you believe these cannibal monsters are still living under the earth?" I was shocked. This man had been laughing about the tale of a hag, but was now telling me that he believed in immortal cave-dwelling fiends.

"I believe in the Devil's ability to mask himself, my son."

I was getting tired, and honestly, I couldn't add more grief to my already worried soul, so I politely thanked him for the tea and for the nice, though gruesome, tale, then moved to other grounds, "Do you know the actual master of Talbot House?"

"Yes, I do. Brandon Cooney of Cork. Well, actually he was born here, right under that roof, but he moved to Cork so long ago that no one considers him one of us any longer." He left his chair and went back to the bookcase. "Plus, there was that scandal."

"What scandal?"

He grimaced sadly, "There were rumors of incest. You see, his family had suffered so many disgraces, one after the other. And the last line of the Cooney was living there, isolated from the rest of the village. I'm not saying it actually happened, but there were some queer happenstances that led to the boy being sent away from here."

He took another book from the library, this one appearing to be a journal of sort. "In this book I have collected all the bad events surrounding Talbot House, from the time of its construction to the birth of Arthur, Brandon's son."

"Why are you doing it?" I asked. Honestly, I was starting to be a bit suspicious of him. Why all this interest about a house he had no claim on? Why keep tab of all the weird stories surrounding Dorchae Bog?

"My son, you are worried about an alleged witch that died more than two hundred years ago. I, myself, have deeper worries. Evil things have happened in and around that house; things that show the work of the Devil." He opened the book on the tea table. It was handwritten and contained dates, names, newspaper clippings, and some pasted documents. "And as a minister of God it is my duty to keep an eye for such things."

"Do you believe the house is under a curse?"

"More or less," he replied, leaning back in his seat and studying my face. "Not really a curse in its traditional meaning, but in that of being possessed – owned, I'd say – by a demon or Satan himself."

"What do you mean? And if so, what can you do to exorcise this *presence*?"

"At the moment?" he scoffed, "At this right moment there's nothing I can do. If what I believe is true, I'm far too weak and old to face it."

I studied him for a moment. "And did you find proof of this?"

"Look for yourself," he pushed the book toward me. "You can stay sure that all that is written, and documented there comes from reliable sources. There are no flights of fancy. All the murders, suicides, and disappearances really happened. Is this enough to say that the Devil dwells in that house? I don't know. But surely too many bad things have happened there. That house, my son, casts an evil spell on those living there."

I thumbed the scrapbook.

Mary Mother of God! The story of Hugh Talbot, as told by Siobhan, was just the tip of the iceberg. Not counting the legend of St. Kevin's slab, the Gruagach, and Dark Annis. All the families that had lived there after the times of Talbot had suffered losses, insanity, and worse. A woman had committed suicide in the attic. Another had murdered her own infant.

Wales pointed to a page, "See? This is what I was talking about: in 1851, Brandon Cooney was sent away to Cork. His twin sister, Victoria, instead, remained at Talbot House. Here," he showed me another page, "here you can read the statement of Mary Willow, who used to work there as a maid before being ushered out by the Cooney. She swore that Victoria was pregnant and that she personally saw Ellie Norris, a woman living in Anniskerry who was infamous for performing abortions, sneaking inside Talbot House at night. And spoke of the screams she heard."

"Well, that doesn't prove the incest." I cocked a brow at him.

"Read further." He sat back, sipping his tea and watched my eyes as they scanned the lines.

"Oh, my!" I exclaimed. "This can't be right."

"It is." He put down the cup and smiled gravely. "Take the book, son. Read it. Then you decide what to make of it. As I said, they are just facts. You can see a series of bad coincidences in there. I see deviltry in it."

"I will bring it back tomorrow," I said, still shocked by what I had read. It was time to go back home.

Before going, I had to ask. "Are there any more accounts of the slab? And do you know if it has been removed or replaced at other times?

He grinned sheepishly, "And why do you think I believe in those cannibals? Of course, there are more accounts. I have been collecting tales and legends about Uath Hole for years. A bunch of highwaymen removed the slab just prior to Cromwell's campaign, at the times of the village of Ballymoin. But after that, no one ever dared to move that stone. It will stay there, until the end of days."

I felt like telling him that – assuming the immortal cannibals were for real – surely there were other surface exits from that underground world, and I don't think all of them are plugged by a blessed slab, but I thought it was not necessary.

After all, who was I to dismiss his beliefs.

April 28th, 1891
Talbot House
Later

Once back at Talbot House I had a quick soup, then I immersed myself into the scrapbook. According to Father Wales' notes, the land of Glencree was granted to the Talbot of Malahide in 1766, but they didn't make great use of it until Hugh, a scholar, returned from an extended voyage through Europe. Construction of the mansion began in 1777 and finished in 1780. At the early stage of the building there's record of an unspecified accident that caused the death of Niall O'Grady, Talbot's personal valet. Father Wales has located the man's grave in Malahide, where he has been laid to rest in a mausoleum along with other members of his family. Apparently, this valet must have been greatly appreciated by Talbot to be granted such privileges. It seems that in the accident, a second man suffered such grievous injuries that he lost his left leg. However, Talbot accused him of negligence and he was sentenced to five years to be spent in prison for manslaughter.

There are no records of the death of Hugh Talbot, except for a note scribbled by Father Wales stating that he died in 1790.

In 1792, the Talbot sold the house and the bog to the Greene family. There's a copy of the deed inside the scrapbook. The new owner didn't last long: Michael Greene was found dead in the moor one year later. On the death certificate, the coroner of Anniskerry declares his *untimely departure due to the attack of a vicious wilde beast*. But what kind of beast, he doesn't specify.

The house stood empty for thirteen years, until William Douglas Greene sold it to a Scotsman, Sir Duncan Campbell. This man renovated and refurbished the house extensively, with furniture and appliances from his native Scotland. He was the one responsible for the creation of the gardens, the livery, and the small cemetery. The first one to be buried there was his uncle, Gregory Campbell, who died of heart failure two months after moving into Talbot House.

Duncan Campbell sold the house and the land to Seamus Cooney of Cork in 1821. The Cooney had made their fortune in the fishing industry, but Seamus was getting old and had decided to invest in the peat trade. He moved here with all his family with bright hopes. As Father Wales had said, his family was plagued by misfortune. In 1824, Kelly, the six-year old daughter of Dermot, the youngest son of Seamus, disappeared in the middle of the night. Search parties were formed, but the girl was never found. Maura, her mother, got the morbs and slowly descended into lunacy to the point of hanging herself from a rafter in the attic. The story was reported by a local newspaper, the now defunct Glencree Post of Anniskerry. Father Wales copied the text from the filed edition of this paper, which can be found at the Anniskerry public library. Wales also visited the County Wicklow Hall of Records and spent time to locate complete birth and death records for the Cooney family.

In 1828 Roy Cooney, Seamus' eldest son, and his wife Beulah, née Quinn, had a child, Andrew. I saw his tomb in the graveyard, however I didn't suspect at that time that the toddler had been killed. My mind had run to the usual causes of infantile death, like pox. Alas, his departure is more tragic.

Though there are not documents attesting the authenticity of Father Wales' notes, the priest had collected rumors among the townsfolk. Beulah had changed after the birth of Andrew; she spent time alone in the moor, walking aimlessly, sometimes only wearing a nightgown. She had been spotted by various hunters and travelers. One night, Mr. Dull recalls – he was a boy at that time, working at the Cooney stalls – he saw her naked, dancing around the henge. Later, she became hysterical and had to take some special medicaments that the Cooney had delivered from Dublin, so Mrs. Yares of the Bridge End Inn says.

In the night of April 30, 1829, Roy Cooney had returned home from Anniskerry, when he found Beulah in front of the great fireplace, her white nightgown reddened by blood. At first, he thought that his wife had tried to kill herself, but when she turned toward him, he discovered the horrid truth. In her arms lay the headless body of little Andrew; his head was burning in the hearth, spreading the stench of charred flesh. No one knows exactly what had happened, but everybody in the village knows that Beulah fled into the bog. And no one saw her ever again.

The following year witnessed the death of yet another member of the Cooney family: an accident occurred to Dermot while hunting in the moor. Or rather, he was accidentally shot by his own rifle. Nevertheless, in Ballymoor, people thought different. They said that Dermot and his brother had a violent argument, and Roy overracted, killing him with a poker. They say old Seamus bought the constable to avoid any scandal and protect his heir.

In the scrapbook, there's a marriage certificate attesting the wedding of Roy Cooney to Angela Reilly. Twenty years younger than him, Angela Reilly was disowned by her own family for marrying a Cooney. In a letter attached to the scrapbook, Constance, Angela's mother, warns her that the Cooney are devil-worshippers for they rarely attended church. This was mostly due to the fact that Seamus and his family were Protestant, while Angela's family was staunch Catholic.

One year later, twins were born out of this union: Brandon and Victoria.

There are numerous newspaper clippings from 1838 to 1854. They are about missing children. Father Wales doesn't explain in the scrapbook why they are there, or what connects these disappearances – which had happened in villages all around Glencree – to Talbot House. I must ask him about this.

Seamus Cooney died in 1845. His tomb is there, in the family plot.

At that time, only Roy, his wife, and the twins were still living in Talbot House. Actually, Roy was more often away than at home, for the peat trade had gone downhill and he had found himself in the dire need of finding a job. Slowly, the Cooney fortunes were eroded by Talbot House. Angela was frequently alone, spending time sewing or knitting in a room on the second floor, while the children knew no one, for their mother refused to let them leave the house. They had a tutor, Mr. Cummings, but he left one day and never returned, so Angela took their education in her own hands, with the help of Mrs. Fowler, an old lady who had been hired by Roy as a nanny. Mrs. Fowler, who now lives in Bray, said that she had surprised the twins engaging in '*obscene activity*' when they were sixteen. She swore Victoria became pregnant from her brother. And she isn't the only one believing that. Father Wales has collected stories from people living in Ballymoor or that were living here at the time of Brandon and Victoria's scandal. When Victoria's pregnancy became evident, all the servants working at Talbot House were dismissed.

Victoria had an abortion. There's no birth or death certificate. Brandon was sent to Cork.

The next year, Angela fell from the second floor of Talbot House and broke her neck, dying on the spot. Roy returned home from an overseas trip, in time for the funeral. Then he went away for six months, to work on a cargo ship. Victoria was left alone in the house and no one in town dared, or cared, to go there to check on her. She never once ventured to the village, and people wondered about her larder.

Her father returned home eventually, but he died of heart failure soon thereafter; his soul sullen by too many tragedies. Brandon, then an attorney in Cork, came back and brought his sister to live with him. One year later, Victoria had a child, Arthur; father unknown. Then, Victoria, completely unstable, was interned in an asylum, where she died of brain fever last year.

From then on, Brandon Cooney has always rented the house. He refuses to come back. A photography of him and his nephew is clipped to the scrapbook. Arthur looks exactly like his uncle. Maybe too much so.

I finished reading the notebook one hour ago. All the time, while I was deep into its pages, I heard the distant howling of dogs. I'm upset by all those stories, but I'm still sure that what torments me is of a more physical nature than a demon.

They want me out of this house.

It is with a great concern that I write these lines. I'm clearly torn. On one side, I think is best for me to leave and spend the rest of my holiday season somewhere else. After all, I have no interest in being dragged inside a local political dispute; I'm a foreigner, I don't belong here.

On the other side, there stands Maggie Blair.

It is evident I feel affection for this girl, but I must also be realistic: we come from very different worlds. Still …

I can't leave her here. With those people.

I didn't really like the way those men were looking at me; the way she was taken away from me …

CHAPTER EIGHT

April 29th, 1891
Talbot House
Early Morning

Queer, when a queer dream helps you find a queer room. Unbelievable as it may sound, the nightmare I had tonight led me to discover a secret room here, in Talbot House.

In dreams, I suddenly woke up in my bed. Somehow, I remembered my previous incubi: the dogs eating Siobhan, and the hag's visitation. The sensation that someone was inside my bedroom, in the dark, invaded me. Temperature had dropped so fast, I could see my breath freezing upon exhalation. Outside, the night stood still.

Then, I heard the low growling of an enraged dog.

Right inside the room.

I couldn't see it, but it was there. I could distinctively hear the clicking of its nails on the floorboards; I could feel its presence just beyond the edge of the bed. But I couldn't see it.

I reached for the lamp and, listening to the beast's movements, lit it up. Warm flames flickered then grew in intensity, allowing me to see most of the room.

No trace of the animal.

Nonetheless, I could hear its hateful growl. A growl that turned into a full, rabid snarling at the sight of the light.

'Bless the sun, for the Darkness cannot stand bright light.'

That line, scrawled on Hugh Talbot's *Ars Goetia*, popped into my mind. I don't know why, but in the dream, I was sure Father Wales had written that note. Maybe man's subconscious is far better an investigator than we give it credit for. Isn't that called gut's feelings by coppers?

Acting instinctively, I moved the lamp forward, toward the source of the snarls. Immediately, the angry growl was replaced by a pained wail. Emboldened by such effect, I dared to leave the bed, and standing firmly on my legs, holding the lamp the way a priest would raise the crucifix in an exorcism, I walked, filled with hope that the Lord walked with me.

Then, a pair of ghostly hands materialized out of the darkness behind me, clapped, and the flames died.

Panic invaded me, and without thinking, I bolted out of the room, while the phantom dog retrieved its courage and started barking after me. I found myself racing through the house, pursued from room to room by the invisible beast. Finally, the ghostly horror cornered me in the library. There was no way out.

As I stood, frozen, my back against the farthest bookshelf, I saw the thing take shape. It was Adair – or Kalie – for what I know, one of Maggie's wolfhounds, only … only, it was somewhat different; there were empty sockets where its eyes should have been, and it looked bigger, almost the size of a pony.

And, incredibly, the dog spoke to me.

"I want Maggie," it growled in a gnarled female voice. *"And ye ain't goin' to stop me."*

My heart exploded inside my chest; my legs slowly lost strength; and, finally, my resolve expired its last breath. I fell to the ground, grabbing my ankles and sobbing like a child. The hellish dog seemed to like it, for it barked and growled at me some more, menacingly.

"Begob!" – "I don't want ye here!" – "Ye're goin' to die!"

It kept going on and on, and I stayed there, cowering, unable to move. I felt so weak, so fallible.

Then, Father Wales' voice echoed in my memories.

I believe in the Devil's ability to mask himself, my son.

Something clicked behind my back. A mechanism, put in motion by some hidden switch, caused the bookcase to slide aside with a grinding sound.

And the dog howled, or rather it cried, something that sounded like a '*Noooo!*' Then, it faded away.

I woke up in my bed.

After the initial shock caused by such a terrible dream, I remembered the secret room, so, overtaken by curiosity, I rushed downstairs. Incredible as it might be, the library's door stood ajar. And I clearly remembered having shut it tight after my last visit. Anyhow, even more appalling was the sight of the dark entryway revealed by the now displaced bookcase. Befuddled, and certainly upset, I peeked inside it. A tight, iron staircase descends into a well of rough-cut stone.

My plan is to explore it later, when the sun will be shining over my head, for at the moment I feel really afraid of the dark.

Still, something – supernatural or else – is leading me.

I will not allow this thing, whatever it is, to hurt Maggie.

April 29th, 1891
Talbot House
Later

There's a new resolve in me. A new strength.

What I have found has shed a new light on the strange occurrences I've been experiencing. Maybe it will not explain everything, but at least it has revealed more about the house's builder's personality.

Indeed, Hugh Talbot was a practitioner of the dark arts.

Although his intentions were noble and he longed for knowledge, he delved into things that honest churchgoers should never meddle with. He was an illuminated man of his times, and like all those men, he dismissed dogmas as fairytales. He thought that a certain 'truth' lay somewhere between the 'accepted faith' and the marvels of science. And he paid for it.

As I wrote before, I discovered a secret passage inside the library. The hows and whys are not my concern right now. What I want to pen down, before this madness completely engulfs me, is the facts – what I found and what Hugh Talbot did.

As soon as the sun revealed its benevolent face to the world, I armed myself with a hurricane lamp (memories of the way those ghostly hands had killed my light in the dream still lingered inside me), and a sturdy mallet, and then descended into the stairwell. The stairs curve two times before reaching the bottom. The secret room appears to not have received visits since the times of Talbot, for it is covered in a thick layer of dust, and I kicked up a lot of it into big, choking clouds. The only window in this small twelve-foot square room is an iris-like glass panel set on the north corner of the ceiling. It is covered in grass and earth on the other side, but it was meant to receive light from the garden. It is a private study of sort, very similar to the library upstairs. The walls are covered in bookshelves, whose books range from astronomy to ancient history, from Celtic culture to Irish folklore. And then there are the occult tomes. Dozens of them. There are scrawls on the floor, and a large table where queer paraphernalia of arcane – or pseudoscientific – items have been completely submerged by dust and cobwebs. Atop a bronze stand, I found Hugh Talbot's journal. It is crumbling with age, but still readable.

I didn't feel like staying for too long down there (what if the mechanism activating the door panel unwound and entrapped me?), so, cautiously, I retrieved it – stand included – and came back up to the main floor.

I made a cup of good coffee, then I started to read it.

This journal reads more like a scientist's or an explorer's log than the annals of an eighteenth-century man.

I'm going to copy here the most interesting parts.

From the Journal of Hugh Talbot, 1788 to 1790

To you who read this, by choice or chance: I am sure you are not going to believe what you will read in this work-journal. Nonetheless, be aware, my sibling in science, that all I am relating here is based on assumptions made after extended research into the very Nature that surrounds us.

At the risk of my own sanity.

I have always been possessed by a questioning spirit; demanding to know the source of every phenomenon, and never accepting it as it is. I have been branded a heathen, and a miscreant; even a devil-worshipper. Yet, I am none. I am one of the enlightened. I believe that the goal of man's existence it to explore the world and the heavens, not to live in ignorance. I will not accept the mystery of the Trinity as much as I will not bow in front of Zeus, or Odin, or Satan. I want proof of their existence before I accept them as real. With this spirit in my heart, I have dedicated my life to the investigation of all occult matters: from the nature of ghosts, to the truth behind mythologies.

In London, once, a student asked me why I was so obsessed with the ethereal and not so much with the terrene. I provided him with the simplest of explanations: 'Remember those times, when you were a child, being afraid of leaving your foot or your hand hanging off the edge of your bed, for you knew something was hiding there, ready to grab it? Indeed, mine was grabbed.'

It was an appalling and disconcerting experience, but it forged my life. I found myself alone, for no one in the household believed me. From then on, I decided I would shed light on the darkness of ignorance; I would spend my entire life trying to understand, and possibly fighting, whatever lies just beyond the veil of our reality. And, partly, I have succeeded. Being of a rich family, I had the opportunity to travel to distant places and investigate with my own eyes legends and occurrences all around Europe. Inspired by the works of Doctor John Dee, I myself have tried to converse with angels and demons. And like Queen Elizabeth's personal astrologer, I have found a scheme, a mechanism, if you wish, behind legends and fairytales.

<next three pages are unreadable>

Each of the stories illustrated here is absolutely, indisputably true. I have tried to depict some of the similarities shared by these occurrences in an effort to demonstrate the truth about what they mean: that there exist entities among us that are not human, perhaps not even a part of the reality as we define it. I call them supramentals. 'Supra' indicating of an external nature, and 'elemental' for they are primeval forces of creation. Ergo, a supramental is a kind of entity from outside our world.

In Ars Goetia, I read how King Solomon tried to cast away all that which disputed humanity's claim upon the earth. Of how he summoned to his side the six greatest sorcerers and magi he had met during his travels. And of the fashioning of the Great Seal. Seven wise men toiled, taking care that every line, mark, or rune was perfectly in place and at the proper angle. The tide of years wore on, and each of the seven attracted young and bright persons that would assist them in their task, and trained them to carry on their work after they were dust. As the completion of their great labor drew near, darkness stirred in a distant land, determined to undermine their efforts. There existed a place, somewhere in the world, that was as corrupt as the pits of Hell. After Lucifer's failed rebellion against the Almighty, the faithful hosts of angels cast the Morningstar down from his place, condemning him and his rebels to the darkest infernal pits. When he fell to the Earth, his lingering presence putrefied the very ground he lay upon, his wounds seeped and festered onto the land, and his spittle caused blight and infestation. Yet, even within his eternal prison, Lucifer did plot to do harm to the children of God. He learned of the great work of Solomon and decided to corrupt it. His whispers emerged from the Heart of Darkness and called upon those whom he had previously favored with gifts and power. And these witches corrupted the seal, so that the enchantment would indeed separate the mortal world from that of the supernatural, yet, at the same time, it would grant them free reign to plague mankind with no opposition. Magic remained in the world. Though weakened, it moved, invisible, among the lands, in twisted and convoluted lines. And where these lines crossed or converged, cracks formed in the Great Seal. Cracks from whence malevolent creatures seeped forth.

Nonetheless, this is just the mere vision of men blinded by faith. For I don't believe in the existence of the Almighty, lest I trust there exists a Satan. Yet, there is some form of verity in the words of Ars Goetia. The Great Seal was indeed created by men of wisdom in the farthest past. And yes, it was corrupted by the forces opposing it. But the powers the seven wise men were trying to isolate were not Lucifer or his fallen angels. They were the 'supramentals': beings so ancient, so unfathomable, that man and his limited mind cannot comprehend; only recognize their existence.

<next two pages are unreadable>

And, thusly, I identified this place in Gorta Cave. Kevin of Glendalough was more than a mere saint: he was a man of knowledge. He knew how to properly draw the Great Seal, and how to etch it in stone, thusly barring the passage to the Morrigan.

<next five or six pages are missing>

On the Nature of the Morrigan:

As it is known, in Irish mythology, the Morrigan is a triple entity: Ana, the Virgin, Babd, the Mother, and Macha, the Crone. Like the Fates of Greek myth, also known as the Moirae (and here you will surely debate about the origin of the term Mor in ancient Irish), the Norns of Scandinavia, and, of course, Hecate. The last one is of special interest to me, for she shares most of the characteristics attributed to the Morrigan. She was said to be the Queen of ghosts, accompanied in her nocturnal voyages by a host of dead spirits and howling infernal hounds. Her approach was said to be heralded by the snarls and barks of rabid dogs. For dogs were sacred to her.

Ana, the Virgin, is the youngest and most fearsome. She is attracted by the insane, she is the suggestress of suicides. Her power is strong, yet her domain is limited and narrow, for she can only approach those whose profound nature has been corrupted. She preys on those whose hearts shake, and whose brains rattle under delusion and fear. She is the Lady of Darkness.

Babd, the Mother, is the middle one. She patrons on the outcasts, the isolated, and the hopeless. She is meek and silent, yet her lure is strong. In her eyes, perished dreams and delirium can be found. Her domain is larger than that of her younger sister, still, she climbs no clouds, nor she aspires for more. She nurtures what she already owns. She is the Lady of Whispers.

Macha, the Crone, is the oldest. Patroness of mourning, grief, and loss, she is the most voluble of the trio: anguished one moment, murderous the next. She constantly weeps, and cries, and laments. She washes blood-soaked clothes at the ford. She was in Bethlehem when Herod's sword stiffened, for ever, little feet of Innocents. Her domain is the largest, and the bleakmost. She is the Lady of Tears.

Together, they are The Morrigan, mother of darkness, the night, the dead, and magic. Queen of ghosts, and dogs, and owls. Infernal, Terrestrial, and Heavenly. Lady of the Crossroads, she who goes to and fro at night.

Yet, to me, she is just a supramental; a thought given form. We gave her power. I will remove it from her. By superstition and wisdom, I will conjure her under my command.

<next two pages are missing>

Indeed, I have resolved to test my craft. Arawn, my faithful companion, will be the host to the Hecatian Hound. I have fashioned the bonds; of a pure element, not combined with any other metal. My blood has been poured into the curling patterns. The Black Bonds will hold the Cu Si forever, as long as the ritual of maintenance is repeated every hundred years. Thus, I write here the ritual, so that future generations will be able to keep hold of the Black Hound. And the means to destroy it, if such a need arises.

I laugh at the thought of poor Annie Carrick. Ha! That ignorant woman thought she could get favors from this dark entity. She only received fire.

<next two pages are filled with drawings – which include the same five-pointed star with the flaming eye at the center in the same fashion as on Kevin's slab, and a series of intonations and gestures to perform>

On witches and the Dark Pact:

From the time the first human clawed his way to the threshold of civilization, Man has shown a terrible willingness to forsake all he holds sacred to sate his lust for power, wealth, and vengeance. It is these lost souls that the supramentals seek. It is from these wrecks that pacts are spawned with the ethereal dwellers.

From greed, wrath, and sadism a corrupted progeny is born, such as a witch. Souls, freely given to the devouring darkness. Alas, these pacts are always deceitful. The supramentals have little concerns about human events, but they do feed on the suffering and turmoil they create. To them, chaos, pain, treachery, and murder are like a delicious nectar. Thusly, though banned from our world, due to the intrinsic weakness of Solomon's spell they are able to send a fragment of their essence to seek out such desperate souls that will heed their call. Usually, the fragment possesses an animal (hence the stories regarding witches' familiars), such as a rat, cat, raven, or dog. Through this vessel, they roam the land until they find the lost and hopeless. And when they find the truly alone and desperate, the supramental talks through them. It whispers, actually. The hate-filled and selfish, who are seeking an easy way to power or revenge, will gladly accept the offered pact. A contract is established between the witch and the entity, a contract to be signed with a sacrifice. Usually, it is the witch's own childe that will be given to the dark. Or, if the witch has no seed, it can be someone's else childe. The pact has to be performed in special places where the borders between our world and that of the supramental are closer. Such places were marked by ancient tribes with standing stones and circles. The bloody deed accomplished, the witch is ready to collect her reward.

That will be the Gift of Power.

The Gift of Power is an illusion through which the witch is led to believe she has been magically bestowed occult powers. The power isn't drawn from some inner strength or knowledge, but comes directly from the master. The supramental projects another fraction of its essence into its pawn, giving her a taste of true power. Truthfully, it is the dark being that holds that power and it can be removed at any time. It is through this addiction that the master keeps the servant at the leash. The supramental will push its servant to darker deeds: to perform more blood sacrifices, to establish a cult in the name of her master, to bear children, and to corrupt them.

Eventually, the master will offer the second reward: the Gift of Union.

The Gift of Union is the ultimate treachery. In this, the witch willingly allows the supramental to share her body, blending the woman with that monster. She still retains her soul, but allows the supramental to share her body with her. Nonetheless, the dark one will soon consume the witch's soul and the master will have complete control of its human body.

<next page depicts a woman standing at the center of a diagram, a queer smoke-like cord at her neck trailing off into the surrounding darkness. Hugh was an excellent artist and his drawings, though morbid, show technique and craftsmanship.>

What have I done! Like Solomon, I have been deceived! Instead of binding Evil I unleashed it! It was Her! It was the Blackness that whispered to me! As Lilith, she seduced me. I have listened to her sweet voice, but her heart is dark. She demands more blood, more suffering. Yet, I will not comply. I will resist and will etch unto me the Sign of Sorrows.

Then, the book becomes a series of incoherent babblings. Except for the same, identical phrase I found on Father Wales' book:

'Bless the sun, for the Darkness cannot stand bright light.'

Later on in the journal, it seems Hugh regained some of his sanity, for here he writes about a woman he has fallen in love with, and about how he intends to marry her. Yet, and I shuddered while reading this, he also seems to be plagued by horrid dreams about a crone visiting him in his sleep. He is sure she is the ghost of Annie Fuath, or Dark Annis, but also formulates the theory that Annie was just the host of something darker: a fragment of the Morrigan. He even believed that the Queen of the '*spawn of Gorta*' (I think he refers to the cannibal queen of the degenerate Cruithni), who was killed at Rathmoin, was a '*Handmaiden*' of the Morrigan, or the Blackness, as he called her later. This Handmaiden was a chosen one, some kind of female antichrist; the human embodiment of the dark goddess (or goddesses). He also believed that the Gorta Queen had transferred her soul, or essence, into one of the sacred stones, and that her spirit lingers on, passing from female to female, whispering in the ears of gifted women until, seduced, they lose their souls. Annie could have been such a host.

In the last passage he wrote this:

Now I know where I failed; the solution has always been there, only, I couldn't see it, blinded by the Blackness in me. I myself have brought this evil into my house. The Cailli stone was the focus, and, in my hubris, I surrounded myself with it. The Cruithni Queen was the host. She was burned. Yet even after death, a portion of her, the one corrupted by the Dark Pact, still lingers within the stone. It was how she beckoned Annie Carrick. And now she will claim my Fiona. I have already seen the changes in her. She spends too much time in the stone circle and her eyes show an evil streak. I will not allow it. Jack told me of Fiona's worriment about Arawn. It is the dog! It has always been the dog! I allowed the Blackness to fool me, believing that that was the path I had to follow to Greatness. Truly, it was the path to damnation. I will kill Arawn, but the right ritual has to be performed, or it will only be its physical form that I banish. I'll go with Jack into the moor. There, Arawn in chains, I will draw the banishment circle and I will pour my own blood on it. A great bonfire has to be lit, for this creature abhors light.

I love Fiona and I WILL stop this thing.

So that's what had really happened. Hugh Talbot had destroyed this Cailli stone, but then had used it in the construction of this house. According to him, the ancient witch of the Cruithni tribe had infused the stone with her essence, and through it, she was able to transfer it into another woman. This way, she had corrupted Annie Carrick. And, maybe, she did the same with Beulah and Victoria Cooney.

Victoria Cooney died last year…

Graceful Lord, Maggie could be next!

That could explain her babbling about *'restoring the land'*.

'Establish a cult in the name of her master'.

That could explain the gypsies' interest in her and the stone circles.

For as absurd all of this may sound, I am now on the edge of saying farewell to reason and embrace the illogical.

I love Maggie and I WILL stop this thing.

CHAPTER NINE

April 29th, 1891
Talbot House
Later

I have decided to face Siobhan and the gypsies. I don't want to use violence, of course, but I will bring along a firearm I found this morning in Roy Cooney's private study, up on the third floor. I had visited the room before, but had never spent much time there. The man's study shows that he was a sea captain, for all the trinkets and memorabilia there talks of the sea: sailing ships inside glass bottles, nautical maps, colored shells and monstrous crabs. There's a large steamer trunk there, but I didn't feel like opening it. However, on the shelves, whose books also speak the mariner's language, I found this large gun, a cap and ball thing, called a Colt Navy. It's a revolver, but I have no idea how to load it, and even if I knew I would still be at a loss for I wouldn't know where to get the balls. There's a kind of spring-loaded mechanism at the front which cracks the gun open, however it looks very different from other revolvers I have seen. It's more similar to those used in the American west. I remember my friend Jonah (the same one who taught me how to properly rope horses in the wilds) talking about this type of handgun, but, for goodness' sake, I just recall that you have to break open the cartridge, pour the powder into the priming holes, then …

No way. I can't remember. Anyway, it makes no difference, the gun already contains two bullets and I do not intend to discharge them. I will just bring it along as a discouraging factor; I will shoot it in the air if the gypsies attack me.

I'm ready to go.

Wait. Someone is knocking at my front door right now. I hope it's Maggie. This would surely make my day easier.

April 29th, 1891
Talbot House
Later

Good news! I've found an ally.

Sadly, it wasn't Maggie knocking at my door, but to my surprise, Father Wales. He is here now, and will stay here in the house trying to exorcise it from the evil that haunts it. Yes, it may sound queer what I'm writing now, and I understand that it requires a better explanation, therefore, I will write down exactly what happened after I opened my door to a grim-faced Earl Wales.

First, he excused himself for the early visit, then, after I invited him in, he told me that he had come to apologize. Obviously, I wondered why, but it was soon revealed to me. He said he had lied to me. Or rather, he had omitted some of the facts. Father Wales is a man of letters and has a very modern mind, something that clashes with his role as the spiritual shepherd of the little hamlet of Ballymoor. He enjoys collecting facts rather than myths, and, as I previously reported in this journal, he has gathered quite a lot regarding Talbot House. More than he had showed me. In fact, he told me that he had been feeling torn apart after our last meeting, for he deemed that he hadn't helped me enough to shed light on the queer events connected with this mansion. With a guilty expression, his eyes looking at the floor, he confessed knowing about Hugh Talbot's research. He had read parts of it in an arcane book that once belonged to the infamous man. Still, he doesn't believe that the spirit of a witch infests these halls, but that something more evil, and more ancient is the cause of all the suffering that happened here. He told me, with unease, that he assumed the cave to be an entrance to Hell; the place where Lucifer himself fell when he was cast out of Heaven. And that the Morrigan, to which Talbot refers, was Lilith, spouse of Satan.

He soon changed his mind.

I decided to allow him to read the true diary of Talbot. I left him alone with it while I prepared one of my strong teas, and when I returned with the smoking brew I found him, his face bleached, deep into the writings of that madman. I guided him along the most salient passages, showing him where everything made sense, and where it connected with the strange story of the Barguest. I could see the shock in his eyes when he read about the terrible pacts between a witch and the dark creature.

"He used the very stone where Annie Carrick was burnt to build this house!" he exclaimed, and his eyes ran to the big, etched slab of grayish-green stone acting as mantelpiece for the large fireplace.

"The man was evil," I said.

He shook his head. "On the contrary, the man was guided by a will to help humanity. Yet, in his hubris, he failed and actually lent a hand to the foulest thing."

I started to tell him the story about Talbot's demise, exactly the way Siobhan told me.

I was halfway through when he interrupted me, lifting his right palm. "That, sonny, is the same story told and retold around here for generations. Yet it's not the truth."

Puzzled, I questioned him. What was the truth? And how did he know it?

"I heard another version from a source I trust. The grandfather of this man witnessed with his own eyes what happened here and in the bog. And when Talbot was shot and killed by Ian Mulholland. Mind you, Ian believed what he saw, so he shot an evil man. I don't blame him. But what really killed Talbot was Arawn, his own dog."

I prompted him to tell me more, but he refused, for he said that if I really intended to reach the gipsy camp and leave this place before sundown it was better for me to hurry up. And he is right, I want to leave Ballymoor before darkness, with Maggie by my side.

Father Wales will stay here and try to bless the house, reciting his prayers to exorcise the witch's ghost from the stone. I doubt he can do that, and I think he doubts it too. Nonetheless, even if reluctantly so, he will try to follow the rites of Talbot, as written in his grimoire. He will wait for me until dark, then he will return home and will warn the villagers and Constable Smale. Should something happen to me, they will storm the gypsies' campsite.

May God stand on my side.

CHAPTER TEN

April 29th, 1891
Gob's Field.
Afternoon

I'm writing this under the shade of Shamna stone, which now, as it is evident, stands upright again. Why I'm here and not back home will soon be explained.

After blessing the old priest for his unexpected help (it feels nice not being alone in this), I mounted on the cart and quickly made my way to the Old Military Road, passing the Pooka hills, until the road descends into a bowl-shaped valley which contains the two lakes. My destination was Lough Bray Lower, where the gypsies were supposed to camp. In fact, as I turned a wooden bend, I spotted the colored wagons, contrasting sharply with the lake's brackish water. As soon as they heard the thumping hooves of Bertha, a pack of rangy dogs started barking loud, alerting the gypsies of my presence. And, as I suspected, I was not welcome.

A band of dour-looking ruffians emerged from the camp, some brandishing clubs, others sporting wicked-looking knives. Though they meant no good, I couldn't deny a fascination for their dashing clothes: colorful sashes, glittering jewelry, and striped baggy trousers. Their jolly appearance heavily clashed with the grim, and aggressive, expression sculpted on their faces. My hand ran to the reassuring feeling of the metal hidden in my coat: I didn't come for a fight, but I was not going to run any risks.

The dogs immediately surrounded the cart, baying and snarling, and I was worried more about Bertha's reaction than their slavering jaws, remembering how she easily goes on a warpath when she is provoked. So I shouted to the men to grab hold of their beasts, for I was no intruder and meant no harm; I was a friend of Siobhan Blair and had come for a visit.

The lead of the group shouted that he knew who I was and that I was not welcome. However, Siobhan, attracted by the commotion, stepped out of a tent and, in her language, said something to the men, who immediately lowered their weapons and started calling the dogs back. Just in time, for bold Bertha had begun to snort nervously and, as always, ignoring that she was attached to a cart, was ready to charge. To be honest, I'm starting to love this ornery creature; she has a fiery temper, like a true Irish.

I wrote before how much I loved Siobhan Blair, and how glad I was to have met her. I spent rivers of words to praise her good heart and explain how she reminds me of my grandma. Alas, that love is lost. She has undergone a change of sort; she's no longer the kind woman I had met on my first day here. I don't know what happened – well, I suspect this has to do to with my closeness to her granddaughter – but she is now different; cold, and distant. Yet, until this morning I still trusted her and I really wanted to be on her good side again.

She came straight to the cart, her eyes icy and boring straight into my soul, without saying a word. I decided to tell her the motive of my visit, but not before explaining her all the things I had discovered at Talbot House. So, I told her we needed a place to talk in intimacy, away from indiscreet ears. She didn't ask me why, she just nodded and signaled for me to follow her to her tent, where, beautiful as ever, Maggie was standing, peaking out of it with a worried face. As soon as I got closer I was taken by the urge to hug her, but, obviously, I refrained myself. Unexpectedly, she didn't smile at me, on the contrary, that worried expression turned into disappointment, and then she disappeared inside the tent. Once we got inside, Siobhan motioned for me to sit down onto one of the fluffy cushions surrounding a short tea table, on which rested some paraphernalia of the kind used by clairvoyants around the world. Maggie was nowhere to be seen; apparently, she had left through another exit. The tent was large and parted by colored drapes which, to me, looked like large Persian rugs, and the entire place smelled of exotic perfumes. Outside, I could spot the silhouettes of the men, ready for trouble. I sat down and waited for Siobhan to speak.

Though the old woman still speaks with her thick Irish brogue, I will not repeat it here, for I don't find it funny anymore after the unpleasant experience I had today with her. I must say I no longer trust her and I think she never was sincere. Yet, at that time, I still saw her as a benevolent figure who cared about my life.

I told her what had happened in the last two days, of the terrible nightmares, and of the invisible dog in my dream. I told her of the diary and the secret room, and of the cave. I told her about the slab of St. Kevin, of the legends and the murder of Squire Douglas. She nodded all along, and never interrupted me. Once I finished, I felt exhausted, yet lighter.

At that point, she lifted her bony finger, admonishing me. "I told you, but you didn't want to listen. I warned you, but you didn't want to leave. No, you stubborn foreigner, you had to act the maggot. And not just that: you had to give the glad eye to my granddaughter, didn't you?"

She must have noticed the puzzled look on my face and explained to me that 'act the maggot' means 'acting stupid' and that 'giving the glad eye' means 'being in love'.

So I confessed my interest in Maggie, and affirmed it was my intention to bring her to safety, for I suspected the witch intended to possess her body. Siobhan exploded into a cackling laughter, making fun of me. "Dear boy, you don't know what you are taking about! She is safer here than with you." Again, she pointed her ugly finger at me. "Do not believe a single word of what Talbot wrote. Yes, there's a danger here. Yes, there's evil in this land. But it was caused by that man, for his heart was full of blackness and his mind was empty. The only one in danger here is *you*. The Barguest is getting closer, and tomorrow night it will be Beltane. Run away while you still have time; the dog has sniffed you, and soon it will be at your throat."

Though her words were meant as a warning, there was a coldness in her voice – as if she was enjoying my terror. I felt at unease and immediately regretting spilling the beans. I wished to leave and forever forget this woman and this place. Still, I had to talk to Maggie before going. As if she had read my thoughts, Maggie stepped into the tent. Again, she wasn't smiling, but her face was stony and pale, as if under a queer spell. "The land will soon be restored and the evil banished. I'm not in danger, sir, but you are. Do as my grandma says: leave this land and …" She paused, her eyes trembled, then a dark shadow crossed them, like liquid darkness, " … forget me."

It was too late. The thing, whatever it was, had taken Maggie, and Siobhan too. Distraught, I left without a word, my heart broken. I decided to go back home, pack my goods, and leave as soon as possible. That one was a battle I could not win.

However, while I was mounting on the cart, I overheard two of the gypsies talking about tracking down Uncle Ben before it was too late.

Good Heaven, I had forgotten about him!

Feigning indifference, and biding my time by fixing the tack and bridles, I listened carefully to what they were talking about. It seemed that the old man had got better and, unexpectedly, had left the camp, Adair and Kalie at the leash, intent on disrupting whatever ritual the gypsies were planning to perform. The flame of hope rekindled in my heart: maybe, if Uncle Ben knew what was happening, and was able stop this darkness, Maggie could still be saved!

The gypsies planned to search for him nearby Talbot House, presumably into the cave, or at Old Luagh, or at the Shamna stone.

I had to find him first.

Realizing that Father Wales was at Talbot House and would surely spot Ben and his dogs, and that Shamna was closer to the gypsy camp, I decided to head for Gob's field and wait for the old man to show up. I had no other choice: I couldn't be in two places at the same time.

So, here I am, sitting under the restored standing stone. And I think this is the right place to wait for him, for the other stone no longer stands, being part of Talbot House, while this one, so dear to the gypsies and to whoever had murdered Squire Douglas, is intact and someone had taken the care to put it back in its place. Honestly, I don't know what this means, but I have a gut feeling that Uncle Ben is coming here. He hasn't showed up yet. Neither the gypsies. To be safe I left Bertha tied to the cart and away from sight. If Uncle Ben left the camp minutes before me he is surely crossing the moor, avoiding the roads. He will have to climb the hill, as I did. Therefore, I'm surely ahead of him.

I will wait for the man here. My pistol is ready in my hand, in the instance the gypsies show up first.

Good Lord, help me.

CHAPTER ELEVEN

April 30th, 1891
Talbot House.
Late Morning

Dear Lord!

I'm doomed. Either my mind is fading away or I'm about to die. I can't believe what happened to me, but I now no longer doubt about the existence of things that should stay dead, yet still roam this world. What a fool was I to not listen to Siobhan's warning. I'm afraid this could be my last day on this earth, for soon the Barguest will burst inside Talbot House and there will be no way for me to escape its slavering jaws again.

Should I die, I want whoever finds this journal to know exactly what killed me. So, it is with a shaking hand that I pen down the horrors I underwent last night.

After I wrote my previous entry, I was caught by an unnatural drowsiness, and afraid to fall asleep, I left the standing stone and went walking around, eager to freshen my mind and regain firmness in my logic. The weather wasn't pleasant, for an icy wind was sweeping over the countryside, chilling my bones and making the experience quite unpleasant. Still, I needed to set some distance away from what I believed to be the negative influence of Shamna stone, so, staunchly I went on to a solitary, but large, oak tree. By that time, the wind had ceased its malevolent gusts, and had died; allowing the feeble sunlight to bring a bit of release to my shivering body. After a quick meal, I submerged myself in my studies, and for almost one hour, I easily forgot about the Barguest, the curse of Hugh Talbot, and all.

However, later on, something disturbed my reading.

To my right, where a thick shrub of wild bramble entwined its thorny stems with nettle and dog-rose, I heard a rustling. At first, I thought a hare or a squirrel was the origin of the noise, but I changed my mind when it became clear that whatever was moving within the wild hedge was far bigger.

It had to be Uncle Ben.

I left my book and stepped closer to the bushes. I couldn't see anything in that chaotic, natural maze of spikes and sleeping buds, but I could hear the thing moving inside it. Whatever was hiding there, unfortunately, wasn't human, as its movements were more akin to a quadruped than a biped or a large bird.

Then, I spotted something grayish. Fur.

Again, my mind went back to the Barguest and my heart started racing inside my chest. I tried, desperately, to dismiss those dark thoughts, yet no matter what, I couldn't help it.

The monster was here to kill me.

The rustling became louder and I could feel the thing coming closer and closer, but, frozen by terror, I couldn't move. I stood there, paralyzed as a deer flooded by a sudden light. Unable to act, my body started to shiver, and cold sweat watered my temples. My eyes, enlarged by fear, stared, in wait of the impending doom, to the now moving bramble, as the thing prepared its final attack.

And it came.

Exploding through the shrubs, the beast jumped on me. The world became blurry as I fell to the ground when the attacker's strength and my own fear-struck legs joined forces. My fingers sunk inside the monster's fur and I could smell the hot stench of the creature's slavering maw as it came near my face. On the ground, I closed my eyes, waiting for the end.

Endless seconds passed.

And then, the hot breath was on my face. Closer.

Oh, my God! It's going to rip my head off!

Like child unable to face their fear, I lay there, pressed on the ground by the beast's weight, my eyes closed tight, my heartbeat growing louder, until it was the only living sound I could hear.

Expecting the sharp teeth to pierce my skin anytime now, it came as a surprise when something softer, yet wet, touched my cheek.

A tongue.

The unknown brute was licking me.

Perplexed, I opened my eyes, slowly turning my head to face the creature, which now, felt more like an affectionate lover than a cold-blooded killer. You can imagine my stupor when I saw that what was pinning me down and licking my face was none other than one of Maggie's dogs. It wasn't trying to kill me. On the contrary, it was showing me affection, wagging its tail and whimpering like a puppy. Terror was replaced by hilarity, and laughter escaped my mouth while the large animal kept lapping at my cheek. This was the same mutt that had scared the hell out of me not once, but twice, and now I couldn't be more happy to see it.

"Good Lord," I cheerily protested, "until yesterday it seemed that I was your worst enemy and now ..." More laughs came out of my parched mouth.

I stood there for a while, slowly gathering my forces while the dog continued its endless show of heart. Then, I gently pushed it away and regained my footing. I looked around for the other one, but it was nowhere to be seen.

"Where's your pal?" I asked, as if the animal could offer me an answer. Obviously, no answer came, but the hound kept jumping around me as if it was eager for something. "Who are you? Adair? Kalie? And where's Uncle Ben?"

I know, my attempt at conversing with a dog might sound silly, but in that moment, that animal – and its inexplicable turn of mood toward me – was a ray of light shining through the thick blackness of the pit where my mind had fallen into. To me, it was more than a dog. It was the savior of my sanity, the triumph of logical thinking over the shadows of irrationality.

That was what I thought at the time.

Unfortunately, as I will shortly explain, I had been deceived again, because reality – as I previously believed it – crashed on me as soon as the sun disappeared behind the hills.

Oh, what a doomed soul am I. I preferred to live in ignorance of the mysteries of the netherworld, deluding myself that the unnatural didn't exist, rather than face the ugly truth behind folktales. Ghosts are real, and what is dead doesn't stay dead if evil fills its being. I've seen it with my very eyes and even now, it's just waiting for sundown to finish me. As I write, I still hear its paws racing in the garden of my mind, a sound of trampled grass, the blunt-clawed feet digging the mud. It's playing with me, the horrible monster! It feeds on my fear, more than on my flesh!

Good Lord! Merciful Lord, let me be calm and keep my hand steady as I pen down my memories, for out of that way lies dementia!

Kalie (for later I discovered she was the female of the pair), kept jumping on me, her paws mudding my clothes, then feinted a run toward the brambles, as if trying to lead me there. I smiled, thinking she wanted to play, but then another shadow crossed my thoughts. What if something had happened to Ben? Maybe, he had had an accident in the bog and Kalie was looking for help. What if he had fallen in a crag? Or had been killed by the gypsies?

"What is it?" I demanded. "Do you want me to follow you?"

Unexpectedly, there came a sharp bark from the dog, and immediately it set for the bushes. Worried, I ignored my belongings (as of now they are still there, under the large oak, except for this journal, and I don't know the fate of Bertha), and started following it. At that, the animal yelped, as if to let me know it was urgent, then it dove into the thicket, ignoring the thorns scratching its skin. It wasn't that easy for me to follow her lead, as the bramble was dry and crossing it was almost impossible. However, I soon spotted a trail, probably made by red deer or that other breed I had previously observed, and, with a certain effort, I crawled through it until I came upon a clearing, and finally was able to stand up again.

Here, in this meadow, grew a large dogwood tree, under whose shadow something furry and disheveled lay, immobile. At first, I didn't recognize it for what it was, as its pelt was caked with mud and blood. Then, when I got closer, I gasped as I saw the mangled carcass of the other wolfhound. The poor animal had been torn to shreds; its throat ripped by large fangs; the rear legs broken and standing at impossible angles. Close by, also torn and chewed, stood its collar: a metal tag identifying it as Adair.

Kalie whined and circled her dead companion, desperately trying to wake him up from his eternal slumber. I shook my head in disbelief as I further inspected the dead animal. I had never seen wounds like that before; so vicious they'd put a black bear's attack to shame.

"Who's done this?" I uttered to no one, looking around. "What kind of beast can tear a large wolfhound to pieces?"

Now the sun was slowly descending and the shadows in the meadow were growing taller as the last rays bathed the world in red. It was also getting colder, for that ill wind had regained its strength. Shivering, I turned to Kalie. "There's nothing I can do, my friend. You certainly know what misfortune befell your pal, but, unfortunately, you can't relate it to me."

Suddenly, Kalie straightened her ears, and without warning, dashed into the woods, on the hunt for something I couldn't see.

"Kalie! Stop!" I shouted, but my order fell on deaf ears as the dog quickly disappeared among the dense trees. I ran after her for a bit, until I realized I had lost her tracks. Vanished. Nowhere to be seen. Yet, the dog now was the last of my concerns as I quickly realized I could be facing a bigger impediment. I had chased the wolfhound down a ravine, and without thinking, had put myself in peril by not taking note of my surroundings.

I was lost.

I tried to trace back my path, but the more I went uphill, the less I could find signs of my passage. I walked for hours under the trees until I found another clearing and, there, I became aware I was on the top of another hill from where I could see the peat bog behind Talbot House. Rejoiced, but still worried, because darkness was fast approaching and I had no source of light with me, I decided that the fastest way home was through the mire, for crossing the woods at night would be foolish and a sure way to get into deeper troubles. I descended the hill at a fast pace, paying attention to the gullies and hidden rocks amid the heather lest I broke a leg. By the time I had reached the foothills, night had engulfed the world, yet, luckily, the moon was almost full and the sky was clear, so there was enough light to see my surroundings. I was at the edge of the bog's north side; beyond, I could see the silhouette of Talbot House, painted in black.

And here my story grows darker and enters the realm of madness.

The wind rose high in a canine howl, then died just as abruptly as it had begun, and the night fell still; not a breath of breeze moved the reeds. After a bit, while I was contemplating a way to cross the bog, a mantle of mist rose from the damp ground, quickly thickening into a cloudy gray, enveloping my surroundings and making my progress even more miserable.

There's indeed a maliciousness in this accursed land; in daylight, it is easy to forget about the dread and gloom this place offers in the wee hours. It seems as if the very land it's alive here; changing its mood, capriciously, to better fit the evil intentions of its haunter. By day, the hills and vale look pleasant, with an early blossoming, somehow defiant of the chilly weather, which invites the sojourner to stay for more. By night, everything changes. Fog smothers the world, and there's a stillness in the air – except when that blasted wind blows through the glens, howling like wolves – as if in wait of something terrible to make its appearance.

I was still there, at the edge of the bog, trying to make my mind on the right path, when a mournful yowling made the decision for me. It didn't sound like that lonely, horrible howl from my dream's phantom hound. No, it sounded as if scores of dogs were howling in unison and coming down the hill, the sound growing louder every minute. Frightened, I looked around for anything I could use as a weapon, and I found a sharpened stake of dogwood sticking out of the mud, so without thinking twice, I unplugged it from the damp ground and quickly moved into the bog. In that panic, I had forgotten about the gun inside my coat. In short time, the fog confused me, as it was so thick I almost couldn't see beyond my nose. Soon, I was lost in a world of sounds and smells. Water dripped from the moss-draped skeletons of ancient trees, which, in turn, creaked and groaned with age. The mire itself gasped and gurgled maliciously. Every light breeze carried the stench of rotting things. And then, that hateful baying of hunting dogs.

Closer and closer.

I fled deeper into the depths of that forlorn place, afraid, jumping at every movement my impaired sight caught. Here, a patch of reeds moved, but nothing came out it. There, something, maybe a frog, jumped into a pool, but to me it certainly sounded as a canine paw splashing the water in its passage. My heart drumming inside my ears, I panicked as the barks resounded nigher, and my haphazard flight led me into thicker growths, my feet slogging into deeper mud. Abruptly, my left foot sunk into a morass, and only the strength given by fear saved me from being swallowed by the bog. Frantically, I dislodged my foot from the deadly quicksand, and as a result, I said goodbye to my walking boot, as I had no time to retrieve it from the muddy embrace, for the sound of barking was now turning into that of panting.

Holy Lord, they were surrounding me!

I crouched, then slithered on the muck, until I found refuge into a patch of tall grass, while the dyspneic breathing of several hounds and the padding of their feet filled the area I had just left. With difficulty, I held my breath and forced my shaking body still as one of the hunters came into view mere inches away from my hiding place.

And the horror – and the impossibility – of this vision chilled me on the spot.

Sniffing the ground with its great muzzle, there stood a large dog, muddy brown in color with splotches of yellow. It was bigger than a wolfhound and of a breed I had never seen before. Yet, what really frightened me beyond belief was its lack of eyes. The thing – for it was a *thing* – only had black, empty sockets to gaze with. It moved around with grace, like a panther, lowering its head to catch scent of its prey, and rising it – along with its pointy ears – to better listen to the tiniest of sounds. Its paws were massive and its short tail never wagged, not like that of real dogs, but it stood firm as if made of wood. And in fact, when the beast came closer and became more visible under the moonlight, I discovered, in incredulity, that the thing was made of straw and mud, its teeth were thorns, and its claws, blunted yet deadly, looked as if sculpted out of rosewood.

And its face, oh, its face!

Big, exaggerated, more similar to that of the sculptured gargoyles of Notre Dame than of the real canine creature it mocked.

How is that possible? A wicker creature, whose flesh is muck and brambles, alive and breathing like a real hound? I swear on my very soul that what I saw is real, though I don't know what wicked magic gave these creatures life.

Yes, creatures. For soon, another one came into my vision, and then another, and another. I counted five scouring the quagmire clearing where my boot had become food for the unyielding bog. All similar in size, all panting like real dogs, yet, none was real; they were just living constructs of packed, decomposing peat.

My mind aflame, my body frozen, I was a living contradiction; my soul wanted to flee the sight of those unholy terrors, yet, my body – wisely – refused to move. I gripped my worthless wooden weapon, ready for a vain defense, and waited for my inevitable doom.

It never came.

Suddenly, another howl resonated from afar. It sounded more similar to that deep, mournful one I had heard in my dreams, and at that, the strange creatures lifted their heads, and in an instant, dashed into the bog, as if summoned by a call they couldn't refuse to answer.

I waited for what looked like eternity before daring to move a muscle, expecting the monsters to come back as soon as I had left my hiding place. However, thank heavens, they were gone for good. Finally, I felt safe enough to emerge from the reeds, and after getting rid of the other boot, I skulked into the night, in the opposite direction to the one the wicker dogs had taken, eager to reach the – relative – safety of my home.

Alas, that was just one of the many frights I had to endure last night.

I waded through the bog, paying attention to every sound, until I reached firmer grounds and paused under a lonely willow to catch some breath. While I leaned on the tree's trunk, panting, a terrible scream came out of a tall patch of ferns, and it was soon followed by the arrival of a stout man, bloodied and muddied, who hobbled out of the grass. His pitiful cries for help were weak and hoarse, and once he stepped into the clearing, he lost his balance and fell face-first into a pool of stagnant water. Immediately, I went to his succor, and helped him to turn over.

He was Uncle Ben.

As soon as he was out of the puddle, he spat foul liquid from his mouth, then yelled, “Oh, my good sir, please, do not leave me to that devil!”

At that, the howling resonated again; this time closer. Without proffering a word, for I was already short of air, I hoisted him off the ground and, together, we moved back to the bog’s shallow waters from whence I had come. We squatted there, hidden by the reeds, holding our breath and listening to the night. I can’t remember how much time we spent there, hiding like rats, fearful of every movement, every light spell. We just huddled together: two strangers against the unknown. Judging by the beast’s snarling and growling, the monster had to be just in front of us; behind a clump of tall weeds. However, I couldn’t see anything.

“It’s there,” the man whispered in my ear, “it just can’t be seen, because it stays invisible until it’s ready to attack. It’s playing with me like a cat plays with a mouse.”

At that time, I didn’t pay attention to what he was saying, thinking the man was magnifying the extent of the creature’s abilities. But I was wrong. I was the ignorant one in this new world of terrors.

After a while, the creature ceased its snarling and the patch of tall grass stopped moving, so I assumed the beast had gone its way, looking for another prey. Grasping my wooden spike tight, I stood up, while my new friend desperately pulled at my jacket, pleading me to crouch again.

“It’s gone,” I mouthed, “we can’t stay here. We have to move or it will come back.” I tried to force him back on his feet, but the man was stubborn and offered resistance. “No!” he almost shouted, then immediately, he lowered his voice to a whisper, “I tell you it’s still there. You fool, get down!”

He pulled again at me, and I, afraid that his yell could attract the creatures back, obeyed. Again, we were squatting among the vegetation, when suddenly, without warning me, the man threw a fist-sized, flat stone to the right of the patch of weeds, where he supposed our enemy was hiding. It ricocheted a couple times then landed inside a small puddle, producing a dull splash.

Nothing happened.

This almost disappointed the little man. I saw in his eyes that he desperately wanted to show me his point; his eyes were darting like those of a madman.

After a while, I managed to convince him that nothing was there, and that we could leave that fetid shelter and move fast to the safety of my house. Reluctantly, but with no choice, he accepted my offer and we waded through the brackish water until we reached the mud banks just at the edge of Talbot House's backyard.

It was at that point that one of those things crashed through the bushes and, with an unsettling cry, jumped on us. In a fraction of a second, it was after Ben Blair; with sinewy muscles made of mucky vines and roots it pounced on him and sent him sprawling into the mud. Triumphant, the unnatural beast unhinged its thorn-laden jaw, ready to sink it into the poor man's flesh. I quickly pointed the gun, and without hesitation pulled the trigger. A loud bang resonated into the moor, deafening me, and a thick black smoke obscured my vision. I heard the man shout despite the continuous ringing inside my ears, and fear gripped me at the thought that I had hit him. I got closer to help him, and I noticed that the large beast was still on him, except it was no longer standing, but covered the man as an old blanket. Luckily, maybe because of the beast's bulk or the short distance, my projectile had indeed hit the creature, and, somehow, had killed it. Still under the shock, Ben made to move, and the carcass of the beast began to issue forth a grayish mist that quickly dissipated into the cold air, while its very body dissolved into straw and mud scattered away by some invisible force. I helped Ben regain his footing and, once I was reassured that he was unhurt, I dared to kick the last piece of the creature with the point of my toes. It immediately disintegrated into a cloud of shuck, dried husks, and vapors.

I was seeing the impossible.

Ben pulled my jacket, urging me to reach the safety of the house, but I couldn't move; my eyes were frozen to the spot where once stood the most incredible of things.

Ben tugged harder, and finally managed to drag me out of my stupor.

Quickly, our eyes scooting from shadow to shadow, we climbed up the hillock to the stone circle, then descended the slope as fast as we could, and finally, we reached the backdoor. I swung it open with such an impetus that it banged against the wall. My companion didn't wait for my invitation to enter, because as soon as the barrier was removed, he sprang into the house with a great jump, dragging me along, and slammed the door against the night. I collapsed to the floor, exhausted, while my new friend kept jumping from window to window, expecting to see the creatures coming back for us.

The house was dark and silent; no fire crackled in the fireplace. I called for Father Wales, but got no answer. Probably, I thought, he had done as he had said and at dusk, had gone back to the village warning the constable of my disappearance.

Once I recovered a bit of energy, I proceeded to restart the fire in the hearth so that our soaked bones could dry in its warmth. And it was at that point that the man calmed down and regained his composure.

"Thanks to you for your kind assistance, my good sir." He came closer to the fire and knelt beside me, "Please, let me take care of this, as you have done enough for me tonight." He gently took the poker from my hand and pointed me to the sofa. "There, good man. Rest, please, and allow me to introduce myself, as these unfortunate events have hindered every possibility to show a proper conduct of myself. I am Benjamin Blair, a Traveller." He bowed in an old-fashioned way, coughed, and then straightened himself.

I also introduced myself to him, but I didn't bow. "I know who you are. In fact, I was looking for you."

"You do know me?" he said, surprised. "How's that? Forgive me, but I can't remember your face. And your accent clearly indicates you are not from here."

I explained to him all I knew, then I queried, "Why did you leave the camp? What were your intentions? And what are those … *things*?" I was full of questions, obviously.

"I left the camp for I was a prisoner, sir. Entrapped into a spell of darkness and deception," he answered, his voice gravelly. "As for my intentions, I meant to stop this curse from growing and save the soul of my niece."

"Do you know how to stop this madness?" I moved toward him, my eyes full of hope. "Is there a ritual we can perform? A counter-magic?"

"For you to understand what I was going to do, I must first explain the nature of the curse. And I have to succeed where Talbot failed, for he never understood that the enemy is Dorchae Bog itself," he said.

"Dorchae Bog? How so?" I inquired.

"That's the local name for Talbot's peat bog. Dorchae is Old Irish for dark, or shadow. My father used to say the name comes from the fact that its peat is darker than usual. Yet, my grandfather had other ideas. He said that the place was cursed. Too many tragedies have happened in it and the very peat is soaked with death and suffering. This always sparked a funny argument between the two, but, I must say, it no longer gives me relief now."

"People say the place was cursed by Hugh Talbot." I went for the drinks trolley – where my precious bottle of poitín had found a new home – poured a couple glasses, and offered one to Ben. He bowed again, then lifted the glass in a silent toast, and quaffed it down as if it were water.

That was just the first of a long series of drinks.

"A woman told me the man was terrible and he was suspected of having murdered his servant … someone named Jack O'Leary." I sipped my glass. I don't have an iron stomach; I enjoy drinking spirit from time to time, but I can't be called a true drinker.

He scoffed, "Nonsense! Sir Talbot was a good man. Yes, he was harsh and demanding, but he wasn't that different from the gentry of those times. And it wasn't him that cursed the bog."

"Maybe you know a different version of the story than the one told to me."

"What do you know, sir?" My guest could not sit still, every little while, he moved from window to window, scrutinizing the night. "For it's true the man had a bad repute, mostly for having been cast off from Malahide by his family, yet it was an undeserved one. I bet it was the Cassidy or the folk of Ballymoor that put out this version of the story. For it was a man named Ian Mulholland that murdered O'Leary."

"Wasn't this Mulholland a local hunter? They say he's the one who found the body." I replied.

"Aye, he was. Aye, he found the body …"

Abruptly, he fell silent; something had attracted his attention. I tensed, but released a sigh of relief when my guest came back to the fireplace, nervously shaking his head. "As I was saying," he continued, "the hunter found O'Leary, but that was just the beginning of the accident. You see, my grandfather was around ten when that bad story happened. And he was there when Talbot died."

I noticed he was eyeing the bottle, so I offered to refill his glass. He thanked me, then, again, gulped it down in one swig. "Here's the story as told by my grandfather, Jacob Blair. May he shine in God's glory."

He sat down beside me, and started.

"As I said before, Hugh Talbot wasn't that bad. Aye, he was harsh and demanding, but his ill repute wasn't deserved. There had been stories of him being a member of the Hellfire club, but nothing was ever proven. He was a solitary man, who loved the company of his books. Still, being a man, he longed for a woman in his life; someone that could give him a son. Nonetheless, having been cast out of his family made his quest for a wife quite complicated, for no gentry wanted to mix their blood with his.

"Now, at that time, there was this family in Anniskerry, the Cassidy. They weren't rich, nor noble, but they had one fortune: Fiona, who was a beautiful flower of the glens. In Anniskerry, Fiona had gained a bad reputation for being as frivolous as a butterfly. I don't know if this was true or not, but it was a fact that she liked to flirt with more than one man at a time, enjoying the fawning and the buzz. Many were lining up for her favors, and there were rumors that she was no longer *whole*, if you forgive me the language. There was much gossip about this man, Ian Mulholland, who had supposedly gone too far and beyond, and that she was so ashamed that her guilt could be seen on her face at Sunday mass. Another story relates that Ian asked the Cassidy for Fiona's hand, but he had been seen coming out of their home, storming and cursing, and Moran Cassidy – Fiona's father – yelling at him and calling him names.

"After this *incident*, Fiona disappeared from Anniskerry, and their parents said she had been sent to their relatives in Galway, but true it is that they sold her to Hugh Talbot in exchange for four casks of his wine. Alas, Talbot, being asocial and suspicious, didn't want to marry the girl at once; he just indentured her as his personal maid, with the promise of taking her as his bride if she proved to be of worth.

"Meanwhile, Ian Mulholland, went desperately looking for Fiona, but could not find her."

Ben stopped again, went for the rear window, and signaled for me to stay silent.

It was still dark outside; the world cloaked in a never ending night where minutes seemed to last hours and the longing for sunlight became a chimerical dream.

Crawling, I approached the other window, while my guest kept his mute vigil. I came to my feet and lurched by the glass, and then, for one infinite moment, I was rooted to the spot, unable to move.

For outside, the world had disappeared.

A complete blackness was hiding the backyard, the hillock, and the sky from my view. It was as if someone, in vein for pranks, had put a black sheet in front of the window. Confused, I moved toward the other window, where Ben stood.

There, the same inexplicable darkness ruled the night.

Then, as if made of smog, it retreated; soon, the stars reappeared, followed by the henge, and the backyard returned. It was as if a gigantic fan had swept away that dark fog, and now, the last strands of it were slowly fading away like snow melting in the sun.

We stood there for a while, not saying a word, while the moonlight highlighted the stone circle atop the hill.

It was Ben's turn again to break the silence. As if nothing had happened, or perhaps because there was not a way to explain the strange phenomenon, he continued his story.

"Time passed, and Hugh started to feel affection for Fiona, and – so my grandfather said – the girl reciprocated. At those times, my grandpa used to come to Ballymoor with his father to help him out with his duties for the Douglas. Being a boy, he loved to sneak away and stick his nose into other people's business. In one of these adventures, he met and befriended Jack O'Leary, the butler at Talbot House. Jack loved children, and he also loved to make biscuits, so he allowed my grandpa to sneak in when the master was absent, and enjoy some of his famous oatmeal and raisin cookies. They would spend some time together, then

Jack would bring the boy back to the village before nighttime. O'Leary always talked highly about his master and Miss Fiona. It was during one of such visits that he saw Talbot proposing to the young lady."

I looked at him as if he was coming from the Moon, out of a story from Jules Verne. He noticed and therefore, smiling, he interrupted his tale to explain.

"You were shocked by that blackness, weren't you, my good sir? And I understand. However, it's not the first time I'm a witness to it. It's a phenomenon connected with the curse. Yet it's a good sign, for usually, when it happens, it also means that it is waning. In fact, that darkness is the *true* face of the enemy."

I couldn't fathom what he was trying to explicate. Somehow, he didn't look scared by the event; on the contrary, he looked relieved and hopeful.

"Do you believe in ghosts?" he blurted, as if that would make everything clear.

"On my honor, I don't know what to believe anymore." I said.

"Some ghosts are just images; reflections of time past. My father – who was a student of these things – affirms that apparitions fall into three categories: departed souls, evil spirits, and projections. Departed souls return to the living world for countless reasons. Some have unfinished business to attend to, a score that must be settled, a sin to be forgiven, a punishment to serve. Often, their mission is a benevolent one, to warn about a danger or to right a past wrong. Evil spirits are the most malign of apparitions. Having no relationship with the victims they torment, aside for their contempt for us, they come back only to cause harm."

This time, without waiting for my assent, he went directly for the poitín bottle, decanted two more glasses and passed one to me.

"Projections – and they are the majority of occurrences – are the least threatening of the three, though no less disconcerting when encountered. They often retell a story of a great tragedy, like the death of an innocent or a terrible accident. As the name implies, they are merely moving pictures; unnatural, rarely frightening, but pictures nonetheless. They have no substance and can't pose a direct threat. They work like those magic lanterns in London, except they seem real and move about."

"So, that blackness ... Was it a … projection?" I couldn't see where the man was going.

"That?" he pointed outside. "Perhaps. I don't know. They only thing I know is that darkness always precedes Fiona Cassidy's parade."

"WHAT?" I cried out. As if phantom hounds, wicker dogs, and unnatural darkness were not enough, this man was telling me that soon the ghost of a long-dead woman was about to appear.

"Do not be afraid, my good host. As I told you, she's not real. She's not dangerous. I have seen her apparition more than once. And I assure you that no harm was ever done to me. It commences here, on that hillock, and then it continues into the bog, where it ends, showing you her final demise." He sipped his glass, this time savoring the whiskey. "However, before it starts, it's better for me to tell you the rest of the story, so that you understand better what you are about to see."

It was my turn to gulp down the poitín now; it burned my esophagus and proceeded straight to my guts. I was astounded, scared, and angry at the same time. I just wanted to flee from this place, to return to the ignorance I had before. I swore that if, somehow, I got out of this situation, I would never again intrude on the unnatural. No, I would spend the rest of my life in cities, away from the wilds and the countryside, where these things mostly occur.

"So on I go with my story," he said. "That evening, at the Bridge End tavern, here in Ballymoor, Ian met Jack O'Leary, who was Talbot's butler. Drink after drink, his tongue loosened, and Jack told him about Fiona. It looked like the master wanted to marry this girl. Hearing about Fiona, Ian became bitter with jealousy. However, he also told him that the girl was terribly afraid of Arawn, the master's dog. She had confessed to Jack that the dog talked to her when they were alone, whispering foul words and promises of queer powers. In fact, Jack had talked to his master about the dog, and, surprisingly, the latter had not dismissed the story as pure fancy, on the contrary, he had grown concerned and had ordered him to help dispose of that dog that very night. Jack was feeling bad about killing that creature, but to be honest, he had never been very fond of it.

"Now, it happened that my grandpa – always a rascal, God bless his soul – snuck out of Mister Sullivan's cart to go get more cookies at

Talbot Manor. I say Mister Sullivan, because that day my great-grandfather couldn't do the trip to Ballymoor, for he was ill. Anyway, the boy went to the manor again, craving more of those delicious treats. But what awaited him there was only death and tragedy."

"On that hill," he pointed, "he saw Jack O'Leary's demise."

"Jack O'Leary was killed here?" I questioned, "Not in the bog as they told me?"

"You see, that night, Talbot and Jack led the dog up to that hillock, intent on killing the dog inside the stone circle. Talbot, in his arcane knowledge, insisted that the only way to truly banish what was inside Arawn was to chain it to the cold iron spike, then slash its throat with a queer dagger he had enchanted. Doing any different would only have the thing move to another host.

"Unfortunately, the beast acted faster; it jumped at Jack's neck and killed him. Talbot, taken aback, was unable to intervene, and quickly the dog fled into the bog. Afraid that the beast could cause more damage, Talbot ran after it, mumbling queer blessings and arcane words. So my grandpa said, for he was there, hiding in the bushes, shaking like a dead leaf on a tree in autumn.

"Unable to leave, afraid the dog would come back and attack him, he stood there, praying the Lord to help him. Then, he saw Fiona climbing the hill, and heard her shriek of terror. My grandpa thought she had just discovered Jack's mangled body, but he was wrong. Soon, the shriek was followed by a shriller one as the woman sprinted in panic, chased by the black dog. For it had indeed come back.

"Now, my grandpa was just a kid, and there wasn't much he could do. Still, he felt guilty for staying hidden, so he gathered his courage, armed himself with a pitchfork he had found in the garden, and ran after Fiona. Just in time to see her fall into the peat."

"Oh, my …" I uttered.

"Indeed." He sipped more whiskey. "Talbot heard her screams and arrived just in time to see her disappear under the mire. Behind them was my grandpa, scared as hell, but unable to leave. He saw Talbot cast about for a branch or vine with which to save her. But it was too late. The woman, bleeding from the hound's bites, was weak. She soon disappeared into the mud and died.

"Ian Mulholland, who had come to Talbot House to confront his beloved, happened on the scene, and believing Talbot had just killed Fiona, shot him right on the spot. My grandpa had never seen such bloodshed before, and the sight of Talbot's head being blasted away by buckshot was enough to send him into shock."

"But what about the curse," I interrupted, "*Bog take my bones and keep them. The hound is forever yours.*" I recited.

"Well, I think that part is just made up. My grandpa never heard her say that. And, if you think about it, she never had the time nor the force to scream that. This is the way legends are told. The one you heard from this lady is probably what goes around. It's easier to figure Talbot as the evil man."

"What was of the dog?"

"It disappeared, or rather it became something else. Or maybe the dog wasn't a dog at all." He winked, then finished his whiskey.

"I'm not following you."

"Let me finish the story, as it is not over yet." He pointed at the bottle, his eyes pleading me for another glassful.

"Be my guest," I conceded. I thought that after what we had experienced out there, we deserved to become a bit arfarfan'arf.

"Later, bitter and shaken about Fiona's death, Ian Mulholland buried Talbot's body into the peat. Then he went back to the village, saying he had found poor Jack dead. The enraged folk of Ballymoor formed a mob and, led by the hunter, stormed Talbot House hell-bent for leather. Obviously they found no one, but spotted the blood on the hillock. They scoured the moor looking for Talbot, but they never found him."

"Yes, this is a different story from the one I know, but how on earth is it going to help us against those things? I see they are vulnerable to bullets, for I just killed one. Unfortunately, I'm left with just one shot and I don't know where to get more. Not in this house." I was losing my patience, I was sick of all those different legends, each one contradicting the other and adding smoke to my already misty mind.

"As I said, my good friend, to banish evil, you must know its weakness. You just killed one of the servants, not the master. That, sir, was not Arawn, or whatever that dog is now, but one of its minions; members of its phantom pack. Unfortunately, I'm afraid the Barguest is made of a different cloth. Yet, while I don't know how to stop this creature, I do know who commands it."

"WHO?"

"Aye, there's a hand holding the leash, the same hand that has controlled it for generations. It is the dark soul of a witch that owns the hellhound."

"Annie Fuath," I whispered, afraid of pronouncing her name aloud.

He nodded. "Her soul is connected to the ancient standing stones of this land. She was the one who seduced Talbot. She was the one who wanted Fiona's body. And she is inside someone else's now. However, she's not at full power. She needs to perform a ritual to rejuvenate and withstand the light."

He paused, then, after scrounging two thick green branches from the wood heap, he started wrapping some old cloth around one of their end so as to fashion a couple of torches. "We need to defile their ritual before tonight," he said. "We must topple, and possibly destroy the stones. All of them!"

"We can't," I protested. "It would take dynamite to do that."

"And we do have the dynamite. We just need to recover it. I had a bag full of it. Unfortunately, I was attacked by the wicker dogs before reaching Shamna stone, and my dogs fled."

"I'm afraid one of your dogs is dead, Ben." I said with a saddened tone. "I saw its butchered body. As for the other one, the female, she disappeared into the woods."

His eyes hardened for a moment, then he continued to craft the torches.

I had a zillion questions crowding my mind, but I couldn't pester this man, who had been so close to death so many times and nonetheless had found the strength to fight back. I just said, "Let me guess, the gypsies are apostles of the witch's coven, right?"

He nodded, then asked, "Do you have any lamp oil?"

I handed him one of the lamps and he immediately proceeded to soak the clothed ends with fuel.

"What are those for?" I asked.

"We'll need them soon," he said with a grin. He changed expression, then shushed me by lifting his index to his nose. That gesture had the power to bring some sobriety back in me. He had spotted something.

"It's time," he whispered.

"Time for what?" I replied.

"Fiona's ghost is here. Don't you see that light in the garden?"

Indeed, from the kitchen, I saw a greenish glow. It was feeble, but I saw it growing in intensity and spreading into the backyard.

I must stop writing now, for I feel weak again. The wounds I suffered last night and the horrible things I saw are sapping my strength. I'm laying in my bed, waiting for the doctor my saviors have summoned.

Saint Patrick, help us all.

April 30th, 1891
Talbot House
Later

No one knows, until they have suffered in the dark, how blissful and precious to their sullen soul the morning light can be. It seemed to me as if God Almighty had pierced the darkness when, at dawn, the sun returned.

I'm awake again, yet no true doctor has taken care of my wounds. I'm at the mercy of my saviors, yet I'm afraid they mean me no good. Like Uncle Ben before, I suspect I'm a prisoner, kept alive only to feed the upcoming darkness.

I will finish this journal and will hide it somewhere, lest my jailors will find and burn it. I also suspect Father Wales is dead, for no one came to my rescue, and my house is full of strangers waiting to perform a ritual tonight. Now I know the true face of my enemy, hidden under the guise of benevolence.

I do not have enough forces to fight it, but I will gather all I have to try my escape. For the horror isn't over. My life is truly in danger and I must flee Talbot House before dark. It has always been at nighttime that the things have showed their powers, and I'm sure they fear sunlight. At the moment, I'm waiting for my gaolers to drop their guard, trusting me to be too weak or naïve to attempt an escape. I'm in my bed, and I know I must take action as soon as possible if I hold my life dear, but I must also keep calm, relax my mind, and think clearly.

Keep calm! Good Lord, how can I keep calm after all the horrors I was witness to?

After Ben Blair had alerted me of the ghostly light, I had hesitantly peeked at the kitchen's threshold. Yet, I saw nothing there; even that pale light was no more. Instead, out of the window I could see something amazing and terrible at the same time: a ghostly vision.

"See? I told you it takes place in the early hours before dawn." Ben said. "Behold! It begins again!"

I gazed out on the backyard as a phantom shimmer arose from the ground. From my safety, behind the kitchen's window, I could see the glow take shape in the form of a young woman, but I couldn't see her face. She looked frantic and erratic, her form quivering as a candle in a gust of wind, yet, solid enough I could discern her antiquated clothing. Suddenly, she turned her head to the right as if someone else was coming into view. At that moment, I managed to see her face.

She was beautiful, though the fading quality of the vision made it impossible to discern the colors, for they had a bleached appearance that made everything about her, including the pale aura, a greenish-yellow color. Nonetheless, I could spot some darker shades – especially on her dress and on her hands – that looked like blood to me. Not hers, as she seemed unharmed, but that of someone else.

There was no sound throughout the unfolding scene, making it even more eerie.

I felt thrilled and scared at the same time: here I was, seeing with my very eyes a ghost. I, Patrick Cahill Conroy, a rational man who had never believed in what could not be proven, had just been shown that myths and folktales about hauntings and apparitions were based on fact; that we, as men of science, should never dismiss as nonsense and superstition that which our illuminated, but still infant, study of nature's laws cannot yet detect. We stand tall in our ignorance, jeering at the uneducated, looking down on the warnings from our ancestors. And yet, we are the most fragile of the lot. For when what we thought as irrational plainly manifests in front of our nose, all of our solidly built beliefs crumble down like a castle besieged by superior forces. Yes, I had already experienced the unnatural before, when I had seen – and felt – those horrible wicker-like hounds, still, my mind had tried to find a reason for their existence. After all, I had not seen them clearly and the whole situation had conspired against me to make me see more than what really was. Maybe they were just natural dogs, of a breed I had never seen before. Or some yet-unknown species of wild canines. I still couldn't explain the quick dissolution of the one I had destroyed, but in my mind I still desperately looked for a natural explanation. It is so easy to rationalize a supernatural encounter after it is over and you are back to the safety of your world. Also, I had doubted the veracity of the dark shroud which had clouded all the manor's windows before, deeming it a child of my intoxication's dalliance with suggestion. But now, I live in a new world. A world where everything is possible, or at least plausible.

As I watched, she whirled to the right, a horrified expression on her face, then, as if she had seen the Devil himself, she started for the hillock, pulling up her ghostly dress and revealing her comely legs. Then I saw the spirit-like image of a huge, black monstrosity, almost the size of a small pony – chasing after her. Its body was regal in appearance; well-formed and smoothly muscled, like that of a Great Dane. However, its oversized head came across as more similar to that of an English mastiff, with its broad skull and flattened muzzle; large dewlap and flews, but its ears stood tall and vigilant like those of a wolf, and ended in a tapered point.

At the corner of the house, where the rear veranda turns southward to join the front porch, I spotted the shadow of a man. I couldn't see the actual figure, as it was hiding behind the wall, but just his silhouette, projected by a phantom light. He was wearing a tricorn hat, like those in fashion a century ago, and the long winter coat of a gentleman. The scared lady climbed the hillock as fast as she could, soon followed by the hound, then she disappeared into the stone circle.

"Look," said Ben pointing at the shadow, "That's Talbot!"

Soon, the ghost ran over the hillock, and he too disappeared at the top. However, the ghostly light was still visible there, moving along with the figures – or perhaps emanating from them – and though fading, while the phantom story of a century old tragedy repeated itself, colored the ancient stones in that sickly hue.

Without warning, my guest opened the door and stepped outside, torches ablaze.

"Come, if you want to see with your own eyes what really happened that night!" There was no longer fear in his eyes, as if he had forgotten the Barguest and all the rest.

"Have you lost your reason, my friend?" I whispered. "I am not going back to the bog. And neither should you."

"It's safe now. I told you," he protested. "Besides, we must recover the dynamite before the gypsies find it." He handed me a torch, and then, without waiting for me, dashed for the hilltop. I couldn't let the man go alone, so I hesitantly followed him.

It was sill dark outside, even if the light aurora of the coming sun was drawing a thin line of lighter blue on the horizon. Reassured by that sight, I ran after the man.

Too late.

How can I describe what is meant to be indescribable? How can I put on paper the horror I was witness to? Still, this *horror* does exist, for I saw it with my own eyes.

The horrible thing exploding out of the henge's shadows was massive and had a vaguely canine form. I said vaguely canine form because, apart from its quadrupedal stance and a pair of wolfish ears, the rest of its features were atrociously distant from any earthborn dog man has ever laid its eyes on. Jet black in color, its skin was oily like that of frogs, and smooth and tightened around the lean body though, here and there, tufts of stringy dark hair cut off its alien texture. And its face! Skeletal and gaunt, as if the beast had been skinned alive, in its bony orbits floated whitened orbs, similar to those of boiled fish. Its ferocious mouth was full of sharp fangs that glistened with drool, and was large enough to swallow a man's head. The thing was surrounded by thick, black smoke, as if it had emerged from the fires of Hell itself, and it was smoldering from the inside.

In an instant, the thing was on Ben Blair. It unhinged its evil maw, and from within sprang out a viscous tongue; impossibly long and more akin to that of a batrachian than of a mammal; increasing its resemblance to a gargantuan amphibian from the netherworld. The man just had the time to emit a shrilling cry before the monster closed its enormous jaws and, with a powerful bite, chomped his head off at the neck. I witnessed a dense red mist spreading from Blair's stump before the body, now lifeless, slumped to the ground.

Then, the creature turned its white eyes toward me.

As I said before, there are moments when every living creature reacts without thinking: flee or fight. My body made the decision for me, for without realizing it, I soon found myself back into the house, slamming the door shut behind me. Then, shaking, I retreated from it, walking backward with the gun pointed in front of me; my eyes darting from doorframe to window, and from window to doorframe, expecting the monster to crash through one or the other at any moment.

I had reached the archway leading to the foyer when the demon rammed into the living room's main window, landing with a heavy thump and a shower of fragmented glass on the wooden floor. I pointed the pistol and exploded my last shot, but it passed through the beast, as if it were made of smoke. I saw the bullet carve a large hole into the leather settee by the window, just behind the creature.

In response, the Barguest sprang that weird tongue at me, and in horror, I discovered that a second mouth capped it when its steel fangs sunk into my left ham. Blood spayed forth, and the mouth pressed so hard that soon, its upper teeth met the lower ones, piercing my flesh like a fastening machine. I yelled in pain, and kicked at the thing, but it wouldn't budge; on the contrary, as a parody of a fishing rod, it started pulling me, forcibly dragging me toward the wide-opened mouth of the monster. Desperate, I clubbed at it with my now spent pistol, and by luck or else, the fiend released its vise just enough for me to dart away from it.

Then, I remembered that phrase from Talbot.

'Bless the sun, for the Darkness cannot stand bright light.'

And I set the torch I was still holding on fire.

Immediately, the beast retracted its tongue, and its already amorphous shape twisted and writhed, reacting to the sudden brightness. It squirmed, moved to the left, then rocked to the right, tying to find a way to avoid the flame. Emboldened by my new weapon, I stepped forward. The monster hissed, spat like a bedeviled cat, then it yelped in pain when a thin sunray, coming through the crashed window, hit its oily skin. I saw black smoke issuing from its flesh, and an acrid smell filled the air.

The sun had returned.

As if it had never been there, the creature faded into nothingness, and I found myself facing, a smile on my lips, the blessed morning light. The feeble warmth of daybreak touched my skin, and with renewed courage, I stepped into it. Immediately, probably due to the blood loss and the extreme stress, I lost my senses.

When I came to, I found myself in my bed, naked and feverish. Someone had dressed my wound, for it was now wrapped in a thick bandage. I discovered soon that Siobhan and Maggie had found me, my life slowly bleeding away on the living room's floor.

Yet, now I know that my rescuers are not here to heal me, for they never summoned the doctor, nor have any intention to. I can hear the gypsies mulling around the house, pulling drawers and tossing items from shelves, and I've heard Siobhan whisper about tonight's sacrifice. I know they are looking for my something, yet I don't know what.

As I am writing this, the sound of many feet and of rustling chains being dragged along is coming up from the ground below. Just before, there was the noise of a cart, probably one of their vardos, climbing the hilltop. I'm hearing footsteps approaching the door, and just now, the grinding of the key in the lock.

I am a prisoner.

My only hope is Father Wales. I pray the man returned to the village and is, right now, leading the constable and armed men to the house, or the camp.

However, I can't count on it. What if the good priest had been killed? Or worse: what if he is part of the conspiracy?

No, I shall not wait for ephemeral rescuers. I shall gather my strength and crawl to the window. Then, in all my desperation, I shall climb it down. Away from this accursed place! Away from this horrible house and its secrets! I shall reach Ballymoor and tell the people what the gypsies are up to.

Better to die while attempting my escape, than at the hands of those monsters.

Yes, it is my only chance. My captors are all atop the hill; I can hear them chant. Nonetheless, before I undertake my foolish evasion, I will leave my journal inside this room along with all my memories of this accursed place.

Goodbye, my loyal companion.

PART TWO: *THE CONFESSION OF FATHER EARL WALES*

OCTOBER 31ST, 1891

CHAPTER TWELVE

31st of October, 1891
St Kevin's Church, Ballymoor, County Wicklow, Ireland.

Yes, I confess that it was I who buried six bullets into my housekeeper's head. Yes, I admit it was also me who burned her body to a crisp in the backyard. And yet here I state that I didn't put an end to her life, but I saved it.

I'd prefer to be called a madman rather than a murderer, for I know no one will believe my confessions. Nevertheless, I owe it to the Lord, of Whom I have been a faithful servant till this last very night. And, even if my hands are red, I know that mine was an act of mercy. The thing I killed was no longer my dear friend, but a puppet of darkness, and I have indeed not murdered her; instead, I have helped her soul, and in so doing, I have temporarily purged the world of a horror whose continual existence has been a blight here in Ballymoor for too long.

Oh, if only I had noticed the changes before! Perhaps, I could have helped her escape the monster's clutches. But I had been too distant, trying desperately to fight off the nightmares of last spring, to put behind me the events that had spawned them. Events that also resulted in the loss of innocent life, for which I feel responsible.

Yes, I feel responsible. And guilty.

I have always been aware of the dark forces lurking in Talbot House. I collected stories, anecdotes, legends, and events surrounding that house. Yet, I never completely understood the true nature of its evil.

Since the beginning, in my first days here in Ballymoor, I have been attracted, and rebuffed at the same time, by the tales walling around that cursed mansion. It all started with that nursery rhyme – *The Old Woman in the Moors*. This ballad tells how Annie Carrick was caught blood-handed and burnt alive for her evil deeds. It is a variant of many similar ballads, the most famous being *Weile Waile* or *The River Saile*, except that this one properly refers to the kidnapping and successive murder of a local infant.

There was an old woman and she lived in the moors, weile weile wee.
There was an old woman and she lived in the moors, down by the Glencree.

She stole a baby three months old, weile weile wee.
She stole a baby three months old, down by the Glencree.

She had a knife long and sharp, weile weile wee.
She had a knife long and sharp, down by the Glencree.

She stuck the knife in the baby's heart, weile weile wee.
She stuck the knife in the baby's heart, down by the Glencree.

There were folks come a'knockin on the door, weile weile wee.
There were folks come a'knockin on the door, down by the Glencree.

They caught the woman lying on the floor, weile weile wee.
They caught the woman lying on the floor, down by the Glencree.

They bound the woman hands and feet, weile weile waile.
They bound the woman hands and feet, down by the Glencree.

They set her on fire and she went crisp, weile weile wee.
They set her on fire and she went crisp, down by the Glencree.

And that was the end of the woman in the moors, weile weile wee.
And that was the end of the baby too, down by the Glencree

I have always been an avid collector of folklore and ballads from all around Ireland, for I feel that in them lies the unity of our people, our heritage, for good or wrong. As a man of the Church, I believe that it is our duty to preserve the cultural treasure buried under the ashes of foreign plantation. Thusly, it became natural for me to look into the story behind the ballad. And it was this way that I discovered Gorta cave and the slab of Saint Kevin.

I remember the day when I got permission from Kevin Yares, the owner of the Bridge End Inn and the person responsible for the rental of Talbot house, to enter the mansion's grounds and take a look at the infamous cave of Annie Carrick.

Houses, like people, do have personalities, and Talbot House clearly shows it at first sight: it is arrogant, and presumptuous I daresay, with its attic spur defiantly askew, as if challenging the heavens themselves, in the way a proud sea captain faces a storm. The gabled windows, which have a haughty expression unto them, seem to look down at Ballymoor as if it is a nuisance. It wants to stay alone, this terrible house; it doesn't like company and doesn't need it. Although capable of accommodating a large family, it has an uncanny air about it that doesn't bide to children's laughter and mirth.

Queerly, Talbot House doesn't lack decorations that would, normally, please the eye. Yet, its arched windowpanes, its rimmed balconies, and the sculpted framework, do nothing to alleviate the malevolence this house emanates. The elegant verandah circling the ground floor, stands constantly darkened by its queer low coverings. The fanlight above the front doors is too small, giving it a decorative purpose rather than an effective use. The stony pilasters at the top of the small flight of stairs appear straight from a distance, but once closer, the observer can't shake off the feeling that they are actually set in the wrong way and are doomed to crumble under the weight of the upper floors. The wormy pediments do not depict cheerful flourishes; on the contrary, they give the impression of writhing tentacles and entwining snakes. Shadows nest on the ugly façade even in broad daylight.

Is it by mere chance that angles and corners meet to form a frightful face on Talbot House? Was giving this house a dreary visage not the original aim of the builders? I honestly doubt it now. For I believe that this evil thing, this ulcerous mass in the shape of a mansion, forcefully willed its own form. It wormed inside Hugh's mind, it slithered inside the thoughts of the carpenters and masons, and violently imposed its own will into the hands of the builders.

Because Talbot House was never meant to be a residence, but a temple to evil and unholy forces.

As I said, I had always dismissed the tales about the house being haunted, for I believed that the Good Lord would not allow a single soul to be left behind. I was more concerned about the works of the Devil. And thusly, all these years, I have allowed the house, and my own ignorance, to deceive me.

Alas, now I know the truth.

Yes, it was in Gorta cave that the vicious disease originated, but it was inside Talbot House that it took shape. And my ignorance, my guilty ignorance, has led to great loss.

My fascination with Saint Kevin's life and deeds naturally attracted me to Gorta cave. There, took place an unknown chapter of the saint's story that no one had heard before. Yet, inevitably, the tale of the cave, and of Talbot House and all those who had lived inside it, enmeshed, and I found myself chronicling the events of various families that had, at different times, experienced tragedies while living in Talbot House. What I had heard, in the beginning, about the accursed house, was merely that people had died or disappeared there in alarmingly great numbers. I first thought, naturally, that the place was merely unhealthy, perhaps because of its location deep in the bog, of the quality of the well and pump water, or of the vicious gases the moray dispels. Yet, the locals insisted that the place had been cursed by a witch, whose immortal spirit had claimed the place as her own since the time of her death. This much I knew before my curiosity led me to embark on to the perilous voyage that finally wrecked, bloodily, in that fateful night six months ago. When, in the end, my persistent research finally assembled the horde of dreadful lore I possess about the house, there lay before me a sad chronicle of deaths and despair with no equal. Convoluted, cold in its logic, and dismally genealogical as most of the material is, throughout it run a continuous pattern of horror and preternatural malevolence which clearly implies a malignant presence. Apparently unconnected events fit together to create a story of obvious vileness.

I will not pen here my findings about Saint Kevin's slab and its related tales, for I recorded them separately, in another personal journal. Here, I will talk about the mansion itself, so that whoever reads my confession will better understand the events that I will chronicle later regarding what happened to Patrick Conroy and the Blair family in the night of the first of May.

The history of Talbot House reveals traces of evil ever since the beginning.

The problems started in 1778 with the topping of the Cailli Stone, one of the menhirs which composed the stone structure on the hilltop behind the mansion grounds. This stone marked the entrance to Gorta cave, and was thought by Hugh Talbot, an alchemist and studious of the occult, to be the focus of the pagan circle's power. He believed that by removing the catalyst – as he called it in his journal – he could trap under his own will the primordial entity that used the magical circle as a doorway to our world. This entity, which he called the Morrigan at first, and the Blackness later, had been, according to him, the source of most of the strange occurrences that had been plaguing the Glencree area for centuries. However, something went wrong and the stone shattered, killing a man and injuring another in the process. Talbot, however, didn't lose his resolve to bind this presence to his own wishes; he commanded the stone to be cut into pieces and for the material to be used as decorations throughout the house; the biggest piece was chosen as the mantel of the main hearth.

Talbot House was finished in 1780 and Hugh moved in at the end of October of that year. However, his occult work wasn't over, for to test his mastery over the entity he performed a ritual to siphon part of the presence into his own dog, Arawn. Talbot believed that the infamous *witch familiar* of folklore is actually a medium for supernatural entities to slowly worm their way inside a human host, which they can ultimately possess and use for their own obscure, if inimical, deeds.

And as it can be seen here, the nobleman's pseudo-scientific notions mixed with the Church's demonology, which easily, alas, floods into demonolatry. In Christian Demonology, the study of demons is regarded as a mean to identify signs of the Enemy's activity. Theologians like Thomas Aquinas wrote about the behaviours which Christians should be aware of, while witch hunters, like Heinrich Kramer, were more concerned on how to find and deal with those people believed to be in league with the Devil. However, there were some, deep inside the Church, who delved into ways to summon and command demons in the name of the Almighty. Such priests, during the Inquisition, dared to commit unholy acts to turn their 'creations' against the enemies of the Church. These 'daemonhosts' were alleged to be powerful creations of terrible and dangerous rituals in which a demon was bound into a living human host's body and enslaved to the will of its creator. An utterly foul act indeed, for I believe the good intents of the summoner don't matter; the goal doesn't justify the means. By the ways of unholy incantations, amulets, and chains, the demon was physically trapped into human form. In these texts, the relation between the binding and the strength of the demon is amply stressed. Demonologists strived to bind the evil spirit three times, for three is the number of God, thinking this would weaken the daemonhost considerably. And some fools had attempted the casting of lesser bindings, resulting in more powerful creatures, yet greater was the chance of the demon to slip out of its master's control. Demonology lists the ranks, names, secret names, myths, powers, and weaknesses of all known demons. In some books, it is believed that they undergo a cycle, going from weak whisperers, to lamenters, to shouters; the greater their power, the louder their voice. Others believe that their powers and ranks are set and never change. Honestly, I don't know which side is right, I only know that demons exist and they are attracted by suffering and iniquity.

There are houses in which husbands have always beaten their spouses, and blades which have taken more than a dozen souls. I do believe that they are more than demon-infested places and things. I do believe they are demons themselves. Because we instinctively know that evil deeds sometimes leave a lasting stain on the world. It's like burning the stew on the stove: the meat is gone, but the sour smell lingers. Often forever. And it attracts more foul stench.

Such is the case of Talbot House.

Arawn the host became the master. And in 1790 it claimed the lives of Fiona Cassidy and Hugh Talbot. After listening to the concerns of his loyal servant, Jack O'Leary, Talbot started to believe that the Blackness was trying to take hold of his beloved future wife and decided to dispose of his daemonhost dog. He certainly saved Fiona's soul from corruption, but his *creature* became totally unbound in the process, resulting in the horror that I personally witnessed last April. I have no proof that Ian Mulholland, who claimed the empty Talbot House for himself for almost one year before being found ravaged to death by a wild animal in the moor, was killed by the unbound Arawn. Or that the demonic beast was responsible for the death of Michael Greene, the first legitimate owner of Talbot House after Hugh's disappearance, two years later. But it's fact that for almost two centuries, the sightings of a dark, phantom hound have been recorded in and around the Glencree valley.

Nonetheless, this phantom hound is just a part of the whole evil, a weapon used by the true enemy against those she can't submit to her will or which strongly oppose her unfathomable works. *She*, yes, for this evil has a feminine nature.

I said previously that it was not by chance that Talbot House was built exactly where it stands now, and that I truly believe that an unknown force gave it shape and reason. As I have stated in my research journal about Saint Kevin's slab, it is recorded that Dorchae Bog was inhabited by a savage tribe of demon-worshipping cannibals. This tribe, the Cruithni, was completely wiped out by St Kevin of Glendalough and an army of faithful Christians. At the head of this tribe stood a witch-queen of sort, the living embodiment of the Morrigan. In Breanainn's chronicles, it is said that such a witch was sent to everlasting darkness when all the survivors of that bloody battle were cast down the pit of Gorta cave. A similar figure resurfaces in Guire mac Domhnall's account centuries later, when Viking raiders joined forces with Gael settlers to defeat a shadow menace from that accursed cave. And it reported that their queen was bound and burnt alive at the stone topping the cave. Centuries later, the taint coming from that pit managed to take hold of yet another corrupted soul: that of Annie Carrick, the so-called 'Hag of the Moor'. The detailed story of Dark Annie and her demise can be found in my journal about Saint Kevin, and there is no need to repeat it here. The important thing is that popular belief asserts that Annie the witch was equally bound and burnt at the Cailli stone. Hugh Talbot knew about it and strongly asserted that the witch had been just a puppet of the Blackness. He was wrong. Annie Carrick had willingly allowed the entity to possess her soul and had become one with the darkness she worshipped. And her will is still so strong that it holds no bounds. For she transferred her essence into the very stone, patiently waiting for a new host body. It was so that she tried to corrupt Fiona, and that she claimed different hosts throughout the passing years.

My conclusions are proved by annotated facts.

I know that many male residents of Talbot House have complained about horrible dreams experienced during their permanence in that mansion. It is recorded that Gregory Campbell, uncle to Duncan, who owned Talbot House for almost twenty years before selling it to the Cooney of Cork, died there of heart failure while sleeping in the master bedroom. Before him, William Douglas Green had decided to sell the inherited house after lamenting the terrible dark dreams he had been having while sleeping there.

It should be noted that Duncan Campbell left no bad accounts of the house, but, essentially, he never lived there, for his intention had been to turn it into a summer residence, which is why he invested heavily in renovations and expensive furniture.

Later occupants, such as Seamus and Roy Cooney, left accounts of the horrible night visits of a crone. Nonetheless, barring the bad dreams, what really identifies Talbot House as a demon-possessed mansion is the series of terrible events which afflicted the Cooney family, which I will later report. In fact, before going into the details of the unfortunate Cooney family, it is better I explain the nature of the beast.

I feel the need to firstly explicate how and when I finally identified the haunter of Talbot House. Up until last April, I had never believed in Dark Annis' tale. Yes, I knew the story was based on true events, but I had dismissed the fact that she had been a witch. When that unlucky American student, Patrick Conroy, showed me the notes of Hugh Talbot, and I saw what stone had been used to make the mantel of the mansion's main hearth, everything came to me with the thunder of revelation.

Some theologians believe in the existence of *Diaboli*: spirits and ghosts that carry a demonic essence. These beings were once evil souls bound to walk Limbo for eternity, until a demon corrupts and twists their nature, turning them into something more diabolical. It is certainly hard to distinguish an evil spirit from a diabolical ghost, yet the difference, although trivial, can help to identify, and to successively destroy, the creature.

Annie Carrick had been a wilful and loyal servant to the Morrigan. She had performed all kinds of evil deeds requested in her dark pact. She had stolen and sacrificed infants and children to her dark goddess. It was said she had mated and got pregnant with a demon from the dark cave, and had later swapped her offspring with one in the village of Ballymoin.

It is of a certain interest the tale of a Samuel Mackenzie which, in 1646, Father Elliot Nicholson, of this very church, described as appearing as a thirteen-year-old boy, yet his birth had been registered just five years before. The whole story can be found in Nicholson's personal memories, in my library, but I will summarise here the most salient parts.

Father Nicholson had just arrived in Ballymoin, in the April of 1641, when he had been urgently summoned by Brian Mackenzie, a farmer. His wife, Bethany, had lost her mind, for she refused to feed her new child, Samuel, claiming that *that* was not her son, but a Changeling – the swapped child of a fairy. She had tried to put the child into the fireplace since it was a long-held belief that the changeling would jump up the chimney and return the kidnapped one, but had fortunately been stopped by Brian. The man had resolved to tie his wife to the bed and had then called up the priest for he wanted him to perform an exorcism because he believed the woman to be possessed. The reason behind this ruckus had been the fact that, according to the Mackenzie, the infant looked different, older and growing faster. In his memories, Nicholson admits the child seemed unnaturally big for his age, and that his body appeared rubbery, and with a somewhat canine cast. Nonetheless, he didn't believe the boy had been swapped, but rather that the poor baby was afflicted by some kind of warping disease or congenital malformation, which was quite a common occurrence in the backwoods. However, what happened next is what caught my attention to the tale, an early ringing bell that made me conscious of the diabolical presence. While the priest had been holding the baby in his arms, the woman had managed to escape her bonds, armed herself with a knife, and slashed her own throat. Nicholson was so shocked by the happening, as he wrote in his notes, that he felt such a pity for the farmer and his child – *"I have never before, in my whole life, encountered a tragedy like this. It fell on me like a big rock, and will stay on me for years to come."* – that he decided to help the man with the funeral, even if the woman had committed suicide and as such she could not receive the final blessings, and personally sent a wet nurse to breast feed the neonate. Five years later, he wrote of how it had become obvious to all in the village that Samuel Mackenzie was not normal. Queer things were already happening in Ballymoin, and the creepy child just added to the atmosphere of uneasiness and dread that was gripping the village. People stood clear of the Mackenzie place and it was rumoured that dogs barked and howled when young Samuel was passing by. Nicholson said that the boy looked overdeveloped, unusually tall, with a muscular body and a strong frame, yet his face kept that canine look. It seemed as though something inside the boy, huge and inhuman, was stretching the child's form to adapt it to its own. He was often spotted wandering, alone, in the moor, as if looking for something. Villagers started to complain about the boy, claiming he was the son of the Devil or else, and begged Father Nicholson to do something. There were also disturbances at the graveyard, and reports of tombs being violated. The priest said in his memories that he had visited the cemetery, and had indeed seen signs of indecent and deplorable disturbing of the dead, but that it seemed to him to be the work of vulgar grave-robbers rather than the work of Satan. Brian Mackenzie died shortly thereafter; though at the prime age of thirty-seven, he appeared to look ninety and beyond on his deathbed.

Another queer accident happened a month later when Patrick Carrick, the elder son of the infamous Annie, was attacked and killed by his own wolfhounds. Two years before, Danny Carrick and his new spouse, Maggie Sullivan, had died in a similar way when their cart had upturned at the river's bend due to a pack of wild dogs scaring the horse. So, it was legitimate that villagers saw a connection between the two instances and, again, demanded the priest to send the devil away. Father

Nicholson was no exorcist, but a simple country clergyman. Nonetheless, to appease the flaring tempers, he promised to talk to Samuel. Samuel sent him away, telling him that he had no time to waste with bumpkin's superstitions and that the loss of his father was a burden heavy enough for him to deal with, for *'the old bastard'* – these were his exact words – had left only debts and sickened stock. The cold reaction of a five-year-old child and his bluntness left Nicholson aghast, but also pushed him to investigate the boy's wanderings further. So, one night, he followed Samuel and saw him disappear under the hill below the standing stones circle. He didn't find the courage to move closer for, according to his notes, he felt an unnatural fear grip his soul and the sounds of howling dogs sent him running back home. Nicholson stopped writing about Samuel after this event, however, in the following years there are notes about more disturbances in the graveyard, queer deaths, and other calamities striking the community.

By 1649 there were greater concerns for Father Nicholson than local superstition; the Irish Catholic Confederation, which had controlled most of Ireland since the times of the Rebellion, had allied with the English Royalists, and this had brought Cromwell's attention to our shores, resulting in the Parliamentarian campaign of invasion and successive conquest. This is one of the reasons for the lack of written documents about what had really happened to Samuel Mackenzie. Some say that after Samuel was accused of kidnapping an infant in the village, folk took the matter into their own hands, tracked him down to Gorta cave, and there, to their shock, found him in an *insanely incestuous embrace* with his true mother, Annie Fuath. Some legends say he was shot dead on the spot, while his monstrous mother was dragged out and burned alive. Others say he died defending his mother. Sadly, there's no way to know the true fate of Samuel Mackenzie. Nevertheless, Father Nicholson's story adds yet another clue to the monster's nature.

It is also rumoured that Annie had admitted followers into her cult, but I have no proof of this ever happening. What I do have proof of is that Annie Carrick became more than a simple ghost once she bound herself with the Cailli stone.

Why her and not others? What was so special about Annie that was not present in the previous hosts? I don't know, and probably, it will never be known. The only way to better understand the relationship between these dark entities and their servants is to dig into the foul pits of their own knowledge, and that, frankly, is something I am not willing to do. As Hugh Talbot has proved, to gaze too deep into Hell is to allow Hell to take hold of you.

My mentor, Father Malone, used to say that the Devil is a chained dog; it can't come too close to us, it is us that get too close to it.

CHAPTER THIRTEEN

The Cooney family have certainly been the most affected by the *'Curse of Talbot House'*.

It was patriarch Seamus that saw in the area an opportunity to profit in the renovated peat trade. Besides, for unknown motives, he fell in love with the house itself, thus in 1821 he bought the house and land from Duncan Campbell, who had lost interest in the mansion. A former successful sea captain, Seamus sold everything he had in the fishing business and moved there to start a new life. What pushed him and his family into this I never found, but I suspect a certain scandal involving the accidental death of child made the Cooney unpopular in Cork. Seamus loved Talbot House so much that he invested a large sum of money in it, expanding the garden, adding the carriage house, the spire-like attic tower, and the great gates.

The first of the accidents happened in 1824, when Kelly Rose, age six, disappeared in the dead of night, leaving no trace. For days, the Cooney combed the moor, desperately looking for their young flower. There were rumours the girl had been abducted and killed by a stranger or a gypsy, but that kind of gossip always surfaces in small communities when a child gets lost. And of these ugly rumours I'm well conscious, for I myself had to listen to many of them when a similar episode happened just after my arrival in Ballymoor. As it can be expected when such a calamity hits a family, the loss of their daughter caused a gloom to fall on the Cooney. Maura, the mother and wife of Dermot – the younger son of Seamus – slowly withered away into madness; a madness that culminated in her climbing the stairs to the mansion's attic and committing suicide by pulling a rope around her neck and hanging herself from a rafter in the attic one year later.

There was another mysterious death two years later on the Talbot's grounds if the nameless tomb in the manse's graveyard is to be believed, yet, whoever this man was and how he died is impossible to find for there are no records of his passage. I collected a rumour that says the man was an Englishman that had been attacked and mortally wounded by the phantom hound, but, as I said, there's no proof of it.

A bit of light resurfaced in the Cooney family in 1828, when Beulah, wife of Roy – the eldest son and head of the family, for Seamus' health had begun to decline – gave birth to Andrew. A light that was soon engulfed by horrible darkness when Beulah became mysteriously ill and irrefutably insane. When the baby was six months old, she used a kitchen knife to behead the poor toddler, then, swearing her allegiance to darkness, she fled into the moor. She was never found, but from then on, every disappearance or death of a child was blamed on her. It is possible that Beulah had indeed become a host for Annie, but it seems that she was not good enough because she was soon replaced by a more sturdy shell: Victoria Cooney.

After the loss of his child and wife, Roy became edgy and short-tempered. He had frequent altercations with both his younger brother and his father, and it was during one of these fits that he killed Dermot. Stories differ on what caused that excess of rage. Some said Roy accused his brother of secretly being happy about the loss of Andrew, the misfortune somewhat levelling his own loss. Others said that it wasn't Roy who killed his brother, but Beulah herself, now a Fuath like Annie Carrick before – she had come while he was asleep and had siphoned off his soul and breath after riding him all night. According to the only reliable witness I have found – Helena Kidman, whose grandfather had been constable of the area at the times of Dermot's death – the two had been discussing by the fireplace about the younger brother's indolence at work when Roy, in a sudden fit of rage, had plunged the hearth's poker into his sibling's left eye, killing him on the spot. Seamus sent for Harold Kidman and paid him off to make the thing pass as an accident; something that good old Kidman regretted for the rest of his life, since he confessed it to his family on his deathbed. This version finds confirmation by the large dark spot on the woodwork by the fireplace, for many a servant and charwoman that worked at Talbot House reported about it during their time of service, and none of them ever found a way to remove it. Even queerer is the fact that this dark spot seems to appear and disappear cyclically, following an unknown pattern. I have seen this spot myself, and when it occurred, it looked to me as if it was newly spilt blood.

Roy remarried two years later. I have letters, a marriage certificate, and some peculiar correspondence between the new bride and her mother. Twenty years younger, Angela Reilly was disowned by her own family for marrying a Cooney. In that letter, Constance Riley warns her daughter about the Cooney family, branding them as devil-worshippers for they rarely attended church. However, we must take into account that the Reilly were Anglicans, while the Cooney were Catholics.

One year later, the couple had twins: Brandon and Victoria.

And here comes one of the most horrid parts in the sad history of the Cooney family. When the twins were five, children began to disappear again around Glencree, all about the same age as the Cooney siblings. Of course, the villagers claimed that Beulah the Mad or Dark Annis had taken them, but the truth was far, far worse.

One day, a worker of the peat discovered the bleached bones of a woman down in the Cooney quarry. She was never identified, but some old folk in the village swore it was the skeleton of Beulah Cooney, apparently swallowed by the mire. The news spread, and soon people stopped blaming Beulah for the youngsters' disappearances, while talks of Dark Annis resurfaced.

As I said before, it seems that Beulah was not suitable as a permanent host to the dark spirit inhabiting Talbot House for, according to her remains, she had died shortly after her escape from the manse. I don't know what happened to her because I never had the opportunity to see the bones found in the bog, and what became of them is impossible to track. Still, after my revelation last April, I'm convinced the woman sunk into the mud, voluntarily or involuntarily, just after her infanticide.

More. From 1838 to 1852, at least thirteen children were reported as missing to the constabulary in Anniskerry, and none of them were ever found. However, the skeletons and corpses of fourteen children were discovered by old Roy Cooney in Gorta cave during a terrible night of August in 1853. Along with a blood-soaked and completely mad Victoria.

This story can't be found anywhere, because it has never been recorded and the only one to know the truth was not willing to share it. Besides, he wasn't even there when this horror happened.

When the twins were sixteen, only Roy, his wife, and the children were still living in Talbot House. Because the peat trade was no longer profitable, Roy found himself forced to return to the sea and the ways of his ancestors. Angela was frequently alone, and refused to let her children leave the house. So she took care of educating them, with the help of the nanny, Mrs Fowler. It seems Victoria became pregnant from her brother. Once her pregnancy became evident all the servants working at Talbot House, including Mrs Fowler, were sent packing. The pregnancy, of course, was never brought to an end; adding more evil to an already evil house. Brandon was sent to Cork as apprentice to a distant uncle. The following year saw yet another death inside Talbot House: Angela fell from the second floor when the balustrade unexpectedly broke away, and she landed face-first into the main room. Well, that is what Victoria said to the constable. The latter ended up living alone inside Talbot House, never venturing to the village and becoming yet another local legend, until she was whisked away by her own brother shortly after the strange death of Roy Cooney.

Brandon Cooney – who is the current owner of Talbot House – recently told me what Victoria had confessed to him during one of his visits at the sanatorium before she died. After the events of last April, Brandon didn't feel at ease any more with his dark secret and thus decided to confide in me what had truly happened the night his father had died. As a priest, I should not divulge the content of such a confession, but I must put this on paper before I die or secrets will add to secrets, and then, they will turn into more legends and rumours. And Talbot House feeds on this. For when I say that the house is a demon itself, I mean it for real. Dark Annis and her hosts, the phantom hound and its wicker pack, the Gruagach and the ghosts, are just manifestations and tools of the same unearthly creature that claims the mansion as its own.

Brandon told me that when his father returned home, after a long trip in the Southern seas, he couldn't find Victoria anywhere. The house stood empty, and the hearth was cold. Outside, in the moor, a search party was looking for Sean Meany, sixteen years old, who had failed to return home after a delivery trip to Moorcrest. Understandably, the villagers feared the worst for it had been raining for days and the roads were tricky, flooded with mud. His cart had been found, but there was no trace of him.

Roy Cooney found his ravaged body, almost cut to shreds, inside Gorta cave.

In the company of thirteen other bodies, all in different states of advanced decomposition.

In the asylum, Victoria had gleefully revealed to her brother how, that evening, the face of their father had turned from red to white at the sight of her *tea party*. For over the years, she had collected many a companion for her games inside the cave. Yes, they were not much to look at, and surely they weren't so good for a conversation, but still it was the only way to appease the Blackness inside her. The house needed souls to feed upon: the Blackness needed them, and once their souls were gone, all that was left were the empty shells, devoid of life, yet a presence to fill her own loneliness. She told him how, once a child, she had used the children's curiosity and spirit of adventure to lure them into the cave. And how, later on, by means of her beauty and lust, she had attracted the boys with promises of soft caresses in the dark. To the villagers, she had said that her father had died of failure of the heart just after stepping into the house. Obviously, she never told them what had caused the poor man's heart to stop.

When I asked Brandon why no one had ever found the corpses inside Gorta cave, he told me that Victoria, afraid to be discovered, had pushed all the remains into the hole, along with her tea service and the wicked instruments she had used to slowly torture to death all those children first, and those boys later. He still doesn't know how Victoria, who was a minute woman, managed to lift Saint Kevin's stone, and the fact is that he never saw the bodies and found no evidence that what Victoria had confessed was true. Yet, deep in his heart he knows it to be the truth, for later, he was himself witness to Victoria's cruelty and to what she was capable of. She killed three men in Cork before, finally, Brandon – brother and lover, protector and later jailer – decided to send her to an institute for the hopelessly insane. The man has shielded his sister's name all his life; he loved and still loves her. The taint of madness and evil Talbot House exudes still clings onto him, and it will stay with him.

Until his death.

CHAPTER FOURTEEN

All those tragedies, all the unnatural events, all of them, could have been averted by a simple act: the destruction of Talbot House. I understand that this would not eradicate the evil spewing forth from Gorta cave, but it will surely trap it there, as Saint Kevin's slab has kept that darkness away for centuries. Looking at the cold numbers, at the chronological statistics, it can be assumed that the glyph placed by the Holy man *had* managed to hold the Blackness in check, until ignorant and greedy invaders were lured by promises of treasure. Yet, even then, the union of two warring people successfully repealed the menace. And again, peace and prosperity returned to the land of Glencree. Annie Carrick, bitter and desperate, allowed vileness to poison her heart, baited by the need for revenge. Once more, the communal spirit of Glencree won, banishing the darkness that had been consuming the innocents. But it was only with the building of Talbot House that the Blackness truly got hold of this valley. Of this I'm certain. It is more than a simple home; it's a temple and a physical host for this impious entity from the abyss. And Hugh Talbot gave a body made out of hubris to this unearthly monster.

It is a given fact that we all have devils inside.

Bruce O'Reilly, he loves to drink. He doesn't care that it makes him rough and aggressive, and that alcohol is going to kill him one day: the stronger the poitín, the better. Mary Anne Dunn likes to break men's hearts. She likes the feeling of power she holds over them. Even men of the cloth, like Father Cassidy of Anniskerry, have their own demons; he believe himself to be so righteous, so perfect, that he condemns anyone he perceives as less strong in their faith.

For sin is like the starving stray dog's snout. By the time the dog puts its nose through the kitchen door, the rest of it will soon follow. Thus, don't leave your door open to Sin, for it is safer to resist the beginnings of weakness.

Hugh Talbot had his hubris. On it the Darkness fed, and through it the Morrigan seduced and then possessed him. Like Annie Carrick before, Hugh had a hole in his soul, a weakness in his armour. For Annie, it had been her scorn, while for Talbot, it had been his pride. Feeling different, misunderstood, and superior to his peers, it was easy for his own demon to lead him to Gorta cave.

And above it, he built his temple to Sin.

Talbot House thrives on all sins. Its gluttony for suffering is endless, and of the same intensity that ruled the Cruithni cannibals. Greed led the Lochlannach to Uath hole, and extremely greedy are the mansion's walls, which seem to expand and wish for more. Envious of the happiness of others – such kind of happiness that only the birth of a child can bring – Annie Carrick wished to destroy that happiness, so that everyone could feel her own emptiness. Equally, Talbot House grieves on Glencree's joy. Thomas Aquinas said that Charity rejoices in our neighbour's good, while Envy grieves over it. That house hates gaiety and will do all it can to smother it. Hugh Talbot's pride and arrogance reflects on the house's façade, where upturned cornices give it an expression of contempt for everything which stands in front of it. Yet, it doesn't want to do its own work – oh no, this evil wants you to do its bidding, like the proverbial Sloth. And it was Dermot Cooney's sloth that caused the argument which killed him, and it was his brother's wrath that struck the blow. And Victoria's lust was as strong as the house's own egotistical urges. Brandon loved his sister, but Love and Lust rarely share the same roof.

Talbot House is a temple of evil. And it must be destroyed.

My first attempt at banishing the darkness failed, for at that time I didn't know the true face of my enemy. And my failure resulted in a terrible loss. But I will not fail this time.

Sins are the key to Talbot House, and virtues the lock.

So, what is the true nature of this blight? What is the Morrigan?

Folk says the Fey originate from the souls of people who died before the advent of Christianity and who were too bad for Heaven, yet not bad enough for Hell. Caught between two worlds, these souls were reborn into new shapes, such as bogarts, sprites, pixies, and red caps. However, the traditional Sidhe defy this categorisation. Here in Wicklow, the Fair People are believed to have been born before man, and, eventually, they faded away from the physical world, making their home within aspects of nature. They are not believed to come from the spirits of the dead, but from a mystical land of loneliness and mystery. Of course, the Church cannot abide this belief, for that would mean admitting the existence of a fourth realm beside Heaven, Hell, and Earth. Nonetheless, the Wicklow people can't deny their presence. The Sidhe embody beauty and horror at the same time, they can be charming and terrible. They can be as beautiful as the emerald sea, and fearsome like stormy weaves. They personify nature. Thusly, it is highly probable, as Hugh Talbot postulated, that the Sidhe and their ilk are just primordial entities, born before the Almighty created man, thus the Shadow Queen – the Morrigan – is part angel and part demon: a fallen one.

What I do now believe is that this Blackness is indeed an ancient entity; it existed in the cold void where the Lord clapped His hands and ordered the Light to be. She is Lamia and Hecate, Hell and Tiamat. Virgin, Mother, and Monster. Birth, Life, and Death. She is bound to devour the spawn of Man for eternity.

As recorded earlier, I received a visit from Brandon Cooney last week. He came to Ballymoor to decide what to do with his unpleasant inheritance. After his confession about Victoria's revelation, I told him of my design to purify the place once for all. I explained that the only way to permanently trap the demon is by the mean of demolishing the house – possibly with fire – sealing Gorta cave, and ultimately getting rid of the stone circle. Of course, it was not something I could do without his consent. More, I needed his help for the second phase of the exorcism; in fact, the house's destruction is only part of it. An unholy place is exactly like my allegory about burnt stew. Yes, the smell lingers, its smoke will stain the walls, and it will attract vermin and pests. However, it can be removed. The pot can be scraped clean or replaced;

the walls can be given fresh paint, and by keeping the windows open and by cooking some good and aromatic meals, the sourness will be gone. All the same, with an act of cleansing first, and an act of repent or moral teaching later, the taint can be removed. My idea was to have a place of charity to be built on the grounds where Talbot House stands: a philanthropic act, a gesture of kindness to a land that has been soiled for too long. In short, I proposed him the construction of an orphanage, in respect and memory of all the children who lost their life there, a ground consecrated to the three spiritual virtues of Saint Paul: Faith, Hope, and Charity. In opposition to the three dark sins of Pride, Envy, and Wrath. And as such, a refuge for the hopeless, the abandoned, and the forgotten, would be the perfect cure for that unhallowed ground.

Sadly, Mr Cooney declined. He said that his current fortunes would not allow for such a big plan. More, he intends to sell his property as soon as possible and use that money to move to America, where – he hopes – nothing will remind him of his family's misfortunes. I rebuked that Arthur – his only son – will be always there to remind them, for I knew the boy to be his and not the fruit of Victoria's tryst with an ephemeral lover who had fled the country, as they told around. At that, he looked at me, outraged, yet in his eyes, I saw that I had hit the nail right on the head. We had an argument and he left, forbidding me to set foot inside his property ever again.

Of course, I hesitated in my plan to destroy Talbot House. However, after tonight's events, I have no other choice than to act on my own. At the risk of my life and soul, I will do what has to be done. I know I'm not crazy, and time is short before the Blackness will call on someone else to complete the ritual for its own rejuvenation. Far too long we have been slaves to her dark crown, and the time has come for us to raise the cross and boldly march in the name of Jesus Christ Our Saviour.

Talbot House is, essentially, an antechamber of Hell, an *oubliette*, I daresay. All the poor souls that have died there, or because of its influence, are trapped into an everlasting torment. The house itself feeds on their pain, keeping them prisoners. Alas, the manor's hunger seems to be endless, for it constantly seeks to add more to its unholy collection. Besides, its spiteful claws extend far beyond the unkempt garden, or the dark peat bog; as capillaries jutting out of a main artery, they intertwine and crawl all over those it has targeted, those it covets.

I myself, after the events of last April, have been visited more than once by the hateful shadow of Annie Carrick. Yet, I was safe from her rapacious talons for I shared my bedroom with a loyal companion that fears her not. Every time, my friend managed to warn and pull me out of the unnatural slumber that precedes the hag's visit. Then, teeth bare and growling in rage, my companion sent her away. For it is true that she has no reign over this breed of dogs until she inhabits and possesses a living person.

Unfortunately, my dog passed away three days ago. I thought the poor animal had been killed by an unseen illness, but I was wrong. Henrietta O'Reilly, my housekeeper, said she had found it dead in the yard and had quickly disposed of the body to avoid me the unpleasant sight of its carcass. She had buried it in the churchyard, under the apple tree. After the dog's death, I noticed some changes in Miss O'Reilly's attitude; she sounded snappier than usual, and her voice was huskier. Already on my toes, last night I decided to have a look at the animal's remains. To my horror, I discovered that its throat had been slit by means of a large knife. And I found that knife in the kitchen, still stained with blood. Thus, this morning, I focussed my attention on Miss O'Reilly when she came for her morning duties. She looked paler and unkempt; queer for such a tidy woman. I asked for some tea, then, once she served it, I asked her to join me for a chit-chat. Nonchalantly, I inquired if she had ever been to Talbot House or its grounds. Smiling, she said that it was quite funny I was asking about it for yes, four days ago she had been there with Brandon Cooney when the latter had paid her to clean the place up. Oh, dear Almighty! She had been there! Perhaps – no, surely – she had even touched that foul mantelpiece!

The monster was inside her now. I was alone. Vulnerable.

I had to act quickly.

That is why I shot six rounds into her head.

CHAPTER FIFTEEN

After my introductory explanation of the motives and the roots of Talbot House, time has finally come for me to bear testimony of the horrible events to which I was a witness on the thirtieth day of last April. This will also better explain the reasons for my extreme act.

On that terrible day, I broke my hesitation and decided to face the evil haunting the moor. I remember my shaking hand as I lifted the door's heavy knocker of Talbot House. It felt as heavy as my own heart. I expected young Patrick Conroy to treat me badly, and with good reason, after I had confessed to him that I was aware of Hugh Talbot's forbidden research. However, as a servant of God, it was, and it is still, my duty to confront the Adversary with faith in my soul.

It was the ghost of a man that opened the door: pale, almost diseased in appearance. Yet, his eyes were different: full of resolve, as if flames were burning inside them. He let me in and asked about the purpose of my visit, which became immediately clear after I told him what I knew. In response, he showed me something he had found, and the way he had found it. He told me that in a queer dream, that night, he had been threatened by an invisible dog, and that, again in dream, he had found refuge inside the library where, by chance, he had discovered a hidden passage to Talbot's secret arcane laboratory. And how, in the morning light, he had discovered the room to be real. Of course, one can imagine my shock at that revelation. He showed me the room and the alchemist's personal journal, and the more I learnt, the better I understood what Talbot House stood for. Later, while the poor fellow was in the kitchen wetting the tea, I clearly saw, at the corner of my eye, a whiff of smoke lifting from the dead fireplace, only for it to quickly disappear into the chimney's darkness when my gaze turned to it. My eyes ran to the mantelpiece, and at that precise moment, I understood how much I had been fooled. I could discern a vanishing glow from the etched druidic symbols, as if that monster had been watching me, unseen, from the moment I had sat down to read Talbot's journal.

"He used the very stone on which Annie Carrick was burnt to build this house!" I murmured. Conroy heard me, for he had come back with his teapot and sat besides me, sharing the corroborating beverage. We told each other everything we knew, and he confessed to me his wish to visit the gypsy camp, down by the lakes, and convince Maggie Blair to leave with him.

Oh, if only I had stopped him at that moment, and advised him to leave Glencree and go back to Dublin, forgetting about Talbot House and all its horrors!

Alas, I didn't. On the contrary, I invited him to hurry and be back before twilight, while I would stay behind and attempt to perform the dispelling enchantment that Talbot never had the time to finish. For in his journal there were drawings of circles and arcane words that he had learnt from the study of Solomon's works; magical formulas meant to banish the evil that he had unleashed. However, as he himself had warned in his manuscript, this Blackness and its lot can be manipulative of senses and thoughts, misleading the arcanist, confusing the abjurer, inserting tendrils of its own essence into the soul and mind of the would-be dispeller. It was in such a way that Talbot was led to give a host body to the demon and subsequently doubt the very person he loved. I had to be careful and not trust everything that I would see or hear. I admit that as a man of faith, I was hesitant to perform a ritual that had nothing to do with God's grace. Yet, asking forgiveness to the Lord for my sin, I decided that I would follow the wizard's words to the letter. And to do that, I needed to find all the pieces of the standing stone. As I sent Patrick Conroy away, telling him to not look for me when he would be back, but to continue for Anniskerry, I immediately set on my first task: I went down into the laboratory and looked for the house's original plans. I found them stacked into a large folio and, to my horror, I discovered the way the manor had been designed. It was indeed meant to be a temple with pieces of the fallen rock as cornerstones.

It was while I was studying the architectural plans that I heard the bumping. At first, I thought Conroy had returned, so I left the laboratory and went back to the living room. However, as I crossed the foyer – my eyes transfixed to the great stairway where Roy Cooney's painting greets every visitor – my hand, instinctively reached for my Bible. Deep inside, I knew it wasn't Conroy making that noise, for it was a rhythmic knocking, accompanied by creaking pauses, as if someone – or something – was rocking, sternly, a chair or another piece of large furniture.

The sound was coming from the second floor.

Hesitantly, I climbed the stairs, holding onto my Bible, mentally praying the Lord to succour me with the courage I certainly needed. I passed under the severe gaze of Roy Cooney and turned to the right, while the bumping sound increased, as if it were some kind of alarm, a calling. And I found myself facing the peeled door of the sewing room. I recalled how this had been Angela's and Victoria's favourite room, where they spent most days alone, surrounded by the silent mansion.

And I shivered.

The sound carried on.

Bump. Bump. Bump.

My heart began to dance with the same rhythm, while my hands threatened to lose their grip on the Holy Book, and like a castaway holding onto a piece of flotsam in the rough waters after escaping the sinking ship, I serrated my fingers on it. I felt reassurance in the contact, and at once reached for the door's handle.

I screamed in pain as my fingertips melted like wax and the flesh was severely scorched by a living flame.

To my shock, I found myself in front of the fireplace, which was now home to a lively fire; my hand extended into it, clutching a burning piece of round peat!

How was that possible? I didn't recall starting the fire, even less so standing by it. I had climbed the stairs to the upper floor, called up by the rocking sound. Yet, here was I, hurting my own flesh unknowingly.

Upstairs, the bumping continued.

Quickly, I went to the kitchen and found relief by soothing my aching hand with cool water.

'You are doubting your faith, Earl', I thought. *'You can't fight this terror if you allow it to get a solid grip into your mind.'*

I recited a *paternoster*, then, after bandaging my injured hand, ran upstairs.

"I'm not afraid of you, fiend!" I shouted.

As if in mockery, the rocking noise increased in speed, taunting me, telling me I was unworthy, calling me a coward. Enraged, I kicked the door open. It crashed against the wall, then bounced back, closing into my face. In the fraction of time of its opening and closing I spotted a dark figure standing inside the room, with long, wild hair, her face pale and creased by an expression of wickedness. Again, my heart raced, but I could not let this fear take hold of me, so once more I reached for the knob.

My hand had no bandages.

I looked at it. It was unscathed.

Intact.

I pressed the palms against my face, my fingers running on my closed eyes.

It had never happened.

Like Talbot before, the house was playing tricks on me.

I opened the door.

Heavy strands of cobwebs covered all the – sparse – furniture in the room except for the tall rocking chair standing by the small fireplace. It was still rocking, although gently so and slowly losing its momentum.

There was no one there.

Pausing to catch my breath, I leant against the door.

And someone screamed.

Then, I heard a dull thump as if someone had crashed to the ground after falling from a great height. Immediately, I rushed to the source, but couldn't find any sign of disturbance. The cry had come from the stairwell, but there was no one. No one at the end of the steps below; no one above. I recalled the way Angela Cooney had died, and shuddered. She had broken her neck by falling from the second floor when, mysteriously, a portion of the railing had broken away. I could see the exact point, for it had been crudely repaired with adhesive resin and iron nails.

From below, I heard the crackling of fire.

This went clashing with the fact that my accident had been an illusion, so I rushed down. Only to find the fireplace dead again.

Then, from upstairs, I heard the door to the sewing room being violently slammed shut.

'It wants to put the heart crossway in you, old dog. And it's quare good at it, for you haven't been as a'scared in donkey's years.' I thought. *'Well, think of it, you're on the right path, for it means that the house wants to distract you. It knows you know.'*

I went back to Talbot's journal to look for what I necessitated. Nothing was going to distract me any more. As I studied the drawings and the materials needed the rhythmic bumping began again, soon followed by the woman's cry, but I ignored every noise. At the edge of my vision, I spotted a dark red substance pooling out of the floorboards exactly in the spot by the fireplace where people said Roy had killed his brother. Simple manifestations meant to scare rather than to cause harm. I realised that the house was powerless in daylight, so I decided to hurry up before sundown, when my permanence could become really dangerous. I needed some cold iron for the spell to work. It has always been tradition, here in Ireland, to place old iron items around the house, especially at the windows, to keep the little people and spirits away. I couldn't see any, so I went exploring. During my search, I found an old sea trunk in Roy Cooney's study on the third floor.

It was inside it that I found the flare gun and the rockets.

I don't know why I picked it up, loaded it, and tucked it into my belt. Perhaps it was God Almighty that whispered in my ear, or I just thought it was wise to have a way to signal for help.

Anyway, in my quest for old cold iron, I ended up in the attic. The place was a terrible mess: dusty crates and ancient trunks – packed with generations of Cooney memorabilia and more – acted as anchoring points for the dense forest of thick spider webs which completely cluttered the room. It would take me days to browse among that junk. Except, I spotted an old pair of rusty shears hanging from a nail on the opposite wall. With disgust, I moved amidst the filamentous network, covering myself in the white strands and spitting dead bugs' shells.

I had almost reached the shears when I felt the presence.

Or rather, I heard it.

Behind me, among the webbings, something cracked its bones. It was the same sound produced when someone cracks their knuckles, except it was continuous, like a stirring, as if something old – or dead – was slowly rising from a long slumber. A waft of cold air lifted the hair on my neck, soon followed by a terrible smell, so pungent that I found myself retching. I refused to turn and face whatever vision the house was playing for me. Yet that became impossible, because a moaning, at first low, then higher in pitch, joined the cracking. I saw a shadow falling on the wall in front of me, obscuring the shears. And fear returned. The horrible odour, like decomposing things, increased tenfold, then something touched my left shoulder.

I made the error of turning.

In front of me, decaying and covered in maggots, stood the corpse of Maura Cooney, the woman who had hung herself here a long time ago. Her face swollen and black, her tongue forced out of her mouth by the rope around her neck, she dangled from the rafters. What had rubbed my shoulder had been her right foot!

My mouth opened, but nothing came out. It was when the dead face of Maura twisted into a wicked smile that I heard myself shout in terror and, instinctively, I jumped backwards, to put as much distance as possible between me and that decaying thing.

This was what caused me to crash into the hidden trapdoor and fall down into Talbot House's secret monk hole, hitting the waiting floor below so hard that I lost my senses.

CHAPTER SIXTEEN

I don't know why Talbot House has a monk hole, and perhaps I will never know. This is just one of the many missing pieces of that horrible house's history. Monk holes, or priest holes, were hiding places for persecuted Catholic priests that were built into many houses at the times of Queen Elizabeth I. Yet, Talbot House was built long after her reign. For what I know, no Catholic priest has ever lived there. I wonder if the place was meant as a hiding place for Hugh for surely it was not added by the Cooney. Because the Cooney never found it, otherwise they would have surely saved poor Kelly. In fact, by chance, I solved the mystery of her disappearance.

I came to with horror from the oblivion I had fallen into and I found myself into utter darkness. At first, I couldn't recall what had happened to me, but then I remembered my drop through an unseen trapdoor in the attic, and, shivering, I understood I was somewhere deep inside the bowels of Talbot House. Also, this brought back the unpleasant memory of the rotten thing hanging from the rafters. You can imagine my terror, and my desperation at the thought of still being in the company of that apparition. As I tried to move from the spot where I had landed, a shattering pain invaded my left leg, and it travelled fast to my head. I levelled harder on it, eager to regain my footing and flee from that engulfing black, yet the ache just increased and I fell onto my back. Blind, my hand crawled to the source of it: something, hard to the touch, yet smooth, protruded from the back of my ham, its sharp ending sunk into my flesh. I felt a liquid wetting my fingers. Afraid of slowly bleeding to death, I gritted my teeth, and almost yelling forced myself upright, then, instinctively, I tugged at the invading object, and pulled it out. The pain was unbearable, and I felt more blood rush out. And at that, I realised I had been a fool, for whatever had been stuck inside my leg, though it hurt, had been acting as a plug. I was now going to die. Slowly. Bleeding.

In the dark.

In Talbot House.

Dear Lord, no! That thought alone redoubled my vigour. Acting fast, ignoring the pain, I tore a sleeve off my shirt, and, pulling it tight about my wound, I managed to slow the bleeding down with the rag. One thousand impelling thoughts invaded my mind: I had to get out of that darkness. How long had I been unconscious? Where was I? Was that *thing* still with me? Was it night time?

Understanding that panic would bring me no help, I decided to ignore all my concerns and focus primarily on my injury. Luckily, I found out that whatever had pierced my flesh had penetrated it close to my left buttock, miraculously missing any important blood vessels and goring only muscles. Yes, the wound was deep, but, at least, I wasn't in immediate danger of death. Having ascertained this, to my relief, I concentrated on the mysterious spike that had caused the damage, so I pawed the ground to recover it from the spot where I had dropped it. And to my surprise, my hands encountered a small heap of similar objects, though they were all of different sizes – some tiny, others larger and longer – and connected together by what appeared to be a rotting fabric of sort. The largest piece, a cage-like affair, was broken at the top, and my touch caused whatever lattice that composed its shape to collapse. I retrieved one of the fallen pieces. In size and texture, it resembled exactly the one I had pulled out of my aching posterior. A terrible idea of what that thing was formed into my mind became certainty when my shaking fingers bumped upon a larger item; round-shaped, with sockets, and whose bottom part was full of teeth.

A skull!

What I suspected was real. I had fallen on the forgotten bones of someone long-time dead. And judging by the size, it had once belonged to a child. And it had been one of its bones that had impaled my leg.

My left hand ran to my mouth, as if to keep it from shouting. What new horror was I witness to?

I touched the skeleton again, hanging desperately to the wish that I was wrong, that those belonged to a cat, to an animal of the wilds, anything but to a child. Sadly, I was right, because the crumbling fabric was that of a little girl's dress and the tiny shoe I found – the foot bones still inside – left no doubt.

A child had died here.

Repulsed, I stood up, and hit my head against the low ceiling. Stars danced gaily around my blind vision, and then faded, also swallowed by the unforgiving darkness. I moved backwards and soon, my back encountered the wall, and there I let myself collapse to the floor, where I cried in despair.

I can't recall how much time I spent in a state of stupor, but when, finally, I got out of it, I decided I didn't want to suffer the same fate, for surely the child had fallen, like me, into the trapdoor and had died there. I prayed the Almighty the poor thing had died on the spot, her skull or neck breaking on impact. Unfortunately, as I found later, that was not the case, for a more horrible destiny had befallen on the disgraced child. Once out of the shock, I moved around the room, crawling and scraping, looking for any unseen exit, and a glint of hope. I found none. Soon, I was overcome by despair again, and I banged on the walls, shouted, cried for help, until my hammering fist impacted against something sharp jutting out of a fissure between the bricks, and I realised, to my horror, that I had slammed my hand against one of the little girl's fingernails. Unable to endure the harsh truth of my entrapment, I crumbled to the floor, and at last, lassitude triumphed against my tumult; I lay my head on the ground, endeavouring to seek a few moments of oblivion, and I fell into a comatose sleep. I slept, deeply, and in it, I was visited by a dream of salvation.

I was again in the attic, following a little girl. Her name was Kelly, and she was six years old. Yet, in the dream, I was like a ghost, invisible to her and floating. I could hear her joyous laughter, her tiny feet running on the floorboards, but could not interact with her. She was playing hide-and-seek with someone. Silvery rays flooded through the attic's window, as it was night time and a gibbous moon hang up in the black sky. Kelly was looking for someone here, in the attic, someone I could not see. Then, I heard someone walking and singing softly:

There was an old woman and she lived in the moors, weile weile wee.
There was an old woman and she lived in the moors, down by the Glencree.

The voice was light, sweet, singing like a mother to her child. It was coming from somewhere, and Kelly was hearing it too. She smiled knowingly and lifted her head like a hound in search of its prey.

She stole a baby three months old, weile weile wee.
She stole a baby three months old, down by the Glencree.

Yet, I could perceive a note of malevolence in that voice, masked by that softness. It was, to me, as if Kelly were a bird lured by the hunter's call. I shouted to stay away from the voice, to not listen to it. But she could not hear me.

She had a knife long and sharp, weile weile wee.
She had a knife long and sharp, down by the Glencree.

The voice insisted. It was coming from the floor, at the far end of the room. And I knew from where: the hidden trapdoor. Kelly rushed to the spot, knelt down, and looked through the now open trap. 'I found you!' I heard her say gaily.

She stuck the knife in the baby's heart, weile weile wee.
She stuck the knife in the baby's heart, down by the Glencree.

I then heard the melody fade, and felt a rushing of cold air pass through my intangible body, while a living darkness consumed everything in its wake. Then came footsteps, and a low, evil moaning. And, finally, I heard the girl scream as she was dragged into the hole.

I found myself there. I became the girl. Alone. In the dark. Afraid. I heard my voice cry, call the *good lady* to come back, and scream that I didn't like that game anymore and that she was scaring me. My head was aching and my limbs were numb. I called for my mother. And father. And Grandpa Seamus. No one could hear me.

A little soft laugh floated around me. 'Mother?' I heard myself say. 'Are you here? Please, let me out!' And around me, the laugh became an unintelligible whisper. Then, I cried in terror as two evil-looking eyes, as red as the flames of Hell, flashed before fading again into the dark.

'Here!' someone said from somewhere. A gentle voice; the voice of a child. And I turned and there was light. I was no longer the girl, but I was back to being myself, and in front of me, inside the light, there stood little Kelly Cooney, like a tiny angel; her fancy dress intact. 'Earl, Earl!' she repeated, then she pointed to one of the cubicle's corners, and I was able to see, there, a patch of differently coloured bricks, and when my hands touched them, I discovered it to actually be a secret panel that, once unhinged, led into a tight, vertical shaft.

'Remember,' I heard Kelly say.

Then, I woke up.

CHAPTER SEVENTEEN

My eyes popped open in the void.

Confused – and terrorised – by the queer dream, it took me some time to understand my predicament. Then I remembered where I was.

"Our Father who art in Heaven, hallowed be thy name," I began praying. "Thy Kingdom come; Thy will be done on Earth as it is in Heaven."

Panic invaded me again. How long had I been there? How long had I been unconscious?

"Give us this day our daily bread and forgive us our trespasses." My voice sounded hoarse and I was feeling thirsty. I dragged myself along the floor, touching the walls of my small prison, as if that contact would help me somehow. My hands ran over the bricks, feeling their solidity, sweeping away every hope for a soft spot, for a concealed door …

Then, I remembered.

'Here!'

Kelly Cooney's voice. In the dream.

"As we forgive those who trespass against us. And lead us not into temptation," I continued while I crawled to the corner the girl had pointed at in the dream. And I felt it. The false wall!

"But deliver us from evil." I finished while my fingers successfully slid between the seams and the panel moved to the left. Immediately, a waft a cooler air crossed my face, and, like in the dream, there was a tight passage. I couldn't see it, but I could feel it. I moved cautiously and, remembering that in the nightmare I had seen a shaft going down from the monk hole, I searched for the iron ladder. It was there. Thanking the spirit of poor Kelly (I promised her to come back and give her bones proper burial and service), I descended the ladder and found myself in another cul-de-sac, for it seemed that the shaft led to nowhere. However, this had to be the exit or the entry point to the monk hole, so I didn't give up and resolutely tested the walls around me. And there it was: another little door with a tiny handle. As soon as I pulled it towards me, a wedge of feeble light slashed the darkness, and I understood that I would make it. I had to duck and crawl to get out of the shaft and into what revealed to be the sewing room's fireplace. In front of me stood the rocking chair. I rushed past it, to the window, and I saw that it was now dark and the stars were shining bright in the heavens. Unable to stay any longer into that terrible room in which I had glimpsed the phantom of Annie and had experienced her mind tricks, I crossed the door and went for the stairs, only to stop when I saw a queer greenish light coming from the living room. I descended the stairs stealthily, afraid of making a sound.

Trickles of grey smoke danced in the air, carried by a soft spell from the large fireplace all the way up to the stairs. I could see the green light emanating from the mantelpiece, the pulsating etchings looking almost alive. Sitting on the very armchair I had occupied before going on my exploration, stood a dark figure, female in size and shape, but whose face was dark and impossible to discern.

"Now you see the dark," she whispered. Her voice sounded like iron spikes grating on a blackboard, yet there was a hidden sweetness in her words.

"Who are you?" I demanded. I couldn't move; my mind wanted to get closer and see the stranger's face, but my body was gripped by fear.

"Me? I'm your mother. I'm your lover. I'm your Angel," she said with a soft laughter, "I'm Eve, and Lilith. I'm Mary and Isis. I'm Hecate, Atropos, Skuld and Megaera. I'm Badb, Nema, and Macha. I'm the Morrigan."

I understood I was in the presence of the foul thing that had claimed Talbot House as her own; a vision, perhaps a projection of the thing in the pit, for I was sure that it couldn't leave its prison, but it could however send out a fragment of itself to manifest at night time. The horror was finally showing its face to me.

"Lord God Almighty, bless Thou this home, and under its shelter let there be health, chastity, self-conquest, humility, goodness, mildness, obedience to Thy commandments, and thanksgiving to God the Father, Son, and Holy Spirit. May Thy blessing remain always in this home and on those who live here; through Christ our Lord." I grasped my Bible and moved into the living room.

An evil laughter exploded from the dark figure. "I see you're not as smart as I'd thought!"

I made the sign of the Cross. "Ecce crucem Domini! Fugite partes adversae!"

The thing that was a woman, yet was not, stood up and pointed a finger at me. "You!"

I continued the exorcism. "I command you, unclean spirit, whoever you are, along with all your minions, by the mysteries of the incarnation, passion, resurrection, and ascension of our Lord Jesus Christ, by the descent of the Holy Spirit, by the coming of our Lord for judgment, that you tell me by some sign your name, and the day and hour of your departure. I command you, moreover, to obey me to the letter, I who am a minister of God despite my unworthiness; nor shall you be emboldened to harm in any way the creatures of God, or any of their possessions."

"You've often gazed into the darkness, but have always turned away because you are afraid of it. I know that deep inside, you want to *know* things, yet, you fear what that knowledge might do to you. Because you know that the truth will make you doubt your precious faith, and by consequence, your whole life. Fear not, my son, for I will guide you into the Abyss; I will show you the truth!"

I ignored her and continued.

"I adjure you, ancient serpent, by the judge of the living and the dead, by your Creator, by the Creator of the whole universe, by Him who has the power to consign you to Hell, to depart forthwith in fear, along with your savage minions, from this servant of God!"

An acrid smell of burnt flesh invaded me as the thing moved closer, offering me her blackened hand.

"Take it and you will never again be afraid of the dark."

I closed my eyes and lifted the Bible, begging the Lord to be merciful and spare me the torment of this beast. Through my serrated lids, I perceived a change in the light and the foul odour vanished, replaced by the musty air of Talbot House. I couldn't hear her anymore, but soon I became aware of another sound, a chanting coming from afar, perhaps from the back of the house. Reluctantly, I reopened my eyes and saw that the living room was once again in the dark, and no green glow emanated from the mantelpiece. The thing was gone. Yet there were lights outside on the hillock, for I could see tiny flickering flames dancing on its top.

And it was at that moment that I heard Patrick Conroy's yell.

He had been roped to one of the stone pillars and kept shouting something that, at the beginning, I could not understand. I thought he was calling for help, but that was not the case. Instinctively, still recoiling from the horrors I had endured, yet at the same time, with a renewed strength in my faith, I opened the back door and ran to his succour. Only to stop when I saw that the path to the hillock was being guarded by armed men. Two of them, bearing clubs and vicious-looking sickles, were standing straight in front of me, their backs turned to the house. Luckily, they didn't see me coming out of it. A third one was right at the top, just underneath the lintel stone. This one, big and wild, seemed to be sporting a hunting rifle or a musket. I was clearly outnumbered and it was obvious that the men, which later I discovered to be gypsies, were in league with the demonic entity. The chanting I had heard before returned. It was a female voice that intoned a litany of sort in old Gaelic. I can't remember the words, nor do I want to report them here.

I had to stop this blasphemy and rescue the poor young man; I could not stand there and be a witness to this. Yet, I could not find a way to. Seeking help from the Almighty, I fished once again inside my pockets, looking for my Bible, and my left hand met the cold metal of the flare gun. I had forgotten about it. Still, it would have been of little use in the cramped space of my previous prison, nor could have helped me against the phantoms of Talbot House. Flare guns have been conceived as signalling tools, they are not meant to be used as weapons. However, I could use it to attract the men's attention and drive them away from

Conroy. Or I could use it to summon help from the village. But deep inside, I knew it wouldn't work. No, I had to find a better plan, and to do that, I had to get closer to young Patrick and know the exact number of my opponents. Thence, I crept toward the overgrown family plot, where the tombstones and the wild brambles would provide me enough cover to move closer without being seen. I was lucky, for the female voice stopped the unholy orison and called for the men to join her at the circle. Thanking the Lord, I swiftly moved below the hillock, and from there, not without difficulty, I climbed the slope shadowed by the wild weeds.

Once at the top, the true horror of what was about to happen unveiled in front of my eyes.

At the centre of the henge, bare as the day she was born, stood Maggie Blair. She seemed enraptured into some kind of charm; her eyes lost into vacuity, she lay on the floor, while an older woman – this one also unclothed except for a horrible headdress made with the skull and the skin of a goat – was drawing terrible writhing symbols on her body and murmuring obscene prayers. Two of the men were removing their own clothes, while the third one was prodding, with the musket's bayonet – for now I could see he was carrying a musket – something locked inside a crude little wicker cage. I remember thinking, at the time, that it was an animal; a goat, or a piglet, I supposed. The truth was far, far worse.

From my vantage point, I could see Patrick Conroy. He was tied to one of the stones, as I said before, and he appeared to have suffered greatly, for his skin was pale and looked weak. I first thought he had been beaten or tortured, but later I found that it was due to a deep wound he had received the night before. He kept yelling Maggie's name, trying somehow to snap her out of the unnatural trance she had fallen into. At first the naked trio seemed to ignore his cries, but when they became too annoying, and too much distractive for whatever ritual the devil-worshippers were performing, the old woman, which now I recognized as Siobhan Blair, stood up and went straight to the young man. Her voice sounded cruel and spiteful as she addressed him.

"You shall stop it or I will slit your throat now!"

Conroy rebuked that he was not afraid, for he knew that she was going to kill him anyway, so now or then would make no difference.

Ignoring her threats, he resumed calling the girl. Thus, the witch ordered the man with the musket to show what was in the cage to Patrick. The big man pushed the box out of the shadow and my eyes widened in terror and rage when I saw what it contained.

Sobbing and screaming, half-naked and dirty, Amanda Douglas, the eight-year old daughter of the murdered Squire, was squirming inside the cage. The hateful witch explained to Conroy that young Amanda was meant to be the real offering to the Dark Mother, while he would be the groom of her new shell – and she pointed to the enthralled Maggie. "She will bear your seed," she said.

I couldn't see Conroy's face, for it was obscured by the undressing gypsies, however, I heard him question Siobhan Blair about why she was doing this to the grandchild she said she loved. The witch snapped at him, "Stop calling me with that name! That woman is no more. I am Annie."

Annie Carrick. Annie Fuath. Everything was clear to me now. Hugh Talbot was right about the *Dark Pact*, for Annie the witch had willingly accepted a fragment of the Blackness inside her, and even after death her spirit lingered on. However, what I could not fathom was the role of Maggie Blair in this. It became clear when Annie herself explained it to Conroy.

The last of Annie's hosts – Victoria Cooney – had died in the Cork's asylum months before, and this had caused her spirit to be ejected and sent back to what the witch called a *philacterium*, a magical receptacle. This *philacterium* was the Cailli stone. She had patiently waited within the stone fragment, unable to leave its confines until she could find a new body to possess. When Siobhan Blair had touched the fireplace's mantel, Annie had immediately captured her soul and transferred her own into her body. However, Siobhan was old and, somehow, imperfect.

Maggie Blair *was* the perfect host.

Thus, that night, she was going to displace the young woman's essence into her grandma's decrepit body and then take hold of her shell. But to do that, she needed the assistance and favours of her mistress. And her mistress needed the blood of innocents so she could manifest into this world.

It was clear. Yet even now, I still do not understand why the gypsies were helping her. I believe Hell to be a place of darkness and full of doors; each one easy to open, for they are unlocked and entice you to cross their threshold. Nonetheless, I am not willing to open any of them, for beyond lies only suffering.

The only thing I know is that I still curse myself for not acting quickly. Yes, I was outnumbered and unarmed, but still, with the knowledge that I now possess, I know I could have at least tried to save Amanda Douglas. Instead, I kept watching the scene unfolding before me, enraptured by the little girl's screams. I watched as Patrick talked to Siobhan – the real one – prompting the woman to fight the evil spirit inside her, begging her to remember the love she felt for her granddaughter.

"Fight it, Siobhan! Don't let that thing get hold of you!"

I saw the woman's faded blue yes change to pitch black, then back again to blue, then again black. It was as if there were an interior struggle going on. Then, with a spine-chilling scream, she went for the cage – brutally pushing aside the gypsy standing by it – and viciously grabbed Amanda by the hair, before pulling her head out of the wicker box. Without hesitation, she slit the innocent's throat with a knife. Blood pumped out furiously from the thrashing little creature, while the woman – who was a monster – threw her head back in ecstasy, as if she was actually feeling pleasure in the girl's death-throes.

I was paralysed with fear, still incredulous of what my eyes were seeing. Then, a superior force took hold of me, lifting and pushing me out of the bushes. I can't recall all the details; it was as if someone was inside me, filling me with a resoluteness I wasn't aware I possessed. I saw myself point the flare gun to the gypsies; I heard my voice command them to stop. Yet, it wasn't me. It was someone else inside me.

"Our Father who art in Heaven, hallowed be Thy name, You who are our Father; ecce crucem Domini, fugite partes adversae! I command you, unclean spirit, along with all your minions, by the mysteries of the incarnation, passion, resurrection, and ascension of our Lord Jesus Christ, by the descent of the Holy Spirit, by the coming of our Lord for judgment, to obey me to the letter, I who am a minister of God despite my unworthiness; nor shall you be emboldened to harm in any way the creatures of God, or any of their possessions."

There was a moment of hesitation among the gypsies before they decided to act, ignoring my threats, and stepped in my direction. Dark Annie turned her face towards me, hissing and spitting like a scared cat, then released her hold of the dead child and crawled beside the comatose shape of Maggie Blair. A wicked smile on her lips, she caressed the young woman's brow. 'She's mine!" she growled.

"Forgive me Father, for I have sinned," I heard myself say as I pulled the trigger and the flare gun came to life, shooting a burning rocket inside the closest gypsy's open mouth. While the flare rocket was not meant to penetrate even the softest of tissues, thus making it unpractical to be used as a weapon, it became deadly when it lodged inside the man's mouth. The man's shrilling screams are still echoing inside my mind.

At that, the other men panicked, and though I couldn't reload the gun fast enough to be a threat to them, they took refuge behind the standing stones, ignoring their comrade's cry for help.

"Nos eriperes de potestate diaboli. Ab omni hoste visibili et invisibili et ubique in hoc saeculo liberetur." I was back; I could feel my body again. Whatever benign force had taken hold of me was now gone. "Begone, you filthy servant of the Devil! In the name of Jesus Christ our Saviour I command you to go back to the pits of Hell where you belong!"

I saw an unnatural darkness take shape above the circle of stones; a horrible void against the backdrop of night, showering down an intense cold and an uncomfortable pressure. It was as if an invisible leviathan were slowly descending on us all.

"You can't do this to Maggie," shouted Conroy, "you love her, Siobhan. Fight it! Fight it!"

And then I saw the possessed woman's skin turn translucent: bluish veins pulsated underneath it, and a blackness, which appeared like living peat, grew and dimmed, moving as clouds of mud in disturbed waters.

"I beg you Lord, through the intercession and help of the archangels Michael, Rafael, and Gabriel, for the deliverance of our sister, who is enslaved by the evil one," I prayed.

Emboldened by the manifestation of their demon, the gypsies came out of hiding. One lifted a sickle, ready to strike me, the other went for Conroy; his face, a mask of lunacy as he prepared to kill the man by bludgeoning him to death with a cudgel.

I went on with my exorcism while the darkness grew around us; coalescing, in a creeping way, into a darker spot at the centre of the stone circle. Then, everything happened fast.

I saw the old woman raise the knife to her own throat and sink the blade deeply into it. Having obviously regained control of her own body for an instant, Siobhan Blair had decided to kill herself rather than deliver her own granddaughter to the clutches of darkness. I saw blood flowing copiously from the profound wound, dripping and splashing into Maggie's face before, finally, life escaped the old Traveller's body and she fell aside, slumping against the central iron spike.

I watched as Maggie Blair came to, suddenly out of the evil spell she had fallen under, and though unaware of her surroundings, she screamed in horror at the sight of her dead grandmother.

I saw Kadie – the Blairs' female wolfhound – dart out of nowhere, jump on the man with the cudgel, then push him down to the ground, where she struggled with him, thrashing his right arm.

And, finally, I saw the thing assume its terrible shape behind the sickle-wielding gypsy. The skeletal head, larger than that of a bear, came first. Its eyes appeared sightless, for they were white, wildly rotating orbs. Its incredible jaws were the stuff of nightmares: bristling with razor-sharp teeth that would put a shark to shame. It emanated a thick black smoke that wafted around the materialising creature as tentacles made of hot vapour. But worst of all was its cruel, spear-like tongue. As I watched, paralysed in terror, the unnameable appendage sprang out, and with a sickening sound, buried itself into the back of the approaching gypsy, then exploded, gorily, through his chest. Blood and bone fragments showered on my face, while I screamed in horror, before the man was violently yanked back, and the great mouth closed on his neck. One of the horror's front paws took form and quickly proceeded to lash at its prey, pushing him hard down to the ground, where he died.

I took that moment of the beast's distraction to run to Conroy.

The last gypsy was still fighting with the dog, but in the struggle, he had lost his cudgel. I didn't think twice and retrieved it from the floor, I lifted it high, then lowered it against his skull. His fight ended. Again, I asked forgiveness to the Lord for I had killed a fellow man.

Having lost interest in her dead opponent, Kadie turned her attention to the monster. Growling and barking, she boldly faced the still materialising thing.

Meanwhile, Maggie, shaken out of her stupor by the demon's wake, had taken hold of her grandma's knife, and was now quickly working at Conroy's binds. An instant later, we rushed down the hillock, while Kadie, somehow, was keeping the demon at bay. It was then that I discovered that this monster cannot suffer the presence of wolfhounds.

We took refuge inside the house, speechless and in shock.

However, it was not over.

While Kadie had been vital to our temporary escape, we had to go away as fast as possible from that place. Conroy insisted that the creature could not stand bright light, so we could either hide until dawn or find a way to fight it.

"The cart!" exclaimed Maggie, looking at Patrick. "I can't remember clearly, but I'm sure the gypsies brought your cart here. It should be just out of the front gate."

"Let's go!" said Conroy, but I saw something that froze me on the spot.

First, I heard the wolfhound's yelp of pain, and then I saw the thing rushing down the hill. There was no more time. Quickly, I started reloading the flare gun with the last, remaining rocket. "You go. I will give you enough time to reach the cart."

They hesitated, but I insisted.

"I have lived in ignorance and fear for too long, my children. And because of this your grandmother died, Maggie." I took her hands in mine. "And an innocent child died." I was shaking. "And many more, and more, and more." I shook my head. "No, not this time. Even if I die today, I will die fighting; knowing that I'm doing what I was ordained for: to protect my flock from evil."

Then, I turned to Conroy. "Go! Bring her away from here. Go back to America, you phoney Irish!"

"It's coming," Maggie Blair whispered, and she instinctively moved to the front door. Patrick Conroy looked at me, tears in his eyes, then, before leaving with the girl, uttered a thank you.

I loaded the gun, turned towards the back door, and waited for the horror to come.

I had never felt so much alive before.

It was only by the will of God that I survived that night; the Lord works in mysterious ways and His plan for me was far from finished.

I remember how the black thing, intangible at first, gradually materialised inside the house. I saw the black smoke rippling into view, followed by the unnatural cold. Shapes, sharp and angular, danced inside the vapour, while from the central mass I could see long, filamentous tendrils extending as if the thing was trying to occupy as much space as possible inside the living room. And then came the head again: terrible, taut with murderous malignity, the maw open, eager to feast on my flesh. All the evil in the universe seemed to coalesce into the vaguely canine muzzle.

I lifted the flare gun, closed my eyes, and fired my last rocket.

Instantly, through my serrated eyelids, I saw a blinding light vanish the darkness, colouring in hues of orange and red the oblivion into which I had taken refuge. And then the beast's cry of pain shook the house.

How can I describe what my ears were exposed to? There is no sound in this world I can compare to that unthinkable piping. It sounded as if a thousand enraged insects buzzed together, then it was followed by the ear-piercing cry of tortured souls, and, finally, it dwindled into a low, guttural moaning the equal of which I have never heard in nature.

When I had enough courage to open my eyes again – fearful that the creature was still there, sadistically waiting to see the terror on my face before killing me – I saw that there was still light inside the room. Yet, no trace of the monstrosity.

I shambled around, bedazzled and dizzy, looking for signs of the beast's presence. Then, exhausted, I staggered and finally fell to the ground where I lost my senses.

CHAPTER EIGHTEEN

I never heard Constable Smale and the villagers coming inside the house. I discovered later that a search party had been organised to look for the missing daughter of Squire Douglas, and that the mob was crossing the moor – the gypsies' camp their destination – when they had heard screams coming from Talbot House.

What they had found was horrible beyond their expectations.

Nevertheless, that was nothing compared to the true horrors I and the two other survivors – Maggie Blair and Patrick Conroy – had been witness to.

As it can be imagined, an investigation into the massacre was soon initiated, followed by the arrest of many gypsies. Not all of them, for some escaped long before the mob was upon them. I was forced to lie to Constable Smale about the happenings, for no one would believe my stories and they would think I was insane. Moreover, Conroy had given his own version of the facts, recounting of how he and Maggie had been kidnapped by the maddened gypsies and how they had been witness to the poor little girl's death. They had told the constable that they owed their life to me, who had courageously faced the villains. I remember seeing in the policeman's eyes a glint of doubt and disbelief, yet it became soon evident that for a quick and logical conclusion of the inquest he had no other choice but to take that story, as absurd as it sounded, as true. Nonetheless, he decided to resign from his position just thereafter, and I have heard that he has returned to his beloved Taunton, in Somerset.

Immediately after that night's events, I was confined to my bed by a terrible fever for more than two weeks, and some villagers began to fear the worst. However, thanks to the cures of Doc McKenna and Mrs Yares, I was eventually back on my feet and able to preach my sermons with renewed vigour.

The last time I saw Patrick Conroy was just before he left. He came to the church, thanking me again for saving his life. He and Maggie Blair were due to set sail for Boston, where, he told me, they were going to get married. We never talked about that night; in our eyes, there was a plead to avoid the subject and focus instead on pleasantries. Still, we both know that what had happened that night has marred our soul forever. It will haunt us until our last day.

I remember asking him what had been of his journal, for I knew how dear it was to him. He told me that he had left it in Talbot House, along with all his belongings. There was no need to explain that he wanted none of the things that had been in contact with that place returned to him. I found the journal later, during my last visit to the house.

Yes, after two months I found the courage to return there.

I had to keep my word. In fact, I had promised Kelly Cooney a proper burial and I intended to hold on to my promise. Which I did: I have buried her bones into the family plot, and have had Mr Kidman cut a tombstone for her.

Of course, I wasn't feeling at ease in that horrible place, but I managed to retrieve Conroy's journal. However, I didn't go there alone. I went early in the morning, in the company of Kadie and of my assistant, Miss O'Reilly.

The wolfhound had survived the demon's attack and had been found, dirty and wounded, by Kevin Yares when he had visited Talbot House to assess the damage. He had brought the dog home, where his wife – who is a lover of dogs and all kinds of wild creatures, except for spiders, which she cannot stand – had taken care of her. Obviously, when I discovered she was still alive, I asked Mrs Yares to give me the dog, for I really owed my life to that bold creature. She had been with me all that time, protecting me from Annie and the Blackness.

It has taken some time for the foul creature to regain its strength, and I feel that her phantom hound shape has been vanished forever.

However, I just won a battle, not the whole war. As proved by its taking of Henrietta O'Reilly.

Again, I have impeded its evil plans, but I have to finish this thing once and forever. Tomorrow, as soon as the sun bathes the valley, I will go to Talbot House.

And I will burn it down.

EPILOGUE

THE GLENCREE COURIER

November the 2nd, 1891

HORROR IN ST KEVIN'S CHURCH

BALLYMOOR: Police have been summoned yesterday by the horrified villagers of Ballymoor after the discovery of two dead bodies inside the local church. The first one, belonging to Father Earl Wales, 68, pastor of St Kevin, was found in his bed, apparently killed by failure of the heart during his sleep. Father Wales had been suffering from a recent illness and the local physician, Mr Angus McKenna of Anniskerry, believes this may have put a strain on his body that resulted in a weakening of the heart. However, what really caused the turmoil was the discovery of a second body in the churchyard, this one allegedly identified as that of Miss Henrietta O'Reilly, 41, a resident of Ballymoor and long-time assistant to Father Wales. Miss O'Reilly appears to have been murdered. Few details have been disclosed, but the Anniskerry constable believes Miss O'Reilly was shot six times to the head before flames consumed her body. In fact, the woman's cadaver has been found, incinerated, by Mr Kevin Yares, the owner of the Bridge End Inn.

It is of note that the area is not new to such grisly findings, for in the beginning of last April, as many of our readers recall, the terrible murder of Sir Edgar Fitzpatrick Douglas, Squire of Glencree, and later of his only daughter, Amanda, caused much turmoil and the arrest of eleven gypsies. As of today, details about the motives of the Moorcrest murders have yet to be given an explanation by the authorities, yet it has been speculated that they may be of a political nature. In fact, Squire Douglas' staunch opposition to Irish Home Rule and his attempts at modernising the Gleencree valley may have led some rebellious firebrand to set a sample. It is also of note that since last April, the British garrison at

Kildare has been put on maximum, in the expectation of further upheavals. As it is widely known, County Wicklow has always been a hotbed for independentists and a perfect hiding place for those wanted by the Law thanks to its vast forests and moors.

Rumours tell of an alleged confession for the murder of Miss O'Reilly left by Father Wales, but at the moment, police denies any conjectures or the finding of such confession. The Glencree Courier will surely keep our faithful readers updated on any further findings.

Jeffrey K. O'Hara

The GLENCREE COURIER

ILLUSTRATED WEEKLY NEWSPAPER

Est. 1833 — Monday, November 2, 1891 — Price 6d

HORROR IN ST KEVIN'S CHURCH

BALLYMOOR: Police have been summoned yesterday by the horrified villagers of Ballymoor after the discovery of two dead bodies inside the local church. The first one, belonging to Father Earl Wales, 68, pastor of St Kevin, was found in his bed, apparently killed by failure of the heart during his sleep. Father Wales had been suffering from a recent illness and the local physician, Mr Angus McKenna of Anniskerry, believes this may have put a strain on his body that resulted in a weakening of the heart. However, what really caused the turmoil was the discovery of a second body in the churchyard, this one allegedly identified as that of Miss Henrietta O'Reilly, 41, a resident of Ballymoor and long-time assistant to Father Wales. Miss O'Reilly appears to have been murdered. Few details have been disclosed, but the Anniskerry constable believes Miss O'Reilly was shot six times to the head before flames consumed her body. In fact, the woman's cadaver has been found, incinerated, by Mr Kevin Yares, the owner of the Bridge End Inn.

It is of note that the area is not new to such grisly findings, for in the beginning of last April, as many of our readers recall, the terrible murder of Sir Edgar Fitzpatrick Douglas, Squire of Glencree, and later of his only daughter, Amanda, caused much turmoil and the arrest of eleven gypsies. As of today, details about the motives of the Moorcrest murders have yet to be given an explanation by the authorities, yet it has been speculated that they may be of a political nature. In fact, Squire Douglas' staunch opposition to Irish Home Rule and his attempts at modernising the Gleencree valley may have led some rebellious firebrand to set a sample. It is also of note that since last April, the British garrison at Kildare has been put on maximum, in the expectation of further upheavals. As it is widely known, County Wicklow has always been a hotbed for independentists and a perfect hiding place for those wanted by the Law thanks to its vast forests and moors.

Rumours tell of an alleged confession for the murder of Miss O'Reilly left by Father Wales, but at the moment, police denies any conjectures or the finding of such confession. The Glencree Courier will surely keep our faithful readers updated on any further findings.

Jeffrey K. O'Hara

ANTI-FAT

The Great Remedy for Corpulence

ALLAN'S ANTI-FAT

is composed of purely vegetable ingredients, and is perfectly harmless. It acts upon the food in the stomach, preventing its being converted into fat. Taken in accordance with directions, **it will reduce a fat person from two to five pounds per week.**

"Corpulence is not only a disease itself, but the harbinger of others." So wrote Hippocrates two thousand years ago, and what was true then is none the less so to-day.

Before using the Anti-Fat, make a careful note of your weight, and after one week's treatment note the improvement, not only in diminution of weight, but in the improved appearance and vigorous and healthy feeling it imparts to the patient. It is an unsurpassed blood-purifier and has been found especially efficacious in curing Rheumatism.

Draught Horse for sale.

In good health. Excellent chestnut horse, 8 years old. Sweet-natured and obedient; can be ridden by a young lady. Travellers do not apply.

Contact Mr. Martin Flanagan, Farmer, Ballymoor

The front page of the *GLENCREE COURIER*, Monday, November 2, 1891

About Jeffrey Kosh

"I live by creation. By pen or by graphics, I summon characters, monsters, and landscapes, like a wizard. Alternate worlds, alternate realities. Yet, I'm more similar to a stage magician than a true weaver of spells, for I don't create them out of thin air, but from the experience of others. I feel lucky in carrying on the legacy of the storytellers, those venerable artisans that created tales and epics to enrich the life of their fellow tribe members. The act of creation requires humility, not arrogance, so I always strive to deliver my stories in a low, hushed tone, raising it only in the scary parts." – Jeffrey Kosh.

Jeffrey Kosh is the pen name of an author of two novels, some novelettes, and a long series of short stories. Perhaps best known for his horror fiction, Jeffrey also writes erotica and likes to experience different paths. His works have been published by Alexandria Publishing Group, Grinning Skull Press, May-December Publications, and EFW. He is also a graphic artist, creating covers for various authors and publishing houses. His various careers have led him to travel extensively worldwide, developing a passion for photography, wildlife, history, and popular folklore. All these things heavy influenced his writing style. His short story 'HAUNT' was featured in the 'FROM BEYOND THE GRAVE' anthology, while 'ROAD OFF' became the lead in the 'SCARE PACKAGE' anthology. His debut novel, 'FEEDING THE URGE' is now at its third edition.

As a graphic artist he is the author of numerous movie posters, notable among them are DEATHDATE, WATERMAN WADE, FIVE DAYS IN CALCUTTA, and PITCHING THE TENT.

ALSO FROM OPTIMUS MAXIMUS PUBLISHING

10.35 AM, September 14th 2015. Portsmouth, England.

A global particle physics experiment releases a pulse of unknown energy with catastrophic results. The sanctity of the grave has been sundered and a million graveyards expel their tenants from eternal slumber.

The world is unaware of the impending apocalypse, Governments crumble and armies are scattered to the wind under the onslaught of the dead.

Kurt Taylor, a self-employed plumber, witnesses the start of the horrifying outbreak. Desperate to reach his family before they fall victim to the ever growing horde of shambling corruption, he flees the scene.

In a society with few guns, how can people hope to survive the endless waves of zombies that seek to consume every living thing? With ingenuity, planning and everyday materials, the group forge their way and strike back at the Hellspawn legions.

Rescues are mounted, but not all survivors are benevolent, the evil that is in all men has been given free rein in this new, dead world. With both the living and dead to contend with, the Taylor family's battle for survival is just beginning.

Book 1 in the Hellspawn series.

OPTIMUS MAXIMUS
PUBLISHING

Made in the USA
Middletown, DE
29 June 2016